"Not safe?" she demanded, and laughed. "Why should I be afraid of the dark, Lieutenant Rowe? I think the only harmful thing this darkness holds is you!"

He gave a bark of laughter. "Do you? Maybe you're right. Remember it, next time you decide to come strolling."

She went to turn away, but stopped as memory jolted her curiosity. "Simone said something about murder, didn't she?"

He reached out and grabbed her wrist. She tried to jerk away, but he drew her inescapably closer until she stood trembling between fear and rage.

"You won't be telling anyone else of these wild accusations, will you, sweet Mary Anne?" he said. *"Will you?"*

Deborah Miles, an Australian, was born in Geelong, Victoria. After much travel, her family settled in New South Wales, and she was educated at Maclean. She began writing seriously after leaving school, with several short stories published in Australian magazines, and two short story prizes to her credit. After living and working in Queensland, she returned to Victoria, and lives in the old gold rush town of Bendigo, where she writes, works for the commonwealth Government and shares a home with her husband and two cats.

HARLEQUIN HISTORICAL

DEBORAH MILES
Sweet Mary Anne

Harlequin Books

TORONTO • NEW YORK • LONDON
AMSTERDAM • PARIS • SYDNEY • HAMBURG
STOCKHOLM • ATHENS • TOKYO • MILAN

Harlequin Historical edition published February 1987
ISBN 0-373-30213-4

Original hardcover edition published in 1986
by Mills & Boon Limited

Printed in U.S.A.

PROLOGUE

THE AFTERNOON had been turning to black ever since two o'clock and now, at four, it might easily have been midnight. The clouds lumbered across the low sky, charging and blustering as the schooner made heavy work of the rearing grey waves. What land Mary Anne had been able to see earlier in the day was now obscured. The spray, blown up by the sudden, gusting wind, whipped the sea into a frenzy of mist about them.

It had been the suddenness of the thing that so terrified her. One moment the sea had lain slightly swollen, the wind playfully tugging at the schooner's sails, the next the tempest had come down on them, a screaming fury, icy from the glacial South Pole.

She had been hovering in the companionway since the first buffeting by the storm. Her one attempt to reach the deck had been thwarted by the captain, who sent her below with a string of choice words she hadn't heard since childhood. Since then, she had remained within sight of the hatch, listening to the wild gale and clinging, as best she could, to the steep handrail.

It was hard to believe, now, how perfect the weather had been from Sydney Town. Only nineteen days before a brisk wind, and they had made landfall at Launceston on a golden autumn afternoon in May 1832.

But Launceston had been too small, for Toby. He had looked for richer pickings in the south, at Hobart Town.

'Just the place,' he'd said, blue eyes shining. 'Full of rich soldiers with acres of land. They call themselves "gentry" and hold soirées. Like Sydney, really. And the surrounding countryside is just chock-a-block with retired squires and squatters.'

'But Toby, we've hardly settled *here*, in Launceston! We've only just arrived!'

'But, Mary Anne,' he mocked, 'you know that even if we did stay here it couldn't be for long. Word would get around, and we'd have to leave. Or, worse, the good citizens would haul us up before the Police Magistrate. No, Hobart Town it must be.'

Her eyes had widened. Police Magistrate had a certain ring to it, a certain . . . menace, that tended to dry up all her arguments for staying.

Toby had smiled, and flicked her cheek. 'Just so. The sooner we set out, the better. I've checked. There's a ship bound south tomorrow morning. A schooner, carrying supplies for Macquarie Harbour, on the west coast of dear old Van Diemen's Land. It's a mite more dangerous, of course, but then life without danger is like bread without the butter.'

'Macquarie Harbour?' she'd repeated bemusedly.

'The penal settlement, girl! Macquarie Harbour, a bay halfway down the west coast of Van Diemen's Land, almost impossible to reach in some weathers. They send the unrepentant and unreformable there. It's called "Hell's Gates", I believe.'

She had been afraid, but he had laughed and teased, and she had given in, annoyed at any suggestion of cowardice. He had bought passages for two on *Infanta*, bound for Hobart Town.

And now the schooner pitched, her knife-like bow slashing down into rolling waves, drawing white blood. Timber crashed to the deck close above Mary Anne's head. There was an ominous creaking of beams. Someone was shouting above the wind, and she strained to hear, her fingers tightening their hold. '*Bread without butter*,' he had said! And he had enjoyed it, too, that nerve-wracking voyage! Slipping round the aptly named Cape Grim and down the west coast of Van Diemen's Land, with its rough cliffs and shrouded mountainous coastline. Sometimes jagged pinnacles had stood out from the mainland, rising like warning fingers from grey, angry water; sometimes what could not be seen, beneath the little *Infanta*, was the more dangerous. The sunken reefs and the wreckage of other, less fortunate, sea-farers. There was fog, too, to shroud them. Thick, damp, depressing fog, swathing rigging and spars, forming continuous rain over the scarred, ridged mountains that watched them glide past.

Macquarie Harbour had been frighteningly beautiful, a wilderness of forest and rock and swamp. 'Hell's Gates' indeed! There could be no escape from here, just as there was none from that other, much warmer, place. The men sent here toiled their lives away, chained with a bitterness heavier than iron. Mary Anne found it horrifying. It brought home to her with a thud just what might be their lot if they ever had the misfortune to be apprehended for their many and varied crimes. The law had no pity upon those who broke its inflexible ranks. There could be no pity.

At Macquarie Harbour, they had spent the few days of their stay on Sarah Island, where the settlement was situated, entertaining the Commandant's wife with tales of Sydney Town. Her life, as far as Mary Anne could see, was as desolate and unpleasant as that of the convicts her husband oversaw. Indeed, no, she had not been sorry to leave Macquarie Harbour. Even the *Infanta*'s captain's information, that the stacks jutting from the water at the harbour mouth were named for the ships they had wrecked, failed to deter her. If she had forgotten, these past few years, how ugly life could be, then Macquarie Harbour and its inmates reminded her.

The timbers groaned. The storm was ripping the little schooner asunder. A man's face appeared in the hatchway, drenched and bloodied, and was gone again. Mary Anne started up the companionway, when behind her a door was flung wide. Toby lurched out as the schooner heeled, his body slamming into the wall. His eyes opened wide, seeming bluer than ever in his green-tinted face. The auburn hair curled riotously against his crumpled shirt collar. He had been vomiting since the storm came up, sicker even than Mary Anne. For her, fear had overshadowed the ducking and diving of the *Infanta*.

The lack of colour in his face aged him, and the freckles on his nose stood out as clear as ink-spots. It was the freckles, Mary Anne decided for the hundredth time, that drew people to Toby, that made them trust him. He had such an honest face.

'God Almighty!' he muttered, trying to straighten his wavering legs as the floor tilted.

'Surely it's the other one *you* should be calling to,' she retorted, but her voice shook. Above, the square of sky in the hatchway was a tangle of snapped lines and torn sails. Salt water dribbled down the stairs. *Infanta* danced flamenco on the waves, her sails flapping like tattered skirts in the fury of the wind.

'Mary Anne,' he said, close behind her. She felt his fingers brush her neck, felt something chill and heavy against her throat. An emerald gleamed balefully, winking up at her. She spun about, to meet his painful smile.

'Yes, it's real,' he said, and bracing himself against the hand-railing, put a finger under her chin and kindly closed her mouth.

'Toby . . .'

He loomed closer, his breath warm on her cold cheek. 'It's our security, my girl. When we get to Hobart, we'll sell it, and set up in style. We'll retire. Really. I'll buy into something honest. Take good care of it, won't you?'

His smile brought tears aching in her eyes. But there wasn't time for speaking. The schooner lurched and suddenly heeled to an impossible angle. Mary Anne screamed on a note as raw as bleeding flesh. She felt herself slipping. Toby snatched at her. She heard voices crying out, and the timbers rending and splitting.

'We've got to get out!' Toby was calling. 'Captain, where are the bloody lifeboats?' And then she hit her head, and everything went black.

Pain. Like light splintering the darkness. A throbbing, wrenching pain somehow connected with the swishing of the water about her. It was the pain which finally brought her back from unconsciousness, and brought her face up and out of the freezing water. Her lungs were screaming for air, and she gasped it in while her body retched and convulsed.

'Dear God,' she said, in a croaking voice, and shivered violently. Her skirts seemed sewn with lead, dragging her down, but her arm was holding her up, though it was sheer agony. She realised, gradually, that she had been lashed to a makeshift raft, made of planking and what looked to be a barrel, and that the rope had slipped, leaving her arm wedged between the two. Evidently the captain had had no lifeboat after all . . . Her eyes widened. She looked about her, at the spars and planks, crates and casks. Wreckage? The *Infanta*!

Fear and grief brought her jerking round, searching the water for that familiar curly head; and the ensuing pain caused a nausea that threatened to send her spiralling back into the blackness of unconsciousness. When she was able to think again, she found that her gown was torn, peeling back from her trapped arm, disclosing blood and lacerated flesh. The sight sickened her, and she closed her eyes under the weight of her dark, loose hair. Her body was numb with cold and pain and shock. Tears pricked, but before she could begin to cry the sea slapped her in the mouth, forcing her face up to the grey sky.

The tempest was past, and a gentle rain mocked at her misery. She was alone, and about to die. Her hand went involuntarily to her throat; the cold stone was still there.

For a moment she felt it to be evil, an ill omen, and dragged at it. But the chain was too strong, and in the end she lost consciousness again, and it was forgotten.

After that, her mind wandered. Toby laughed at her, her mother raised a shaking hand, screaming, 'You wicked bitch!' in some dirty alley. What had she done? Spoken to the Corporal on the wharf? Spoken to another bloody lobster?

'You mustn't speak to soldiers,' Toby was saying, gently, smiling. 'You know your mother doesn't like it.'

A particularly savage slap in her face brought her chin up again. 'Bloody lobsters,' she muttered. 'Bloody soldiers,' her voice rasping in the rough, drawling speech of childhood; before Toby had come, and she had learned to pretend to be a lady.

Her eyes opened, surveying the scene through a haze of pain. And she saw him.

At first she thought him an illusion: a mirage sent to taunt her. Or maybe this was death, coming personally to claim her. Poseidon himself, god of the sea and the dark underworld. The idea took hold, and when he had drawn closer she asked him, in a polite, drawing-room voice.

The drenched, sunbrowned face split into a grin at the suggestion, disclosing very white teeth. The voice was rather breathless, clipped and deep. 'Not yet, anyway.'

Then he *was* a mirage! Her eyes closed. But pain shot them open as quickly. Her arm was being wrenched and jolted, and pain jarred. The mirage had a knife, and was sawing at the ropes that held her.

For a moment the throbbing agony threatened to curtain her mind, and she concentrated desperately on the sky. It was not nearly so dark as it had been, and the rain had stopped. There was a line of sunlight along the horizon, like the gilt rim of a teacup. Her eyes travelled about the edge, and she blinked. There was land—

surely there was land? Hills misted with fog, trees like
daggers, and, further back, the jagged escarpments of
the rugged land beyond the inhospitable coast. Was she
not to die, then, after all?

Warm, strong arms slid under her, supporting her as
she lay half on the flotsam and half on the water's
surface. Her arm was free, dully aching. He had bound it
across her breast with a strip of cloth he had torn from his
shirt. A face swooped over hers, blocking out the sky.
Fair hair plastered to a frowning forehead, and eyes
absurdly like the storm. 'You're safe enough now,' it
said. 'I've got you.'

And, strangely enough, she felt safe. Despite everything. Water and salt might sting at her mouth and eyes,
her skirts might pull her down, her body might be stiff
and frozen. But he was holding her, and it was only very
vaguely that she realised they had left the shelter of the
flotsam and were moving towards the land.

'What a hell of a day to choose!' he said. 'Jesus,
woman, couldn't you have waited until it was warmer?'
He was talking to her; she struggled to understand. 'I
suppose I can be glad it's autumn and not midwinter. Lie
still!' She had tried to straighten, to see his face. She
wondered if he were mad.

The face swooped over her again, the grey eyes
searched her own. 'Do you speak English, then? Not
French, I hope? I've a mind to take you right back to
your raft, if you're French.' His teeth were chattering,
she heard. She stared at him wide-eyed, and tears
blurred her vision. 'Well,' he said. 'Well, maybe not.
The war's long over, after all. Lie still. Not far now.'

The movement, or lack of it, lulled her. Her eyes
flickered and closed. The cold made her weary. Toby
was laughing at her again. 'Don't you trust me?' he
mocked her. 'You're always worrying, girl! There's
nothing to worry about. You're like . . .'

'. . . A little girl in the dark without a candle.'

'A what?'

She stared back at him, aware that she had spoken aloud.

And then he said, 'There you are, my beauty,' and she felt sand beneath her feet. Coarse, gravelly sand. She blinked, focusing painfully on the beach and, above it, the steep, forest-covered rise. And the faces.

Hard, white faces. And chains. She sought wildly for the face of her rescuer, but could not find him among them, and when she tried to stand, her legs gave out on her. The world went dark again. The approaching gallop of a horse along the beach echoed the thundering of her own heart.

CHAPTER ONE

SHE WAS a child again. The past had reclaimed her. A poor, despised child. So very poor. The thought mocked at her from the darkness of her mind. She focused on it, and saw her mother. The face was as clear and intense as if she stood there. As if time had gone into reverse. How she had loved her mother, and how she had hated her! When she had had the gin, her mother used to beat her. A mindless, mechanical violence. As if there were a sore inside her, that could be drained only by hurting her child. And yet, at other times, she would have given up her own food so that the child could eat, given up a blanket so that she could be warm. Given up her life—so that Mary Anne could do better in hers.

Mary Anne tossed and turned. The darkness whispered all round her, taunting her. Chains rattling. Chains like those at Macquarie Harbour. Chains weren't new to her. She'd seen the road-gangs in Sydney Town, and the convicts on the wharves. She'd seen the scars of men who had been chained. Her mother had those scars. She'd been so certain, as a child, that everyone had worn chains, that she'd asked her mother what the Governor of New South Wales had been sent out for. Her mother had laughed until she wept, rocking back and forth on the cask that served as a chair, the light from the window drawing grotesque shadows in the damp, smelly room.

'The Governor and his kind are a different breed,' she had said at last. 'Altogether another breed.' Her eyes narrowed, became sly. 'The Governor and his breed need money, so's they can buy all the soft luxuries. They need such things, to keep them alive. But us . . . we just

13

have to be strong. If we're not, there's no money to keep us living.'

Her mother had survived much—life in the slums of Clerkenwell, London, transportation for petty theft, and life in the slums of the colonies. Like all her class, she was bitter, full of baffled hatred and anger. And she had passed it on, an inheritance for Mary Anne. There were 'us' and 'them', to Mary Anne's way of thinking. And where was the harm in stealing from the latter?

'They lie and cheat us. And they hate us as much as we hate them.' Her mother again, her face all bruised, her lip cut. Someone had beaten her again. Embittered men took out their frustrations, their futile rage at life, on their women. It was the way of the world. By the time her mother died, Mary Anne thought it was the way of all men. She still did, deep inside. All men except Toby—he alone could be her friend.

Toby.

When her mother died, Mary Anne had had no alternative but the streets. What more was there when a girl had no money and no home? Still, the thought had horrified her. Her mother, in her way, had kept her safe; away from the worst of the slum life. Her days had consisted of the endless laundering her mother took in, her nights at the inn and its relative peace and safety. Her mother's going had changed all that—she was alone. Laundering was out of the question; she was far too young. No one wanted to look twice at her when she went for work at the market. Who wanted to hire a grubby, thin bit of a girl who could offer nothing but 'I'd try hard'? It had been the streets, and if Toby had not come along when he did . . . She shuddered. But he had come, and found her in the darkness that first night, and taken her to his room. To a big fire and a tray with bread and ale, and a bed soft as the waves along the shore. He had been so kind and gentle, and then so angry when she tentatively offered him the only thing she had to give. He had been the brother she had never had, and she had stayed with him.

So then had come to her initiation into Toby's trade —trickster and confidence man. Together they had lived precariously up and down the country, but mainly in Sydney Town, where there was more scope, as Toby put it. And in due course had come the fatal evening, and their flight in darkness from their rented lodgings to take passage from Sydney Town to Launceston in Van Diemen's Land.

It had been all her fault. Why had she opened her mouth at that fateful supper? Why hadn't she stuck to the plan they'd agreed upon? Just for once? And yet, it had seemed such a harmless little lie—it always did. There was nothing harmless, however, about the consequences.

'A little lie?' Toby had mocked, eyes gleaming appreciatively. 'That the Chief Justice was your cousin?'

'How was I to know that the vulgar woman with the emerald was his aunt? You should have warned me.'

He squeezed her arm. 'Oh, Mary Anne, I never know what you're going to say next. How can I watch your tongue?'

'And so we have to go into hiding, is that it?'

His smile had told her the worst.

'I'm sorry. I really am.' She was always contrite, after the deed. 'You meant to make such a killing at the supper. All those "pure merinos", all those exclusionist blue-bloods.' She sighed. 'And all that sparkling jewellery. I'm sorry.'

But Toby had merely smiled, and though she had wondered a little at his smugness, she had not had the heart to question him.

It hadn't been until the last moments on the *Infanta*, when he produced the emerald—the Chief Justice's aunt's emerald—that she had realised why he had smiled. He had relieved the woman of it, no doubt, when he had been explaining to her later in the evening what a disappointment Mary Anne was to her dear parents.

The darkness swirled, chilling her so that she moaned. The past receded again, becoming the present.

There was the feel of a warm hand on her brow, the salty taste of soup on her lips. Her eyes fluttered open and were drawn to the light. Lamplight, shining like a little sun. It hurt her eyes; she closed them again. But the very fact of being alive and on steady land was too exciting to ignore for long. At least, she hoped she was on land . . . She peered through her lashes. The lamp was not so bright now, and beyond it lay the room. A small, shadowy room with a ceiling that sloped down at one end. An attic room? Her eyes opened wide, and she said the first thought that came to her mind. 'Toby?'

She seemed to have been saying it all her life. Toby, where do we go now? Toby, what's to be our next plan? Toby, tell me who we concentrate on next? Some little backwater, perhaps, where we can dazzle the inhabitants with our city polish and then creep off in the night with their savings. Life, such as it was, had really grown exciting only with the advent of Toby. Before him there had been fear and pain and poverty: all the bad things, the dark things. Toby had been a giant in comparison. A man who did not hurt her or frighten her, who was kind and, in his own careless way, protected her.

'Where's Toby?' she said, and her eyes—big, brown, dreaming—searched for and found the room's occupant.

A woman, broad-faced, who smiled uncertainly and with sympathy, and said, 'I'm sorry, but they're all gone. Your ship went down beyond the entrance to our bay. We hoped your captain would turn in before it was too late, but he couldn't have seen . . . When the weather calmed, there was only you still afloat. It's been a week since then, when Lieutenant Rowe pumped the water from your lungs.'

The speech was breathless, the woman hovered, frowning. As though Mary Anne were an added duty she begrudged. But Mary Anne hardly noticed her. Toby was gone. The shadows approached her from the edges of the room, lumbering like the storm-clouds towards the bed. They crowded over her, hiding the lamp, pressing her down into the soft mattress. Toby was dead.

When she woke again, she was much calmer. Somewhere in her restless sleep she had come to terms, faced the truth about Toby's death. He was gone, she was alone and must somehow survive. As she had survived once, before he came. Perhaps, in Hobart Town, there would be something. She would find work, of any sort. Her fingers slid automatically to her throat, and she sighed. The emerald was still there. The thought of it, and Hobart Town, brought her mind back to more pressing questions. Where was she now?

Macquarie Harbour.

She jerked up at the thought. She had watched the men there working, chained together in gangs. They had been chopping down trees along the side of a ridge, slipping and sliding on the spongy ground as they dragged the logs down to be floated out into the freezing water of the harbour, ready for the ships to load. The scene had appalled her. The sight of those heavy, clanking manacles befouled with grime and mud. Worse, so much worse, than those chain-gangs she had watched often enough in her native Sydney Town.

Manacles. On the beach. Faces looking down at her, unmoved by her condition or her pain. She almost screamed at the sound of the latch. When the door opened beneath her widening gaze, it was only the plain woman, her brown hair neatly coiled on her crown in an old-fashioned style.

'You're awake,' she said unnecessarily. But the voice

was low and soothing, rather deep for a woman.

'Where am I? I must know, I . . .'

'You're at Etwall.'

'Etwall?' Not Macquarie Harbour then, thank God, thank God!

'We're some forty miles south of Hell's Gate,' the woman said, as if reading her mind. 'The only other settlement worth the name on this coast.'

'There were convicts, on the beach.'

A smile for the fear in her eyes, as though an adult soothed a child's fear of monsters. 'Did you see the timber party? We have convicts working for us, but this is not a place of punishment. You've no need to fear them.'

The woman had moved to the window, to draw aside a curtain. Mary Anne watched her uncertainly, taking in her appearance automatically, judgingly, as Toby had taught her to do. She was quite tall, and broad with it, with bones large and well-covered. Her age was perhaps midway between thirty and forty, and her profile, stark against the light, was regular and broad with a chin receding a little towards a wide neck.

'You can see our harbour from here,' the woman said. 'Only a dint in the coast, really, but it's sheltered enough when the weather comes up as it did a week ago, and ships can anchor there when they come for our timber.

Mary Anne turned her head to look. Her window faced into a small cove. Her eyes followed the shore round, beyond a half-moon of sand, to black rocks, and further round to a jutting headland. The water seemed smooth enough, but dark and glowering. Toby lay beneath water such as that. Dead, drowned, gone.

The woman turned with a rustle of dull skirts. There was a trimming of white, rather limp lace about her sleeves and bodice. The dress was wool, longer than the fashion, the sleeves narrower. Etwall, obviously, was no Mecca of the rich and fashionable.

'This is my husband's house,' she was saying, in her deep, slow voice. 'The timber camp is round the bay, above the beach. He's there at the moment . . . My husband, that is.' A pause, and she let her eyes rest on Mary Anne's. 'Who was Toby?'

Mary Anne started. The woman's eyes were blue, and kind enough. Not so blue as Toby's, of course, but . . . It came to her, in some cool part of her brain, that she would be wise not to tell the truth. Toby always avoided it where possible, just in case. Besides, lying was second nature to her now.

'He was my husband.'

The woman tut-tutted. 'Have you relatives in Hobart?'

'No, I . . . That is, my husband and I were travelling on business. He was thinking of investing, or some such thing. I never took much interest in his affairs.' She bit her lip at the word, but for the woman it had no sinister connotations.

'You're from . . .?'

'Sydney Town.' Well, that at least was a truth.

'There'll be no ship due here in the immediate future, I'm afraid. The last one was only a fortnight ago, so there is no need to send one to us for at least another month. Probably two. This time of year the weather is so uncertain, as you have cause to know.'

'What will I do?' Her voice betrayed her. The blue eyes, which had turned a little cool, warmed again.

'You will stay here. Indeed, there's nothing else you can do! There is no way out of Etwall, apart from a ship.' She plucked at her collar, twisting the lace. 'What is your name?'

'Mary Anne.'

'Mary Anne . . . ?'

'Mary Anne Gower.' That, too, was best suppressed. She had known a family called Gower once; for the moment she would adopt herself into their bosom.

'Have you any family in Sydney Town?'

She slowered her chin on to her chest. 'My father died last year. I was his . . . sole heiress. There is no one else.' They had clothed her in a white and voluminous night-gown, she noticed. Toby would have called it hideous, but no doubt it made her look very pathetic. The woman had actually condescended to pat her hand.

'Now, now,' she said in a gratingly cheerful voice. 'Rest, and after your supper my husband will . . . will . . .' But what he would do seemed to elude her, and she merely smiled and turned to leave.

She was halfway through the doorway when Mary Anne roused herself enough to speak again. 'It wasn't a dream, was it? Someone did pull me from the sea?'

'No,' the long fingers twisted a moment on the brass doorknob, 'it wasn't a dream. The timber party were lopping trees when the storm came up. They caught sight of your ship; there's a rock halfway up the hill that runs into that part of the bay. It juts out from the trees, a sort of spur, I suppose. From there they saw the wreck and, when the storm had passed, you. My husband wanted to put out a boat, but his brother knew how dangerous such a thing must be so soon after the storm . . . Storms in this part of the world have a habit of returning as suddenly as they leave.'

'Was it your husband, then, who swam out so far?' Her eyes were wide for such courage.

The woman's mouth twitched in amusement. 'No, Ralph can't swim more than a yard without sinking. It was one of the timber party—Lieutenant Rowe. You will be able to thank him personally when you are better.'

Then the door closed. Mary Anne lay back in her bed and shut her eyes. It was all very strange; her head ached with thinking. Perhaps it was best, as Toby sometimes said, to take things as they came.

*   *   *

In fact, it was another day before she was considered
well enough to have any visitors. The woman, whom she
had learned was Bessy Etwall, came back that afternoon
to change the dressing on her arm and tut-tut over the
pink, bruised flesh and the weeping of blood and fluid.
'It is mending, but you'll have to keep as still and quiet as
possible,' she warned.

'It will heal?'

'Salt water is considered excellent for cleaning
wounds, and there's been no infection.'

The arm looked ugly to Mary Anne, but she said
nothing. Better than death, after all; and what was a
little scar? She had plenty enough inside. Still, the
removal of the bandages had made her feel sick, and the
long sleep had given her a heavy head.

'Simone is bringing your supper. You'll be famished,
no doubt.'

Anything but, Mary Anne thought, and yet she
looked up with interest when there was a clatter outside
the door. Bessy hurried to open it, and an untidy girl
came in, precariously balancing a tray on which was
arranged some pretty china.

'Very nice, Simone,' Bessy nodded. The girl flushed,
her pale cheeks colouring to dusky pink. 'At least the
tray is neat,' Bessy added with meaning, and the girl
flushed even more.

With cause, Mary Anne decided wryly. The girl's
uniform was creased and the hem damp—as though she
had been running through dewy grass. Tangled strands
of hair escaped a rather grubby white cap, her nails were
dark rimmed. 'The cows, madame,' the girl whispered,
her accent thickly French.

'Of course, the cows.' But Bessy's eyes were hard, and
the girl made haste to bend over the tray and set out the
invalid fare with trembling fingers. Now that the flush
had died, Mary Anne saw that her skin was clear as milk,
the nose a little curved at the bridge, the eyes, flickering

beneath tawny lashes, a bright, bird-like yellow. It was an interesting face.

'Unlike Sydney Town,' Bessy Etwall said coolly, 'at Etwall we must make do with what we can find.'

Simone bobbed a brief curtsy, and went out. Bessy clicked her tongue. 'The girl was the wife of one of my husband's men—a free man, I might add. He died last autumn. An accident, I understand, involving the felling of a tree.'

'Involving the felling of a tree?'

Bessy's mouth thinned with annoyance. 'It fell on him,' she said bluntly. 'Unfortunately he was the foreman at the time, but we've found another, so things haven't worked out too badly. And Simone is useful in the house, if a little . . . "touched", since it happened.'

'Poor Simone!' Mary Anne could pity someone like that—her destitution and her sudden inability to cope with life. Luckily she herself was made of sterner stuff, she had had to be to survive as she had.

Bessy was at the door again. 'I'll have to leave you, I'm afraid. Ralph will be home, wanting his dinner, and I have to dress.'

Mary Anne's eyes widened a little, but her face was schooled to remain straight. Dress for dinner, in this place? It seemed absurd. But then, how did one survive isolation except by pretending that beyond the dining-room was civilisation, of some sort.

'I suppose you will find Etwall very boring, after Sydney Town.'

It was said conversationally, but there was a hint of something else beneath the politeness. Jealousy, perhaps, or bitterness.

Mary Anne smiled. 'Oh, life is very exciting there, of course. But, at the moment, I think I prefer solitude.'

Bessy's hand rested on the doorknob, the lamp shadowing her face. 'Yes,' she said, 'I understand that.' A pause. 'My brother-in-law, Nick, will be pleased with your company, I know. He has so little opportunity to meet . . . respectable young women in this part of the world. He was in Hobart until just recently, you know, but now he's back again.

Mary Anne forced another smile. 'I shall look forward to meeting him.'

The door closed, the steps faded away. Mary Anne bit her lip and lay back against the pillows. The meal was cooling swiftly in the chill evening. Had she been wrong to give an illusion of wealth? Would Toby, dear Toby, have acted so? She longed suddenly to be up and out of bed, out of this restrictive little room. Even the view of the sea was denied her—Bessy kept the curtains drawn. She sighed and picked up her spoon, looking vindictively at the boiled egg and bread and butter. Tomorrow she would meet Ralph, who could not swim a stroke, and perhaps Nick who had lately been in Hobart, and that paragon Lieutenant Rowe, who had saved her life and whom Bessy detested.

She was proclaimed well enough, the following afternoon, to leave her bed, and, with a gown wrapped round her from chin to toe, was helped to a chair by the window, where there was a patch of very pale sunlight.

The bay lay smooth and glassy, the sky a pale, cloud-studded blue. The house sat on a rise close to the shore. To the left the land curved round like a protecting hand, dense with trees and scrub, the shoreline lying low and marshy at the water's edge. To the right was the little beach, and the distant sweep of the land, dark with rock, some of which jutted far out into the water at low tide. Above, in the forest of trees, was a trickle of smoke. Tall, tall trees, dark and forbidding, so thickly grown that she could hardly see into them. The land dropped to the cove steeply, making deep shadows as the sun swung around. It was not much different from Macquarie Harbour, only much smaller, and there was no river to wash down the brown, swollen waters from the high escarpments. Mary Anne found it all fascinating. A frightening beauty. Men didn't belong here. Man had no right to be cutting down these ancient grandfather trees for furniture in somebody's drawing-room.

Bessy came to change her bandages. 'I suppose it is pretty,' she said, with an uncertain flicker of her eyes. 'Much of the country inland is as yet unseen, at least by white men.'

'It must be lonely for you,' Mary Anne murmured.

'It is lonely.' The woman looked for a moment out of the window, watching the wash of the water on the sand. 'And dangerous.' The blue eyes swung back. 'The weather and the isolation. And there are bolters—convicts who have absconded into the bush and make their living by thieving and killing.'

'But surely, here, you are safe from that!'

Bessy returned to the bandaging. 'We have our own convicts; there is always a chance one of them might take to the bush. They should have more sense, of course. There is nothing there. Only death. The forests are impenetrable, the mountains unclimbable. It is always wet, you see, and the plants grow so quickly, and so thickly.'

Sometimes death, Mary Anne thought, was preferable to being chained. Obviously Bessy would not understand that. To her, it seemed the forest was the most frightening thing of all. Etwall was a haven, safe and secure. Anyone who wanted to leave it was beyond help. Instead she said, 'You have soldiers here, to watch over you?'

Bessy's expression cooled with alarming rapidity. 'Yes, there are the soldiers. They are not needed here, but who are we to argue with the powers in Hobart?'

The dressing was finished, and Bessy rose, smoothing her skirts. 'Ralph will be home soon,' she said. 'And no doubt our gallant Lieutenant will wish to speak with you.'

There seemed little to say to the sarcasm. Mary Anne smiled, and when the other woman was gone, sighed. The sunlight had gone, fading with the evening, turning the sea to grey again. There was a mirror above the mantelpiece, and with some difficulty she struggled up from the chair. By resting most of her weight on the bedside table, she could see herself in the glass. For a moment she wasn't sure it was herself, and shuddered. What a sight! White-faced, hollow-cheeked, her eyes shadowed with smudges the colour of plums. Of course, she had not had a proper meal for over a week, and had been immersed in sea water for God knew how many hours. She touched her nose, found it still small and straight, her chin was as unfortunately square and stubborn as ever. The slanting black brows needed plucking, but somehow she doubted Bessy Etwall had the necessary implement. The brown eyes stared back at her mockingly, larged than ever. She made them sad, compressing her lips to stop a smile. The arm in white bandages was a nice touch, too, and the sling Bessy had insisted she must wear.

Toby used to say that one glance from Mary Anne's eyes, and any man worthy of the name was lost. But Toby had been a one for flattery. Still, time would repair the pallor and the shadows. She would still grieve, of course. But she must look to herself, to her future, as Toby would have wanted her to do. And she had the emerald.

The tap on the door startled her, and she jerked her arm, hurting herself and making her face all the paler. The evening had crept further into the room; outside it was growing dark. In haste she regained her chair, tucking her feet under the hem of the gown, and calling whoever it was to enter.

The door opened. She knew before he opened his mouth that it must be Ralph Etwall. 'Mrs Gower? I'm not disturbing you?'

'Not at all. I was just . . .'

'But it's almost dark in here! Let me.' He fumbled with the tinder-box and lamp, and while it caught and was turned up, she had a chance to survey him.

Where Bessy Etwall was broad, Ralph was slight. His clothes were old, well-worn and patched. His boots, too, were old and dulled with work. His face, bent to the lamp, appeared serious, with lines etched deep into his brow. Perhaps he sensed her study, because when he turned at last to her, his eyes, though tired, sparkled with something warm she found she liked.

'I've offered you no condolences,' he said softly. 'I do so now.'

Mary Anne nodded, and folded her hands in her lap. She felt like crying, and knew she mustn't. She needed all her wits about her now. The Etwalls must be drawn out, and formally ranged on her side, in case she should ever need their full support.

'I wish we could get you to Hobart, where at least you would be near people who might be able to help you, or get in touch with someone who can, but . . .' A smile, as weary as his eyes.

'Your wife told me you depend entirely on ships.'

He looked as if he knew very well his wife's feelings in regard to Etwall, but refrained from replying. A moth fluttered against the windowpane, and he drew the curtain.

'You must see Etwall for yourself, to make judgments,' he said at last. 'I find the isolation peaceful. The clatter of towns was something I gave up long ago. For my wife, I know, it has been difficult. She has forgone much.'

Mary Anne smiled sympathetically, a flicker of lips and lashes.

Ralph cleared his throat. 'My brother, now, is entirely different from myself. He lives for a town's clatter. He loves the bustle.'

'Your wife told me he's only lately returned.'

The curve of his mouth was somewhat sarcastic. 'Needs must, as they say.' His face creased in its well-worn lines. 'You've no idea what your arrival has done for us, Mrs Gower. Life is pretty dull for most of those living here; so you'll have to prepare yourself for being the centre of attention for a while.'

'How long have you lived here?' she said, after a moment.

He scratched his head. 'Over ten years now, since we first started the settlement. Not much to show for it, I suppose, but then timber-getting is a slow business, and perhaps not very exciting.'

'My husband owns a mill,' she replied, and watched his eyebrows go up.

'A mill?'

'For cutting timber. I suppose it is mine now.'

The tap on the door stopped him from asking how much else was hers, and she hid a smile as Simone peeped round, her hair as untidy as ever.

'Madame Etwall says that Lieutenant Rowe is here.'

Ralph nodded, and glanced at Mary Anne. 'Our Lieutenant is very conscientious,' he said, with a pretend smile. 'He wants to satisfy himself as to your well-being.'

'Indeed,' she murmured, wondering at the hidden sting of his words.

Ralph shrugged, 'Etwall is under his military control. He may wish to ask you some questions.'

'I suppose, then, I must satisfy his curiosity.'

Simone's eyes flickered to Ralph and, when he nodded, dropped as she closed the door. There was a silence, before he said, 'I must admit that we were most surprised when the Governor decided we needed some military men stationed at Etwall. We've managed well enough by ourselves for the past ten years, and there's rarely trouble at the timber camp. One or two of the convicts we get in from Hobart are trouble-makers, but we handle them well enough without military interference.'

She understood his feelings. What right had the military to interfere? she thought indignantly. What were they, anyway, but fools in red coats, prancing about a parade-ground like tin men? Corrupt and power-seeking, they were to be neither trusted nor liked. And officers were the worst of the lot!

Ralph, sensing her sympathy, added, 'And now we have Lieutenant Rowe deciding what we feed them and where they are to sleep. It's annoying, to say the least.' He smiled at her nod of agreement. 'Still, by all accounts, they were as eager to be rid of Luke Rowe as we were loath to welcome him here.'

Mary Anne lifted her eyebrows, and bit back her curiosity about exactly what he meant. 'Mr Etwall, I have no reason to love the military,' she said at last, cautiously. 'My father disliked them intensely for reasons I shall not elaborate upon.' Her own dislike showed in her voice, for more reasons than Ralph Etwall would ever understand—or, come to that, anyone could know but she and her mother. She rarely let it show, for most of the people she and Toby used their wiles upon were the richer army officers and their cronies.

Ralph Etwall seemed, indeed, to provide a sympathetic ear. He leaned forward eagerly, his tired eyes bright. 'Perhaps, when you get to Hobart, Mrs Gower, you would do us the great favour of putting those opinions to the Governor. Obviously you have connections . . . If you could only get the Lieutenant removed, life would be so much the better for us all.'

Mary Anne's face remained smiling, but inside she shuddered. Lord, what had she got herself into now? Well, Toby always said her mouth and her mind were not connected! Still, Ralph Etwall thought her a friend, and that might yet stand her in good stead.

There were footsteps outside; heavy, determined

steps. Ralph, with a grimace, rose to open the door. There was darkness beyond, a shadow with no substance. 'Mr Etwall,' a voice said, a voice she remembered suddenly and vividly. The memory supplanted the dislike that had been growing with Ralph's words and her own memories. This man had saved her life, after all, and risked his own doing so. Officer or no, he deserved her gratitude.

'Lieutenant.'

He came in, ducking beneath the lintel. A man above medium height, wearing the tight white breeches, black boots and red coat of the military, creaseless over hard, well-muscled flesh. The fair hair was a little untidy, the grey eyes were exactly as she remembered. He smiled at her, one side of his mouth curving more than the other, but the grey eyes remained cool and somehow assessing. The look disturbed her—as though he looked right past the gown, and all her sweet pretence, to the gutter child she in reality was. Not a pleasant feeling, and for a moment she made no response.

But he had already come forward to take her unhurt hand and to execute over it a slight bow. 'Mrs Gower,' he said in pleasant, deep tones. 'I trust you are feeling much better than when we last met.' It was the voice she remembered berating her so ridiculously.

'You saved my life,' she said, her smile strained with memories. 'At risk to your own. I must therefore thank you, Lieutenant Rowe.'

'I'm sure he counts it a pleasure, Mrs Gower,' Ralph stepped out from the shadows. Lieutenant Rowe acknowledged his words with another slight bow. The smile still played about his mouth; for some reason she had begun to find it irritating.

'Without risks, life must necessarily be dull,' he retorted, reminding her of Toby. The grey eyes narrowed against the light, and surveyed her with insulting openness.

She mightn't have minded so much, perhaps, if she were looking her best. However, she was very sure she looked her worst. Her chin lifted, and she met his eyes coolly. Toby always assured her she had the presence of a duchess when she was offended. Why, then, was Lieutenant Rowe's smirk broadening into a grin?

'Mrs Gower and her husband were on their way to Hobart. I've explained to her the difficulties with continuing her journey.'

The Lieutenant lifted his eyebrows at Ralph Etwall, who continued, 'She'll have to stay here with us until such time as the ship arrives.'

The grey eyes slid back to Mary Anne. 'She has no choice. We must hope your wife doesn't find the strain on her supplies too great. Even though the army has sent extra for myself and my men, there never seems to be enough.'

His voice was dry, tinged with mockery. Ralph's tired eyes shone a moment with something that flickered and danced like fire. Anger? Or hatred?

'Truly,' Mary Anne murmured, sweet as honey, 'it wasn't my intention to be a burden to anyone.'

Ralph made no comment. Lieutenant Rowe said, 'I've yet to offer you my condolences, Mrs Gower, on your loss. I do so now.'

She bowed her head, wondering if he were aware he had uttered almost exactly the same words as Ralph not thirty minutes previously.

'You're from Sydney Town, I believe,' he went on.

'Yes, my husband was a . . . a merchant.'

'Dealing in timber? He owned a timber mill, you said,' Ralph put in.

'Yes. But he traded in other things, too.'

'A free man, then,' Lieutenant Rowe stated. 'He was no ex-convict?'

'Indeed not!' Mary Anne spluttered, flushing.

'There's little in the way of polite society at Etwall.'

'Indeed.'

'You'll soon be mourning your friends. Still'—and his tone was smooth enough for anyone less experienced not to notice the underlying note of distaste—'I suppose this is an experience for you, Mrs Gower. You've probably never been this close to a convict settlement before.'

'I'm sure no one would envy me that,' she retorted with a little laugh. She had heard the real Mrs Gower give just such a laugh, and flutter her lashes just so. 'Besides, you forget,' and now she let her lashes drop, shielding the tears, 'this visit was none of my doing, sir.'

'Rowe, you forget yourself,' Ralph Etwall hissed. 'Mrs Gower has lost her dearest husband, man.'

'I have offered her my sympathies, such as they are,' the Lieutenant said evenly, not to be shamed. 'I was merely concerned that, when Mrs Gower was feeling more herself, she would grow bored with us all. But perhaps she could fill in time by teaching us something of the polite society I'm sure she graces with such perfection. I'm sure there is much she can teach us, hmm?'

Her lashes rose, and Mary Anne looked at him with dislike. His own eyes were gleaming with something she should recognise but was too tired to attempt. Her arm was aching, her head was aching, and all this detestable man could do was make barbed fun of the woman he imagined her to be. She longed suddenly to throw the truth into his undeniably handsome face and watch it pale. 'Why, yes, Lieutenant,' she would say, 'all one needs is a mobile face and a quick wit. It's easy enough to learn the movements and the motions. All that remains then is the voice. You'd be amazed how a person can get away with just about anything, with the right voice. Who taught me, you ask? Some actress Toby was friendly with. Once I learned the voice, everything else soon followed. Conscience? I had one once, but it grows less demanding if one remembers the alleys and the

gutters, alive with their gleaming foulness in the slums of
Sydney Town. Crawling with unhappiness and misery,
as well as vermin. A girl must live, after all, and if she
prefers lying and play-acting to walking the streets, well,
so much the better for her . . .' God, how she hated the
military! Maggoty apples, the lot of them. Why did it
have to have been a soldier who had saved her miserable
life?

Ralph had been speaking, but she heard only the last
few words. Something about the convicts. Lieutenant
Rowe's grey eyes were scanning her coolly, his face
grave. Hypocrite, she thought. Liar!

'You must be weary, Mrs Gower. I'll leave you to your
rest. Perhaps we will meet again tomorrow.'

Not if I can help it, she thought. But she smiled,
shielding her dark eyes coquettishly with her long lashes.
Ralph Etwall pressed her hand and wished her a good
night. The door closed on them. Soon Simone would be
coming to help her to bed, and with any luck, to sleep.
She sighed. Perhaps tomorrow would bring fresh hope,
and with luck the redcoat would stay well away.

Her fingers stole up to the emerald and drew it up on
its chain. The green stone caught the light balefully.
Their future, Toby had called it. There would be enough
from this to set her up in fine style, for a time. Until she
found something else, something better. But at least she
had a choice . . . a chance to pick and choose.

The door had opened before she knew it, and she
stared at Lieutenant Rowe in startled surprise. 'I'm
sorry to intrude again, Mrs Gower,' he said, 'I . . .' His
voice trailed off, and his brows drew down. He continued to stare as he came forward and, bending down,
gently took the emerald between his fingers. 'May I?'
but he already had. He studied the stone, still frowning.
He was too close. Good God, she could see the fine,
fair stubble where he had missed shaving! And smell
tobacco. His skin was smooth, made dark gold by the

sun, almost the colour of his hair. This close, his eyes
weren't so dark as she had thought, but a lighter grey,
with darker lashes . . . With a shock she realised he was
looking straight at her.

'Quite flawless,' he said softly. 'Indian, is it?'

'I—Indian?' she whispered, stammering like a fool.

'Yes,' he weighed the stone in his hand. 'Someone
once described something like this to me; he had seen it
in Madras and brought it back to New South Wales.' He
seemed to lean even closer. 'It is yours, isn't it?'

'I . . . My husband gave it to me.' Well, that was near
enough to the truth!

His breath stirred her hair. 'He must have been a
remarkably wealthy man. I've only ever heard of one
other like this.'

'Oh?' she murmured, trying to portray interest. She
could feel the perspiration beading her top lip and
longed to wipe it away. But he held her effectively by the
chain about her neck.

'It belongs to a Mrs Winifrid Scott,' he said. 'I've
heard it described minutely.'

'Oh?'

'The friend I spoke of found a ready purchaser in her.
I would have thought you had seen it too, seeing as your
husband was such a leading light in Sydney Town.'

'I . . . She . . .' She must be weaker than she thought
to act such a fool! If only she had been prepared for this
cross-examination.

His mouth twitched. 'Oh?' he mocked.

He was making fun of her. She tried to pull away, her
eyes filling with tears. But he held the emerald still, and
she only hurt herself on the chain. He was looking at her
curiously, and as suddenly as he had lifted up stone, he
let it go.

'Perhaps, though, you find her company as boring as
my friend did,' he said blandly. 'She speaks of nothing
but her nephew the Chief Justice. Still, when one's as

rich as she, most will put up with boredom.' He smiled, and gently wiped his forefinger over her top lip. He had straightened before she could move, and strode again to the door. She held her breath as he turned, his face suddenly grim.

'It would be a difficult thing to sell, though, a stone like that. Especially in that setting. And the penalties for such a theft must be very high. Still, perhaps you should keep it in a safer place.' Again he smiled. 'Greed sometimes over-rides all fears of punishment.'

Rage, effectively silent until now, flared up. She rose, oblivious of trembling legs and her attire. 'There could be no safer place!'

He laughed, and still laughing, shut the door.

She stood turned to stone for a moment, and then fell back into the chair with a cry. Oh God, oh God, he mustn't know! He was guessing, teasing, tricking. How could he know? Her act was perfect: there was no way they could know she was lying. She closed her eyes. She had been right about the stone; it was an ill omen. If she didn't need the money so desperately, she would take it to the window now and throw it out into the sea. It was only as she lay in her bed at last that she realised Lieutenant Rowe had forgotten to tell her exactly why he'd come back so abruptly into her room.

CHAPTER TWO

BESSY HAD had Mary Anne's only dress washed and pressed, but it would never again be the same. Tarlatan was not a cloth that benefited from a prolonged soaking in salt water. Besides, the sleeves had had to be shortened because of the tears and rents. Still, for the moment it must do, and she had worn worse. As well as the dress, there were borrowed stockings, and some shabby shoes purloined from Simone. Hairpins for her hair, and a hand-woven shawl to pin about her shoulders.

The final effect was unusual, to say the least. She stared back at herself from the mirror, a sparkle lurking in her eyes. At least, she thought wryly, the bloody Lieutenant hadn't dimmed that sparkle, despite his threats and half-threats. Of course, what she should have done was order him out of her room, deny all and, maybe for good measure, faint. Still, it was no good fretting on the past. Time enough to deal with him before it was time to ship to Hobart.

Bessy came to frown at her uncertainly. 'Are you sure you're quite well enough, Mary Anne, to be out and about?'

'Quite well enough.' The room had become a prison, a prison she longed to escape. She had grieved for Toby and, inside, always would. But she must now start surveying her surroundings, deciding on her future. Her life depended upon it.

Her room was in the attic. The landing was narrow, made even narrower by a row of shelves pressed to the wall. There were three doors giving on to it. The stairs, hard to the wall, were also narrow, and steep. The

shadows were darker here, away from the views of the
sea, and Mary Anne picked her way carefully down the
rather shabby carpet. The walls, too, were faded. As
worn and old as Ralph's boots.

The narrow stairs ended in a hall, with doors leading
into rooms which led into each other. The effect was of
space, when in fact the rooms were rather small and
crowded. But Bessy seemed so proud as she showed her
through, that Mary Anne forced honeyed compliments
to her tongue. It would seem merely churlish to mention
ungainly furnishings and shabbiness of curtains and
chair-covers. The Etwalls were a long way from
civilisation, after all.

Beneath the windows were odd raised circles in the
wall, and when Mary Anne bent closer she discovered
them to be actually circular covers fixed over holes to the
outside.

Bessy's voice sounded close to her shoulder. 'Every
isolated settlement here knows the value of preparation.
We're aware of the dangers; we must be ready. If the
house were ever attacked, we would fire our rifles
through these.'

'Surely Lieutenant Rowe would take control, in the
event of an attack of some sort.'

The blue eyes flickered to the window. 'His past
record doesn't promote confidence.'

'His past record?'

But Bessy had moved away, saying, 'If you're not too
tired, I'd like to show you our garden.'

The garden was at the marshy side of the house,
protected by a shoulder-high stone wall. The ground was
soft and seemed good; Bessy explained that it had been
brought in to cover poorer stuff. There were some
vegetables and a small herb patch. A wooden gate led
out to the surrounding flat grass-covered land. Mary
Anne saw a wooden barn and a pen, and a number of
small cottages huddled together further towards the

marshy side of the bay. Beyond, the coast jutted out and
hid the opening to the sea. This place, at least, offered
some shelter from the savage storms and the Antarctic
winds. There wasn't much cleared land, and fewer
crops. A few cows and a goat or two were tethered on the
patchy grass, and there was a horse closer to the cottages. Otherwise nature held sway. The trees started
where the hills began to slope towards the sky. The
marsh was tree-studded too, wiry, black-looking trees,
twisting together in a silent agony. On the other side of
the house, beyond the beach, were more trees and
scrub, where rocks did not prohibit the luxuriant
growth. A sort of track seemed to run along the fore-
shore, but the sun was still to rise far beyond the hills,
and the shadows hid it from Mary Anne's gaze.

Bessy led her round the outside of the house. It was
sturdy, a flat façade with small windows. The roof was
sharp, to rid it of snow in the winter. 'We've planted
some apple trees here, and pear trees,' Bessy called.
They grew a little way further on, a bare-limbed orchard
set well back from the shore. There was a well-worn
track here, wide enough for a cart. Mary Anne could
now see that it ran two ways, one of them following the
shore, the other vanishing up into the trees.

The sound of someone whistling drew her eyes back
towards the house, and a man digging the turf. Bessy
followed her look.

'That's Perkins,' she said dismissively. 'He's useful
round the house, when he wants to be.'

The man must have heard her, and yet he played deaf.
Mary Anne watched him curiously. He was a little,
wizened man, shabby in a worn shirt and trousers. The
flesh on his arms and face was dark, leathered by cold
winds and the outdoor life. His eyes, when Bessy's
commanding call reached him, were dark and narrowed.
He had the face of a thief, sly and untrustworthy. Mary
Anne watched him approach somewhat uneasily. 'Like'

recognised and was drawn to 'like'; it was a well-known fact.

He walked with a stoop, and when Bessy introduced her as 'Mrs Gower', he jerked his head in recognition, ignoring her outstretched hand.

'Got to get down to the beach,' he said, looking past them to the bay. 'There'll be pickings washed up by now.'

'Pickings?' Mary Anne whispered.

The black eye lifted and caught hers, shining with its slipperiness. The wrinkles on his cheeks creased up, a strand of grey hair fell from under his faded, oily cap. 'Pickings from the wreck. There's always pickings. That's always the way of it. The rich get the prize, and the rest of us make do with the pickings.'

'The prize?' she repeated after a moment. The eyes slid away, the slit of a mouth quirked. He ducked his head and hobbled on his way, while Mary Anne stared after him.

'I'd have him thrashed,' Bessy said, her frown ageing her by ten years. 'But he's so used to the lash, it no longer causes him any hurt.'

'I suppose one *would* get used to . . . to the lash.'

Bessy's eyebrows lifted. 'By the way, Mrs Gower, it's not the thing—one does not offer one's hand to a man of Perkins's standing.'

Mary Anne flushed. 'I'm sorry, I . . .'

But Bessy waved her hand, obviously satisfied with making her point. Mary Anne stood for a moment, watching. Beyond her, Perkins had started down the track along the shore. There were two men in red coats coming towards him, and when he reached them, they paused. One was tall, with red hair flaming against the grey hillside behind him. The other was smaller and darker. Perkins waved his arm, and they all turned. They were looking at her. The small, dark soldier laughed.

'McDonald and Hagetty,' Bessy murmured. Her voice was edged with impatience, but Mary Anne pretended not to notice. She had already been ticked off once this morning, and once was enough.

'Are the soldiers billeted in the house?'

'Thank the Lord, no. Lieutenant Rowe has a cottage. Over there.' She waved towards the trees up from the beach. 'The other two bivouac where they please.'

The three men were still talking. About her, Mary Anne was sure. And the 'pickings'. The 'prize' was evidently meant to be her. Horrible little man! Still —her lips twitched—she liked him, in an odd sort of way. He was a scoundrel, and you knew where you were with scoundrels.

Bessy brought her back round the house, to the land side. There was a stone building at the back, joined by a covered-in passage to the house itself. The kitchen quarters. Bessy informed her. The distance of the passage was because of the chance of fire. Presumably if the kitchen and cook went up in flames, they could deal with them more easily without fear of the house going up too.

'Perkins's daughter cooks for us,' Bessy said.

'Oh?'

'His wife died in Hobart. Or so he says. He and his daughter are of a kind.'

Which sounded ominious, Mary Anne decided, as Bessy opened the heavy door to the kitchen. The heat of the place hit them with force, and she realised suddenly how chill it was outside. The wind tossed at her skirts and hair, making her eyes water, and drying out the soft, damp ground. The bay was ruffled with white frills, and down on the track Perkins's hat went flying. Mary Anne was smiling, when Bessy closed the door again.

Perkins's daughter was big, with a voice to match. She greeted them with a loud joviality that obviously grated on Bessy. But her frowns and the occasional sarcasm, which worked so well on the more sensitive Simone,

were wasted on Joan Perkins. She wrung Mary Anne's
hand with a will, her eyes gleaming. 'Someone up there
must have been lookin' out for you, Mrs Gower.'

'Amen,' murmured Bessy coolly.

'I mean, to be saved like that from such a storm. It's
not often anyone is.' The woman shook her big blonde
head and pounded bread dough as if it had insulted her.
Bessy clicked her tongue, and disappeared into the stone
pantry to check the supplies. Simone was in the far
corner, peeling potatoes, her untidy hair curtaining her
face. The kitchen was made of stone blocks quarried
from the rough cliffs beyond the beach, or so Bessy said.
There were rough wooden shelves near the fireplace,
and a variety of buckets and pots and utensils. A carcass
hung close to the pantry door, ready for spitting.

'Wallaby,' Joan said, jerking her head at the creature
in much the same way as her father. 'Davey shot it day
before yesterday.' For a moment the fleshy face
softened. Davey, obviously, was special.

'You don't starve here, then?'

'Oh no! We make do. A lot of the stuff we try and
grow goes rotten, of course. Too damp, you see. But we
make do, while we wait for the ship from Hobart to
come.'

The kitchen reminded Mary Anne suddenly of childhood. The heat, the loud voice, the smell of food
cooking. Even the line of unwashed grime above Joan's
collar reminded her of the past. It startled her, when
Joan spoke again.

'Of course, the Lieutenant had more than a bit to
do with it.' The dark eyes were sly—indeed she was
Perkins's daughter!

'Your being saved!' Joan added impatiently, seeing
her blank look.

'He seems to believe so,' she sounded prim. Joan
grinned, and went back to her dough.

The smell of the place was soothing; Mary Anne

allowed some of the tension to drain out of her and closed her eyes. The inn her mother had frequented had been much like this. Cosy and warm, with the glow of a fire. She had crept closer to it, and warmed her grubby hands and feet, while her mother slouched in the corner over her mug and drank herself into the wretched state she found so necessary for living. At least, they had called it an inn, but now that she knew what an inn truly was, she found it a poor comparison. A one-roomed cottage, filthy and squalid, kept illegally with a hundred others, down the dank alley of the Rocks. The inn-keeper had brewed his own liquor, a mixture of vitriol and gin, affectionately known as rot-gut.

She blinked suddenly. Joan was talking again, her eyes shining like ebony. She had plaited the dough and was wiping floury hands on her apron. '. . . disgrace, they reckon. Only place they could think of sending him next to being dishonourably discharged.' She smiled, or perhaps it was more of a leer. 'Still, he's a man and a half, is what I say. A man and a half, and I'm one what knows!'

Simone giggled, and hid her face in her apron. Mary Anne wrinkled her brow. 'Disgrace?' she repeated, trying to hazard the subject of the conversation she had missed.

'Ay! Something he did to the Governor in Hobart, or didn't do, maybe. Bloody Arthur, I say. Hard as rock, he is; doesn't care a damn what happens to anyone. But, then, who does? Look out for yourself, I say. No one else will.'

Mary Anne thought it best to remain silent.

'That's what my old man says, any rate. And he should know. He's seen enough rock to last him a lifetime,' she laughed at her joke. 'The roads, I mean,' she added, seeing Mary Anne's carefully blank stare. 'The gang. Built more roads than any man, me dad.' She laughed loud and long.

The fire spluttered. There was an elaborate arrangement of pots and pans resting on a grid over the flames. Bessy returned, keys jingling at her waist. 'We're getting low on salt,' she announced in a crisp voice, blue eyes accusing on Joan Perkins. 'Still, we've enough salt meat to see us through the winter. If need be, the soldiers will just have to shoot their own rations. I'm not wasting good food on them.'

'Why should you, indeed?' Joan murmured, winking at Mary Anne. 'Just because the army sends special supplies for 'em doesn't mean we have to give it to 'em.'

Bessy snorted; she had already reached the door.

'Still, I wouldn't like to tangle with our Lieutenant,' Joan went on, smiling with, Mary Anne decided disgustedly, fond memories. 'He's a man and a half, that one!'

Outside, the air was twice as cold. It stung Mary Anne's pale cheeks to pink, and whipped away her breath. 'Joan Perkins thinks she's indispensable to us,' Bessy was saying. 'Rattle-brain! And convict blood in addition. Unfortunately, the isolation of Etwall does not appeal to those with a free will.'

'I should think it pays well. Doesn't the money attract decent men and women?'

Bessy looked approvingly at her. 'Decent' had been carefully selected for that purpose. If Bessy liked her, Bessy would talk. Mary Anne needed respectable people behind her.

'The timber, of course, brings in a fair price. The colony is crying out for it, especially our famous Huon pine. But we are so far away and everything costs so much more to ship in and out.'

Toby, Mary Anne thought, would have spoken now about profit and loss and the intricacies of balance books. But Mary Anne knew little of finance. That had been Toby's side of the partnership: he had always been the one to unpick human locks, to open the closed ledgers. For Mary Anne, the flirtations and smiles and the distraction. As Toby had said often enough, she was the sweet syrup into which the flies blundered, the succulent morsel tempting the victim a little closer, and a little closer, until it was too late, and the spider had them. And Toby was, of course, the spider.

Only Toby was gone, and she was alone.

Mary Anne had a headache when they went back into the house. It was a relief to lie down in her small room and close her eyes. Her arm hurt, too, and though Bessy seemed satisfied with its healing, she longed to take a peek at the bruised flesh, just to be sure. And there were other worries. A whole list of them, to torment her as she tried to sleep.

The future, looming so uncertain; the length of her stay at Etwall. Perhaps she need not leave, if she found everything to her liking. And there was Nick, the brother, who liked the clatter of the town and yet had retired to the solitude of the timber settlement. Nick might well be a replacement for Toby . . . at least a replacement for part of him. And then there was the Lieutenant and his insinuations—from what Joan hinted, he had as many dark secrets as she. So what right had he to threaten her over the emerald?

Her fingers stole up to the chain, satisfying themselves it was still safe. It was. She sighed and settled more comfortably into the mattress. Perhaps it was all a mistake. It must be. He had been guessing—it amused him to be cruel. He was a rogue, like Perkins, and a disgraced rogue to boot. It was a mistake, and she would not think about it any more.

Simone came with the growing shadows, and silently proffered one of Bessy's dark woollen gowns. It was too big, and old-fashioned, but a tuck here and a flounce there might make it a little less uncomfortable. Mary Anne was used to good clothes; they were a part of the trade. Why should she be ashamed of enjoying the feel of silk and satin, the whisper of creamy skirts, the tap of pretty slippers over soft stockings? She loved to dress for her part. It was just a pity her part at the moment involved pathos.

Simone helped her to dress in silence, and a comment on the weather met with a faint, far-away smile. The girl was curious enough, however. Mary Anne turned and found the yellow eyes on her more than once, but when she tried to hold them with her own, they slid away.

Her head still ached. The sleep had done little to relieve her worries. She was tempted to say she was too ill to come down, and go back to bed. Still, it was best to see the lie of the land, and if that meant playing a part, the show must go on. Besides, the only way to prove bloody Lieutenant Rowe wrong was to face him, and that she must do.

Simone led her down the stairs to what Bessy grandly called the parlour. It was small, with chairs and a writing desk. There was a whale-oil lamp on a side table, and Bessy was sewing by it. She laid the stitchery aside, however, when Mary Anne arrived in the room. Sparse, practical stitchery, without frills—like Bessy herself.

'I will have some gowns dyed for you,' she said crisply, eyeing Mary Anne's appearance. 'And Simone can take some tucks here and there. The girl's well enough with a needle, if you tell her what to do.'

'Dyed?'

'For your mourning!'

'Oh!' She bowed her head. Toby would laugh at that. Mourning for such a smooth-tongued liar as he? He had lived his life to the full, so why should anyone mourn him? Still, she owed him more than *her* life. Mary Anne smiled grimly.

There was the sound of hooves, she realised, outside on the soft ground. The jingle of harness, mingling with voices calling. Bessy rose again, setting her stitchery aside and smoothing her dowdy skirts. Her eyes flashed to Mary Anne; her smile was uncertain. In the hall, boots echoed, coming closer. Someone laughed. And then the door was opened.

Ralph looked as tired and rumpled as before. His sparse brown hair stuck to his brow, where he had washed over-hastily. Behind him, another man, taller, with black hair more luxuriant than his brother's. His features were similar, but sunburned, and a nose hooked a little like a hawk's beak above thinner, smiling lips. Mary Anne met his eyes, and watched his dark brows rise slightly in acknowledgment of her own smile. 'Nick,' Ralph was also smiling, 'you've yet to meet our . . . guest. Mrs Gower, my brother Nicholas.'

'My pleasure.' His voice was deep and smooth, and he bent over her hand with practised ease. His eyes were blue, like his brother's, only harder, and the flesh round his mouth was scoured with two deep lines. He would be thirty-seven at least, and he looked what he was—a rake.

She recognised the type instantly, and at the same time the pieces clicked into place. Nick had returned from the clatter, Ralph had told her, because 'needs must'. He had run out of money, and been forced to come to Etwall. Debts were pressing, and what safer place to escape them than Etwall? The man was a gambler, a user of other people. Life was to be squeezed for all it could yield, and then tossed aside like a wrung sponge. And yet such a man could be a fine companion, even a finer husband, and they were often able to make incredible fortunes in even more incredible periods of time.

Nick had stepped aside, his lazy smile lingering as his eyes slid round to Bessy. His stance was a little derogatory, but Bessy was oblivious to it. Her blue eyes blatantly adored him.

Beyond Nick was another man. 'Mrs Gower.' Grey eyes full of dying laughter. The red coat was creaseless over his shoulders, the buttons shone. He nodded at her with a briskness she found insulting, and irritating. Last night, seated, she had been more at ease. Now, standing before him, she felt threatened. The eyes assessed too coolly, too fully. Whereas she could cope and hold her own with Nick Etwall's smiling glance, she found herself disarmed by the Lieutenant.

Because I don't know what he's thinking, she told herself severely, and I should. I should!

'I see you're wearing your emerald, Mrs Gower,' he said.

She touched it, despite herself. 'Is there any reason why I should not? There was little else I saved from the *Infanta*.'

He feigned surprise.

'It was a gift from my husband. I told you.'

'A fine, sober and upstanding man, I'm sure.'

It was said softly enough, in a manner most people would have believed sincere. But Mary Anne saw the devil in his eyes and knew it for mockery. 'A better man I have yet to discover,' she said rather breathlessly, her anger beating in her breast.

The eyes observed, mocking, and shifted away. Bessy cleared her throat. 'Joan has dinner ready now. Shall we go into the dining-room?'

Nick offered Mary Anne his arm. The blue eyes scanned her face with admiration, and she smiled. Nick's hand gripped her arm the tighter; she felt the pulse under the harsh stuff of his brown jacket.

'You have my deepest sympathy for your affliction, Mrs Gower,' he said, bending close to her.

She lowered her lashes and sighed, the sadness moving like a shadow over the gaiety of her heart.

'We must do all we can to make the burden easier.'

'You're very kind,' she murmured, and smiled again. 'Very kind.'

The black brows rose, giving her the impression of a

bird of prey. Apt, she thought grimly. He certainly meant to prey on her, but whether for her body or her money she had yet to ascertain. Still, she was not averse to a little flirtation—it kept her in practice!

The dining-room was narrow, quite long, with thick curtains to close out the darkness and muffle the force of the wind against the shutters. It had sprung up with night, and brought with it the wail of the sea. A bitter, salty wind. Was Etwall, she wondered, always so bleak?

Simone served the meal, efficient in her silence, her untidy hair restrained beneath a white cap. The girl's yellow eyes rested upon them all—like all servants, she saw and heard everything. Life lived second-hand, Toby used to say of them.

'Even at Etwall the formalities are observed.'

The comment was too soft for the others to hear. It was meant exclusively for her. Mary Anne turned her head stiffly, coldly, to return Lieutenant Rowe's stare. He was seated beside her, a fact she had discovered to her dismay as they took their places. She would have preferred Nick Etwall—at least she knew how to parry his barbs.

The grey eyes mocked her, too close for her liking, and reflected the light of the lamps, one at either end of the table. 'Don't you find it a little ridiculous? To sit down to all the trimmings, when outside . . .'

'We'd be no better than the savages without the formalities, Lieutenant,' Mary Anne retorted.

Bessy was straining to hear their conversation above that of the two brothers, who were deep in some other topic. 'I trust there are no savages left at Etwall,' she said now, staring coldly at him.

The man smiled; that one-sided smile Mary Anne so detested. 'Don't you find it a little meaningless, Mrs Gower?'

'Meaningless?' Bessy demanded.

'The Lieutenant perhaps is more used to living
"rough", as they say,' Mary Anne said swiftly. 'I believe
some people do feel awed by silver cutlery and finger-
bowls.'

He laughed at that, a low laugh of pure amusement.
So she amused him, did she? She gritted her teeth until
he finished, and Bessy's polite smile faded. Nick, across
the table, was watching them, tapping the fingers of one
hand beside his plate. The blue eyes rested on the
emerald about her throat. How often had she seen Toby
look just so?

'Perhaps you're right,' that mocking, laughter-filled
voice said at her side. 'Perhaps you should cling to the
conventions, Mrs Gower. They're your only protection
in this place.'

She pondered that a while, but dismissed it to compliment Bessy on the meal. It would have been more to the
point to compliment Joan, but that would not be the
done thing. The cooking was plain but perfection. She
let her eyes wander round the table. Nicholas was
bending attentively to Bessy, his lined face full of polite
interest. He caught Mary Anne's glance, and smiled.
Women, for him, were for taking and leaving. Still, he
had his own attractions, and if he was a replacement for
Toby . . . Not a replacement, she reminded herself
sharply. Never that.

Ralph and Lieutenant Rowe were discussing convicts.
The Lieutenant looked stern, almost grim. '. . . human
dignity,' he was saying. 'Surely brutality breeds like?'

Ralph sighed and shook his head. 'What will you have
of us? Crime must be punished, and the harsher the
punishment, the less likely crime is to thrive.'

Simone had come to take the plates and serve the fruit
syllabub and thick cream. Nick flicked her a bored
glance, and turned back to his brother. Lieutenant
Rowe winked at her, sending colour scudding into her
pale cheeks. Mary Anne sniffed in disgust and turned

her shoulder. One didn't need two eyes to see for what reason the Lieutenant was in disgrace!

'Simone and I help each other.'

She stared attentively at Nick and Ralph, trying to follow their conversation. Something about timber hauling. But the voice she was beginning to hate at her side would not be silent.

'Are you interested in commerce, Mrs Gower?'

'I find it enthralling,' she retorted, not looking at him.

'Good Lord, don't tell me I rescued a pinch-penny! Better I had left you to the ocean, madam.'

She was so surprised she turned to stare, and he met her eyes. He had meant her to look, of course. Baited the hook, and caught her. The grey eyes danced with the victory, and suddenly he leaned closer. 'Mrs Gower,' he murmured, 'do you know your eyes overshadow that emerald you wear?'

The look in *his* eyes brought the colour aching into her cheeks, and when she managed to drag her gaze from his, her hands were trembling. Did the fool actually imagine . . . Did he really think that she would . . . Good God, he was more of a rake than Nick Etwall threatened to be! Disgraced, Joan had said. Disgraced and sent here in preference to being cashiered. The man was mad, and, moreover, a soldier! She'd rather be dead than let him within ten miles of her. How dared he?

She managed to steady herself enough to look up at Nicholas. 'Tell me,' she said, her voice strengthening. 'Surely the logs are too big to load on a ship?'

The black eyebrows lifted a little mockingly, as she had expected. 'We saw them up first, Mrs Gower. There are saw-pits, and two men do the sawing. One stands on top, and the unlucky one stands beneath, in the pit, and they each work an end of the saw. When the ship comes, the pieces are floated out and hauled aboard. I don't think I've missed anything, have I, brother?'

'I think not,' Ralph retorted, smiling.

Mary Anne smiled back, 'Oh, I see.'

'I suppose life has been very different for you?' Ralph offered kindly. 'You haven't had to worry about saws and trees and the like.'

'Very different!'

'You must educate us about the ways of the polite world,' Nick retorted, mock-serious, and she laughed.

'Minx,' Toby had said once. 'You play them all against each other like counters in a game. Or are you paying them all back for your childhood?'

She had refused to believe him at the time, but perhaps, after all, it was true. Had not some nameless, faceless man given her life and left as easily as he came, reducing her mother to such a sodden lump? Had she not learned from that same mother that men were the source of all pain and bitterness in her world?

'But I want no vengeance,' she had told Toby. 'I don't feel glad . . . except for a job well done.'

Toby had laughed at her, flicking her cheek. 'All to the good. Otherwise I might lose you to some handsome young money-bags. Keep your heart to yourself, girl, and you'll always be safe.' Sound advice, even if he had ignored it himself. Always in and out of love, was Toby. Always breaking hearts, his own included.

'Sydney Town,' Nick said.

She shook herself out of her reverie. 'Do you know it?'

'I've been there. I've been most places. Where did you live?'

'Oh, Woolloomooloo,' she said enthusiastically. 'Such a fine view down over the harbour! Of course, my childhood was mostly spent out in the country. My father owned land, and . . . do you know of him? He's almost as famous as John Macarthur, in Parramatta, you know. It was he thought of the idea of merino sheep. Not Mr Macarthur, as everyone would now have us believe.'

'Indeed?' Bessy's blue eyes were alive with admiration.

'Yes, he was. He decided to import sheep from somewhere or other across the seas, and interbreed them and build a better . . . strain, I suppose. They were most successful. My father always told me it was his idea first, and of course everyone there knew. I remember Mr Macarthur visiting, when I was a girl, and my father being so cool towards him. For, of course, he had taken all the credit. This was before I went to school. Misses Pinkerton's Academy, in George Street.'

'The Misses Pinkerton?' Lieutenant Rowe's grey eyes were quizzical.

'Yes.'

'In George Street, you say?'

She frowned. 'Yes.'

'I must admit the place escapes me. I spent a number of years myself in that town, and . . . in George Street? You're quite sure?'

Her face was cold—inside her heart was colder. Her tongue had run away again; an audience, especially an appreciative one, tended to have that effect. 'Yes,' she whispered.

'Near the corner of Elizabeth Street?'

'I . . .' She looked away, but everyone was intent upon her and there was no escape. No Toby to laugh and change the subject, no Toby to extract her from this mess. 'I don't remember.'

'I think I know the one you mean.' He frowned with thought, then abruptly hit his palm on the table, making her jump. 'I do! A large, red-brick building.'

'I believe . . . Yes.' She was so relieved that she beamed at him.

'Or was it sandstone? No, red brick. And a portico, with steps leading up.'

'Yes.' Her smile wavered. 'With great doors and . . . and, I think, a bow window.'

'Bow? Are you sure?'

Nick Etwall laughed without humour. 'I'm sure we're all very interested in the Misses Pinkerton, but . . .'

Lieutenant Rowe ignored him. 'You're right, of course,' he said. 'A bow window it was. It was the older Miss Pinkerton who ran the place; the younger was an invalid.'

She said nothing to that, and after a moment Nick took up the conversation again, leading it to Britain, and politics. Mary Anne sat dumbly in her chair. He knew. He was playing with her, tormenting her like a cat a mouse. What now? What was she to do now?

After what seemed a lifetime, they rose from the table and returned to the parlour. Lieutenant Rowe opened the door for her. 'What a pleasure it is,' he said softly, 'to find someone who remembers Sydney Town as well as oneself.'

Her glance was vitriol. He smiled.

The three men brought out some cards, while Bessy took up her stitchery again. Mary Anne was invited to make a fourth, and gladly joined. Concentrating on one's game left little room for light conversation. She was a passable player, relying more upon intuition and luck than careful planning. Nick let her win several hands, and Ralph let her win at least three. Lieutenant Rowe beat her at every turn, and when they played for coin, totted up his winnings in a totally ungentleman-like fashion. He was brisk and practical. Crude, she decided —and hated him intensely.

'My game again, I think.' The grey eyes mocked her. He knew what she thought, without her uttering a word. He had assessed her and labelled her, and there was no escape. He knew. The dismal hope she had allowed herself to entertain, that perhaps he was lying about the emerald, and perhaps there really were Misses Pinkerton in George Street, was crushed. He knew, and would no doubt in time, when the fancy took him, when his lust for cruelty had wearied, expose her for what she was.

The game was pointless. She rose, excusing herself with commendable steadiness. Nick gave her a lingering goodnight, and Lieutenant Rowe followed her.

'There's no need,' she said sharply, as he opened the door.

His expression was grim. All trace of mockery and humour gone from his mouth and eyes. 'If I knew your intentions, Mrs Gower, I could perhaps help you to steer clear of more . . . dangerous waters,' he said in a clipped voice, very different from his previous tones.

A pause, then she took a breath. 'I have no idea what you mean.' Her eyes were hard—hard with fear and hatred, the hatred of an animal cornered.

He scanned her face for a moment that seemed an age. 'Your dislike means nothing to me,' he said finally. 'I deal in facts, not feelings. Remember it.' He nodded briskly and turned away, her enemy.

She climbed the stairs wearily to her room, wondering what that warning had meant. Had he been offering help? He? As if she would even consider it! The military were not to be trusted, never to be believed and certainly not to be helped by. She wished suddenly, fervently, that she could learn to hold her tongue.

CHAPTER THREE

SHE WOKE to the morning and someone laughing. The sound echoed above the twitter of the birds, and she started up, her hair in disarray. Outside, mist was creeping over the ground, swirling like milk in the rising breeze from the sea. The bay, too, was white-covered, secret. The cottages close to the marsh were barely visible, the smoke from their chimneys hanging still and grey.

Mary Anne stretched her arms and smiled. As if on cue, the sun slid from beneath a bank of clouds and set the world alight. All problems seemed capable of being solved today: her head was clear, her arm wasn't throbbing. The laughter came again, and she looked down over the front of the house. Joan's fair head bobbed up over the slope to the water's edge. Her face was pink with exertion, and when she had scrambled to the safety of the bank and stood panting a moment, another head appeared. The black one of Hagetty. He, too, was laughing. Abruptly, Mary Anne drew the curtains, her happy mood fading a little. It seemed that everyone had someone, except her.

Ralph and Bessy Etwall were in the dining-room. They looked up and greeted her so warmly that, just for a moment, something inside her twisted. As if, for that moment, she truly was what she had pretended herself to be. As if she truly belonged here, with these people, in their world. The illusion was shattered as swiftly as it had grown. She was a slum child, and a bastard. If they once smelt that fact . . .

'There was no need for you to come down,' Bessy was saying. 'Simone was to take you a tray . . .'

'I can't lie in bed all day! I'm used to being up and busy.'

'But you're our guest,' Ralph admonished gently.

She smiled. 'Well, now I'm down, I may as well stay down.'

Nick wasn't there, and Mary Anne felt a little disappointed. She rather enjoyed sparring with him. She felt she already knew him, as she had known Toby. Still, perhaps it was as well not to push herself at him. Time enough for that—the ship was still a long way away.

Ralph left her with Bessy, who immediately launched into a conversation on his 'unworldliness' as she called it. 'Etwall is the only thing he thinks about these days,' she said, lines of discontent drawing down her mouth. 'He's a good man, I know, but sometimes he doesn't seem to know what's happening under his very nose.'

Was anything happening? Mary Anne wondered idly. She had seen Bessy looking adoringly at her brother-in-law, that was all. But then looks did not mean deeds, and Nick had seemed bored with her. Never had she seen a place with so many undercurrents as Etwall. But then she had never experienced so isolated and insulated a place.

'He tells me,' Bessy went on after a moment, 'you think as we do, about Lieutenant Rowe's intervention in our affairs.'

'Indeed I do!' Mary Anne could not quite suppress the dislike in her voice. But Bessy seemed to approve of it, and nodded.

'The man becomes more insufferable by the moment. I'd refuse to speak with him altogether, only I'm afraid that would make him worse. He's the sort who would turn to petty revenge, and as things stand there's little he couldn't do. And always with the support of the Governor, while he wears that uniform.'

'But if he's disgraced, surely a complaint in the right quarters would have him removed?'

Bessy sighed. 'We've written already to friends. Nick has a number of contacts in the government in Hobart. He was in the army himself once, you know. But he sold out. Too deadly dull, he says.' She smiled a little at the memory. 'So, you see, he has friends there he can write to and request our deliverance from this man.'

'But he's still here.'

'Yes,' she muttered. 'He's still here.'

Mary Anne knew what was coming next. As Bessy opened her mouth to repeat her husband's request, she plunged desperately into a story of her father's similar troubles with the army, in the form of the New South Wales Corps. Bessy, impressed, listened in flattering silence. By the time she was done, Lieutenant Rowe was forgotten, and breakfast was long finished.

'I forgot!' Bessy started up. 'I meant to visit Leah Connor. Her husband's one of the timber workers. She's ill again.' She shrugged. 'She's always ill.'

'Poor woman,' Mary Anne murmured.

'Perhaps, now you're up, you'd like to come with me?'

The Connors' cottage was one of the several grouped together near the marshy shore. Smoke drifted up from roughly-made chimneys, and hens ran squawking before them. Leah was in the furthest, a slab cottage, small and compact, with bark jammed into any cracks that might let in the cold draughts. The ground was trampled hard at the door, and inside too, contrasting sharply with the spongy ground elsewhere. A fire burned in a fairly large fireplace, with a pot suspended over the coals. It seemed crowded, and over-warm. For Mary Anne it was a reminder of the hardship and poverty she had left behind.

Mrs Connor lay on a bench that served as a bed, her cheeks flushing like a child's at the sight of Bessy Etwall. A slight woman, delicately boned, with fine fair hair. Her abdomen was distended with her unborn child. It was as if, Mary Anne thought, the life within was

burning away the life outside. Two other children,
sturdy boys, stood suspiciously by the doorway.
Neither returned Mary Anne's friendly smile.

'I'm not well,' the soft voice complained. 'Not at all
well, Mrs Etwall.'

'I've brought you some eggs and milk, Leah.'

'Thank you, you're very kind. Ah, so kind.'

The voice was subservient. Almost grovelling. No
matter how poor she had been, Mary Anne had never
grovelled, and she found it distasteful to listen to Leah
Connor. Instead, she glanced about her. The windows
were small, and shuttered with wooden slats. Faint light
trickled through, thick with dust-motes. A table leaned
dangerously to one side, and a bucket stood in the
corner, its function sending Mary Anne's curious gaze
darting back to the bed.

Leah Connor had heaved herself into a half-sitting
position, her soft, pretty face turned in Mary Anne's
direction. 'Mrs Gower, is it? Ay, they said you was a
pretty one, and so you are.'

Bessy clicked her tongue, but Mary Anne laughed.

Leah Connor's own pale lips smiled, the eyes bright
and a little anxious. 'You take care now, Mrs Gower.
Things aren't safe.' Her eyelids, flickered, and she lay
down again. 'Mrs Etwall?' she murmured.

Bessy stepped forward, bending closer. They spoke a
moment in low voices. Mary Anne wandered outside,
ignoring the sullen faces of the two boys. The mist had
cleared, the bay stood softly ruffled with a strengthening
breeze. Seabirds, over near the rocks on the far side,
shrieked like tormented souls, their cries muted by the
distance. They sounded like echoes of those Mary Anne
had heard aboard *Infanta*. She wrapped her shawl closer
about her shoulders, and turned again towards the
untidy cottage.

The whole group of dwellings smelt of poverty, as
though the occupants were used to struggling to live and

expected nothing more than struggle. It seemed a shame that the Etwalls could not have built something more stolid and comforting for their employees.

'There's cold weather coming,' Bessy said, close beside her. She flicked a practised glance over the scene. A pause.

'Is Mr Connor a convict?' Mary Anne asked.

'The next thing to it. He's got his ticket-of-leave, but he was a convict. Poor Leah has had a deal to burden her besides ill-health. Still, she's brought much of it on herself. She insisted on coming here with him, when Ralph hired him. I would have thought she'd be better off back in Hobart with her two sons, living on the money he sent her, instead of living here at Etwall, among rough and tumbles like Joan Perkins and her father, and bearing more children to the man.'

It was bitterly said, and Mary Anne wondered whether Bessy herself would have liked a child. She asked, 'Who else lives here, in these cottages?'

'The ticket-of-leave men, and the free men live here. The actual convicts remain up at the timber camp. There are quarters for them there.'

'I should very much like to see the timber camp.'

Bessy smiled. 'Nick will show you, I'm sure, if you ask him.' Her smile broadened. 'Ralph and I are so glad to have him back again. Poor Ralph. His idea of controlling the convicts is to close his eyes to them. If it wasn't for Davey, the foreman . . . But Nick knows about such things. He knows about discipline.'

'Indeed?'

'Fear is the only way to keep a man in line. Fear and pain. Without them, there would be nothing to deter him from refusing to work.'

It was obvious that Lieutenant Rowe knew all about fear and pain. He had caused Mary Anne enough of both. In fact, she couldn't see why the Etwalls so resented him, when he was very good at his job.

They started back towards the house. There were a few women about now, in drab old skirts and shawls, to whom Bessy nodded without speaking. They lowered their eyes, in mock-respect, but there was nothing of respect in their set faces and thinned lips. Mary Anne was not surprised. Conditions were hardly rosy, and Bessy's lady-of-the-manor attitudes didn't help. They must loathe her almost as much as they loathed Etwall!

They had reached the walled garden, and were about to go in through the gate when Bessy paused. Her shoulders stiffened, her fingers tightened on the basket she carried. Her breath hissed out between her lips. She was, Mary Anne thought uneasily, like a badly startled cat not sure whether to pounce or turn and run.

'Jezebel!'

For a moment Mary Anne imagined Bessy was using the biblical name as a curse, and didn't reply. But Bessy spun round to face her, the colour drained a little from her face.

'She's come to satisfy her curiosity about you. I didn't think it would be long.'

Frowning, Mary Anne looked beyond her. It seemed absurd, and she blinked a little, expecting to see a monster at least. But it was only a woman. A woman with red hair and a blue gown, making her way towards them from the direction of the sturdy barn.

'That's Jezebel?' she said in puzzlement.

Bessy bit her lip. 'Yes.' Her eyes, turned suddenly to Mary Anne, were hard with triumph, a gleaming, almost malicious satisfaction. 'And this time, Mary Anne, I hold the trump card.'

The woman was close enough now for her to make out details. Mary Anne did so, curiously. An oval, creamy face framed by abundant red-gold hair. Blue eyes, soft and pale, like a dawn sky just fading from gold. She was beautiful, her figure moulded by the cloth of the gown, the halo of her hair against the grey sky. There was a rustle of petticoats as she drew to a halt in front of them, and pale pink lips curved over sharp white teeth. Freckles sprinkled her nose, like gold-dust.

'I came to see the mermaid,' she said, almost a purr.

'Mrs Gower is tired, Belle,' Bessy replied stiffly. 'I was taking her back to the house to rest.'

Belle's eyes scanned Mary Anne. 'She should think herself lucky to be able to feel tired. Those other poor souls will never feel tired again. But then, when Luke sets his mind to something . . .' she shrugged her shoulders '. . . it's as good as done. Don't we know that?'

'I am most grateful to Lieutenant Rowe,' Mary Anne said carefully. The smiling face made her uneasy, as if at any moment it would begin to snarl.

'Grateful?' Belle's lips stretched further over her white teeth. 'Given some time, Mrs Gower, you might start to wish he'd let you drown. Luke Rowe has a habit of demanding payment for any favours he does.' She sounded cool, and yet beneath her smooth tones was a hint of something more. Anger? Or perhaps a threat.

'Mrs Gower doesn't associate with the likes of Luke Rowe,' Bessy said sharply, and suddenly she, too, smiled. 'She finds the company closer at hand much more congenial.'

There was a pause. The dislike Mary Anne had been aware of at the beginning of the conversation had grown apace.

'Your husband was an elderly man, Mrs Gower?'

'Not at all.'

'You must be . . . grief-stricken.' But the eyes said otherwise, and when Bessy suggested they'd best hurry if she wanted to rest before lunch, she readily agreed. Belle seemed amused by their rush to escape her and, with a smile, turned away towards the cluster of cottages. She wore, Mary Anne noted, red petticoats that gleamed like silk. The dress, too, was soft and well made. And yet, in contrast, Jezebel's voice had been untutored, her nails dirty.

Bessy said, 'That woman causes more havoc than the rest of them put together.'

'But . . .'

The blue eyes flickered to her. 'The girl, to put it bluntly, is a slut. I speak plainly to you; you're a married woman. The girl is a common whore. My brother-in-law was foolish enough to bring her with him from Hobart. Since then, she's caused nothing but trouble. She found a fitting partner in Lieutenant Rowe for a number of weeks, but unfortunately Nick proves richer game. She's set her sights on him, despite the fact that he no longer . . . cares for her.'

A pause, the wind tugged at their skirts, forcing the grass to bow before them as they stood by the gate. The large, flat area behind the house, before the forest rose brooding, lay green as the emerald around Mary Anne's neck. Some cows were cropping, picking their way steadily towards the more succulent patches near the barn. A stunted tree stood to one side, trunk bent with the constant beating of the wind from the sea.

'Poor Nick,' Bessy murmured. 'He has so little sense where women are concerned. But at least he's seen through Belle, even if it is too late to send her packing. She wanted much more than he was prepared to give her. Marriage. That's something we are all agreed must never happen.' Her face was as grim as her voice.

'But if he loved her?'

Bessy's mouth curled in scorn. 'Love? She knows nothing of that. She wants his money. And she's a slut—a convict slut. Her blood is tainted. If Nick were fool enough to marry her, it would mean social ruin for us all.'

'I see that.'

Bessy heard only the fervent agreement in Mary Anne's voice, and nothing of the bitterness in her heart.

She reached out and opened the gate, only to pause again, her eyes searching the girl's a little desperately. 'May I ask something of you? A favour?'

'Of course!' She hoped it was not beyond her capabilities!

Bessy smiled. 'I know how you must feel, about your husband, but would you spare some time for my brother-in-law? Talk with him, perhaps, draw his attention away from Jezebel. He won't listen to me, and although I doubt he would marry Belle now, she still has some influence with him. Could you do that, Mary Anne?'

Nick Etwall, handed to her on a plate! It was amusing, and her lips twitched. 'Of course,' she said, with deceptive gentleness. 'I will do everything in my power to help.'

How Toby would have laughed! After all, Bessy, in trying to save her beloved brother-in-law from the clutches of one fire, had merely eased him into another. Still, in a way, she admired Bessy for it. The woman obviously loved him, and yet she was willing to watch as Mary Anne sought his interest. Unselfish, indeed!

Simone came breathlessly to help her to dress for dinner. 'I'm sure I could dress myself,' Mary Anne said, but the girl shook her head violently, and clutching her chest, drew a long breath.

'I was late because of the cows, that is all.'

'The cows seem to cause you a great deal of trouble.'

'*Oui!* They must be milked, and I must bring them into the shed, and they do not always want to come, you see. And I must clean the shed. The cows are a great deal of trouble, madame.'

'I suppose you wish them to the devil.'

The yellow eyes flickered shyly. 'I wish them to Jezebel, madame. It is the same thing.'

Mary Anne laughed, and glanced at herself in the mirror. Lunch had been uneventful, and she had spent much of the afternoon resting. Now she felt fit and strong to face anything fate could throw at her.

Nicholas Etwall was already in the parlour when she arrived, and rose to take her hand and lead her to a chair by the window. His smile was charming, just the right flicker of the lips belying the interest in his eyes.

Oh, he was an artist indeed, thought Mary Anne. And, by all accounts, a fool where women were concerned. Was it possible a man could be blind to Belle's hard eyes? And yet had she not played that same game so many times? Men like Nick Etwall were fools where women were concerned, and clever with money. No doubt he already had some plan or other to make his fortune and returned to the clatter of the town. And if she played her cards right, she might be accompanying him.

'I was thinking about what you said about Sydney Town,' he was saying, stroking his chin with one long, brown finger. 'It sounded so full of life. I can barely remember it now. It's many years since I was there.'

'Was that when you were in the army?'

The black brows rose and he smiled his dangerously attractive smile. 'With the army, as you say. That was my brother's idea. To steady me down, do you see. The army, to steady one down!' He laughed softly, and she joined him. Their eyes met again—she felt the pull of attraction, the locking of like minds. Nick Etwall would do, he would do very well as a substitute for Toby.

'Etwall must be a marked change for you, then. After the army.'

He grimaced, taking the bait. 'Five minutes of it is enough for me. There is now one consolation, however. You.'

She glanced down without answering, her dark eyes gleaming beneath the long, curling lashes. A ringlet of dark hair lay on her shoulder and she plucked at it, smiling. 'You're very kind.'

'I'm not kind at all,' he retorted. 'And you know it.'

He was going too fast. It was one thing to know something, another to say it aloud. Don't rush a thing, Toby used to say. Go slowly, make certain of what you're doing before you do it. Build a solid wall, testing every inch of the way, and there's less chance that it'll topple down on you.

'I envy you,' he said suddenly. 'The world opens its arms wide to the rich. The rest of us most hover about on the outside, hoping to strike on some scheme to gain entry. But few ever really do.'

She laughed. 'A rather depressing philosophy, Mr Etwall!'

'But nevertheless true.'

'I should think you could think of any number of schemes to gain entry to that sort of society. Besides, there is much more to life than money, surely?'

The blue eyes slid over her lips, down to her white bosom. They lingered a moment on the emerald, before rising again to her interested gaze. 'Beautiful women, perhaps? And good wine? Not much else. I have no wish for a home and brawling brats. Nor do I long for famous paintings and fashionable décor.'

'Let me understand you correctly, then. If you were to find a beautiful woman, who was rich and owned a cellar of rare wines, you would be satisfied?'

'Ah, you know me already,' he said, and bending closer to her, added, 'I'm beginning to think I've found her.'

The words startled her. She had forgotten, for a moment, that they imagined her to be rich. More complications. It was as well, perhaps, that they didn't know the truth about her, and yet the lies would confuse her growing relationship with Nick Etwall. She struggled for a path out of the maze and was almost glad when a deep, well-remembered voice spoke her name.

'Mrs Gower.'

She looked up, the colour flying from her cheeks. Nick Etwall rose to his feet. 'Lieutenant.' Something in the blue eyes changed and hardened. Luke Rowe must have seen it, for he too allowed his gaze to grow cold. Or perhaps he had overheard part of their conversation?

'I've been waiting for a word with you,' Nick said, a belligerent note creeping into his voice. 'I believe your men spent this afternoon searching the camp. My brother was most upset.'

'It's my duty to be certain there are no concealed weapons.'

'You might at least have asked my brother! I call that insolence, not duty.'

A silence. Ralph, too, had come in, and was watching them with narrowed eyes. Mary Anne could feel the tension in the room, the great dark thunder-cloud ready to erupt. They did not like Luke Rowe, these Etwalls. Even hated him, perhaps. She could not really find it in her heart to blame them one jot.

'I feel,' Lieutenant Rowe said at last, 'that I must remind you that, although I am billeted on your property, I answer to the Governor.'

Nick's sallow skin flushed. 'Isn't it a little late to make a pretence of duty? You weren't sent here to do the Governor's duty, after all. They wanted rid of you as much as we do.'

The Lieutenant's mouth tightened. For a moment Mary Anne thought he would strike the other man. They were of a similar height, although the soldier was the younger by some years. Still, Nick Etwall was wiry and probably not averse to using any means at his disposal to win. She waited, excitement bringing the blood to her cheeks. If only Nick would floor the bloody redcoat! Floor him, as she longed to do.

The grey eyes dropped abruptly, and met hers. For a moment his mouth tightened even more, and then he relaxed. That detestable smile curled his lips, he hooked his fingers into his belt and said, in an almost drawling voice. 'Mrs Gower thinks you mean to demand we meet with pistols at dawn.'

Nick also looked at her, his expression one of comical dismay. So comical in fact, that Mary Anne laughed. 'Not at all,' she retorted. 'I wouldn't expect anything so . . . gentlemanly from you, Lieutenant.'

He scowled. Evidently she had touched even his steely heart. The grey eyes scanned her face insultingly, but she bore it. 'Beautiful women seem to think they can say anything, and remain so,' he murmured at last.

'Beautiful?' she repeated mockingly. 'You are mistaken, Lieutenant. If you want to speak of beauty, you'd best look at Jezebel.'

'And what do you know of Belle?' His tone was sharp, no longer lazy.

She pretended surprise. 'Only that she's a friend of yours, sir.'

Anger came to his face, sharp as a whip, and she was relieved when Nick claimed her attention and she could turn away. Good God, such a man as that shouldn't be angry at such an insignificant slight! He was a rake, a disgrace even to the Hobart barracks. What was that pale barb to him?

'So you've met the incomparable Belle,' Nick said, smiling. The anger had gone as swiftly as it had come, his eyes were warm again. 'She's best left at a distance, let me tell you. I'd not wish harm on you.'

She returned his look. 'I'm sure no harm can come to me with so many people to protect me!'

Behind her, Luke Rowe laughed harshly; a sharp, jarring sound. She ignored it, and him, as far as she was able, and took Nick's arm into the dining-room.

But the Lieutenant was not easily ignored. His very nearness was a threat, and though she tried to converse with the others, her tone had a note of desperation to it. As she feared, he was not to be ignored.

He mocked her over the first course. 'So you've found a niche for yourself already, Mrs Gower.'

The grey eyes were cool, but not the cold of the evening before or even the anger of earlier. There was a gleam of scorn in them. She was to be the butt of his mockery, evidently, in revenge for her dislike.

'The Etwalls are very kind to me.'

'Oh yes, they're kind.' His smile was not pleasant.

He taunted her over the dessert with, 'No more stories to tell us about Sydney Town, Mrs Gower? I had hoped . . .'

Insults trembled on her lips; but she bit them back.

'For someone who holds such contempt for the military, you were remarkably keen to claim the redoubtable Mr Macarthur for a friend.'

She turned to him in dismay. 'Mr Macarthur?'

'Didn't you know? He himself was of the New South Wales Corps until he had the sense to sell out.' He scanned her quizzically, but whatever he meant to ask was interrupted by Nick, who leant across the table with his warm, calculated smile to offer her one of the carefully preserved apples from their summer stock.

After the meal, Ralph and Nick went over some books, while Bessy spoke of gardening at great length, and all the things she couldn't grow at Etwall. Lieutenant Rowe stood by the window, staring out into the darkness of sea and sky. Mary Anne found herself puzzling, with some surprise, about why she hated him so violently. It was not in her nature to be quite so extreme, and he had saved her life, after all. Saved her from the cold arms of the sea, and Toby. He was a soldier, of course, and yet . . . He knew things about her that were dangerous in an enemy. It would be best to keep him as a friend.

Bessy wanted to speak to Joan, and when she had gone out to the kitchen, Mary Anne took the opportunity to make her way across to the window.

Nick looked at her as she passed. 'I'm sorry to leave you to your own devices, but Ralph insists on my listening to his latest plans.'

'Not at all.' With a smile for Ralph, who had treated them to a look of impatience, she moved on, reaching the window, where she stood beside the Lieutenant and gazed solemnly out. She felt him glance at her, a brief look. He wished her away, no doubt, but she determined at least to try. Enemies were dangerous, Toby always said, and unnecessary. An enemy could make life so very uncomfortable.

'Do you find life at Etwall tedious, Lieutenant?'

For a moment she fancied he meant to ignore her. She tilted her head to one side in her most appealing manner. He didn't even look at her. 'I do my duty, Mrs Gower, tedious or otherwise.'

'How very commendable.' Sarcasm there; she bit her lip on it. 'I should have thought you pined for the gaiety of Hobart.'

'Hobart is well enough.' He looked down at her, seeking something. She fancied whatever he sought he didn't find, and was amused at his frown. 'You know that I'm in disgrace,' he said abruptly.

She thought it best not to reply to this, and smoothed her skirt with her fingers.

'Aren't you worried about your reputation?' he went on softly, mockingly.

'You saved my life,' she retorted. 'That must cancel out all other considerations.'

For a moment he seemed stunned, and then he had turned again to the window. 'You must please yourself, madam.'

She took an impatient breath. 'I'm trying to be polite, Lieutenant, but you make it very difficult.'

She fancied his mouth twitched. 'Because I saved your life?'

'Why else?'

An eyebrow lifted, and he looked fully at her. 'The Misses Pinkerton, perhaps. Do you regret my offer of assistance now? I'm afraid it's too late. Anyone who is a friend of the Etwalls is no friend of mine.'

'You pompous . . .'

'Do you know how to fire a gun, Mrs Gower?'

The change of topic threw her, and she widened her eyes at him without pretence. 'A gun?'

'We're a long way from civilisation here. There are perhaps eight people at Etwall without the convict "taint", as it's so charmingly called. The rest are convicts or ex-convicts, and they have no love for their masters. Even you, self-centred as you are, must see that. The situation is potentially explosive.' His clipped voice was lowered, for her benefit only.

'I should have thought it your job to protect me.'

He made a harsh sound. 'Three men? And one of them roped into the army out of the Campbell Street Gaol? No, Mrs Gower, you must protect yourself. Can you use a gun?'

'Toby . . . My husband never imagined that . . .'

'Ah yes, the millowner-merchant.'

'I'm sure it can't be true, what you're saying about the the convicts. They are too well protected.'

His glance was pitying. 'Open those eyes at something other than Nick Etwall, Mrs Gower. Why should those protecting them have any more love for the Etwalls? Ralph Etwall, for instance, who doesn't give a damn; and Mrs Etwall, who won't concern herself with anyone's welfare but her own.'

'That's not so!' she cried, then, lowering her voice, 'It's not so. Today she went to visit Mrs Connor, and took food to her.'

The grey eyes mocked. 'And why would that be, Mrs Gower? Not love for the woman, by God. Leah Connor's husband has been trying to buy himself a share at Etwall for years, but he's a ticket-of-leave man. Not good enough. Leah Connor has been passing on what her husband tells her . . . for a price.'

She didn't believe it, and told him. 'Besides, why should she? What could Mr Connor have to say that is of any interest to Mrs Etwall?'

'You'd be surprised what there is to interest Mrs Etwall in the gossip, Mrs Gower. But don't expect me to enlighten you.'

'You're making it up!'

'Not at all.'

She sniffed, and didn't reply.

'And as for Nick . . .' he began.

Behind them a skirt brushed the floor, and Bessy said, 'One of your men is here to speak with you, Lieutenant.'

They spun round as one. Mary Anne's face went pink, Lieutenant Rowe's pale. The door into the hall was open, and in the shadows flamed the uncompromising red head of Private McDonald. Behind him, Simone twisted her hands in her apron.

Lieutenant Rowe bowed to Mary Anne, the grey eyes distant, hard. He murmured something to Bessy, and went out. The door closed. Mary Anne watched the latter exchange a glance with Ralph and Nick, and then Ralph had risen to his feet, stretching tired muscles and saying it was time to retire.

Nick came to stand by Mary Anne. 'Now that our gallant Lieutenant has gone, Mrs Gower, you'll find us more talkative.'

She smiled with an effort. The 'gallant Lieutenant's words had disturbed her more than she cared to admit. Why should they? So there was danger at Etwall? So what? There had always been danger for her and Toby, wherever they went. Why should it matter to her that the Etwalls were so pure and almighty, they cared nothing for their enforced labour? Because, she admitted bitterly to herself, she felt kinship to that class and was betraying it for the glitter of gold.

'You have secrets, then?' she said at last, forcing a broader smile.

The full mouth curved, the eyes teased. 'Perhaps we do. At least, we do from him. The man is not to be trusted.'

'I can see he would make life difficult.'

He laughed loudly. 'Difficult! You have no idea. I think, personally, the army sent him away because he was too officious, not because he did something disgraceful. My God, I've never met a man so determined to treat scum as flesh and blood. Would you believe it? He once had Davey to dine at his table, and that was only after my brother had refused to have him at ours. There is a limit to such things, surely? To have a convict to supper? It's laughable.'

'Yes.' Laughable. The man was a fool! Everyone knew convicts were lower than cattle, to the gentry. Good God, one could be hung for the stealing of a cow or sheep, while the murdering of a convict carried little more than a fine. She dipped her gaze, avoiding Nick's. So that was his 'disgrace' . . . showing favour to convicts. Disgrace indeed, in the eyes of the army. She could picture him, vividly, showing favour to the lowly Davey. But life was not like that! People were not. To go against the grain was sheer social suicide. The man must indeed be a fool.

CHAPTER FOUR

BESSY WAS busy overseeing the churning of butter and cream the next morning, and Mary Anne, alone with her thoughts, wandered out into the orchard.

The sun was out, a little wan but pleasant in the chill of the morning. The breeze was strengthening, and whipped colour into her cheeks. It smelt of the sea, and tasted of salt. The bay lay grey and sullen, and, where it met the shore, lashed against the rocks and pummelled the beach. Even the trickle of smoke from the timber camp, hidden up in the trees, was whipped away inland with the wind.

It had rained in the night, and though the puddles had dried, the ground remained damp and spongy. She picked her way between the trees. Perkins was digging again. He leaned on his spade and watched her approach, the black eyes narrowed against the glare.

'Mrs Etwall wants some bulbs in here,' he said abruptly, and jerked his head at the neat rows. 'Not that they'll come up, o' course. Everything rots in the ground here. And on top o' it, too.' He laughed at his own joke, his face creased like brown paper. She smiled. The black eyes slid slyly over her. 'You've met Joan?'

'Yes. She's very like you.'

'She's a fool. No sense at all. A man only has to beckon, and she goes like a lamb to slaughter.'

'I don't think . . .' she began, glancing round.

'Nobody to hear us,' Perkins retorted. 'Besides, I think you'd prefer plain speaking, Mrs Gower.'

She said nothing. He saw too much. It wasn't safe.

He held out his arm suddenly, and for a moment she frowned at him, uncertain what he was about. 'See the

72

scars,' he said softly, shaking the gnarled, muscle-corded limb. The wrist was marked with white, purplish-tinted scars.

'I see,' she said, as softly.

'You've seen the like before,' he murmured, and dropped his arm. 'And you don't care. I can see you don't care.'

'Mr Perkins . . .'

He laughed, shaking his head. '*Mr* Perkins? Not here, I ain't. This is a bad place, lady. A right bad place. There's misery here. You can feel it.'

'Mr Perkins, Lieutenant Rowe told me that . . .'

The old face hardened. 'Lieutenant Rowe is misguided.'

'You don't like him?'

The black eyes shone. 'Do you?' And when she coloured, he laughed. 'My daughter calls him a man, but she's a fool. There she is now, waving her arms at us. Go over to her. I've got the bulbs to put in.'

Mary Anne picked her way across to the kitchen door, where Joan was standing in the patch of sunlight, a short-stemmed pipe in her mouth. 'I've something to show you, Mrs Gower.'

The kitchen was steamy from the fire, and the smell of onions overpowered everything else. Mary Anne followed the cook's jerk of the head. Simone was peeling vegetables again, and looked up with a smile. The cake stood on the table, richly iced. Mary Anne approached it cautiously, and Joan chuckled at her expression. 'For you, to celebrate your escape.'

'You're very kind.'

Simone smiled; Joan laughed. 'Little enough cause for celebrations at Etwall, love. We make the most of those we do have.' The black eyes met hers squarely, and Mary Anne felt a prickle along her spine. Lieutenant Rowe was right: danger was brewing. Had been for years.

'By the by'—Joan frowned at a mark on the table and rubbed at it with a grubby nail—'I've a piece of advice for you, Mrs Gower. I've taken a liking to you, so I have, and . . .' She smiled, disclosing big white teeth. 'Mind yourself. People aren't what they seem. You're too trusting, I think. The same as me.' The teeth flashed again. 'Only I've been here long enough to know.'

'You mean the Etwalls?' she ventured.

A snort. Joan banged her pipe out on the chair back. 'The Etwalls! They're what they seem, all right. Did you know, Simone, that the rations for the convicts and ticket-of-leave men have gone down again for the winter. Seems Hobart ain't paying as much as they hoped for the last lot o' timber. So we're the ones that suffer.' The black eyes came back to Mary Anne. 'You've met Belle? Ay, well, take warning from Simone here. The girl's no angel. She was at poor Simmy's man before he died, and she's been at most of the rest. Not good honest lust, like me. But playing with them, leading them on. You know what I mean. And now Nick Etwall's making eyes at you . . .'

'I'm not afraid of Belle,' Mary Anne retorted.

'Don't say you weren't warned,' Joan said, turning away. She began to berate Simone almost sharply for clumsy fingers.

Mary Anne left them to it, feeling amused by the warning. She was more than a match for Belle, even if the other woman wanted to harm her. And why should she? Because of Nick? Well, Mary Anne was prepared for a fight, if it came to that. She had fought and won before, and had no doubts as to her superiority.

A sound distracted her, and she shaded her eyes. The rumble of cart-wheels drew nearer. A heavy, cumbersome conveyance, with thick, unspoked wheels on wooden pins and axles, had come up from the track along the shore and was heading towards the house with steady revolutions of the great wheels. She realised

suddenly that where there should have been horses
harnessed to the vehicle, there were men doing the job.
They were bent forward, heaving the cart along, truly
beasts of burden.

Her eyes moved on, to the beach. There were more
men down there, one of them stooped over something.
Perkins had gone from the garden, his spade un-
attended. There was something about the scene which
sent prickles down her spine, as if she already knew it
would give her grief.

Where she stood now, she was obscured from the cart,
and she watched unnoticed as the men approached. As
far as she could tell, the back of the cart was covered in
with a tarpaulin, caked with mud and ragged at the
edges, where it had been lashed to the sides. Even as she
watched, the vehicle veered off to her left, towards the
barn, some of the men from the beach beginning to
move after it. They were in brown serge, like those who
pulled the cart—the uniform of the convict. Their ankles
were chained; the clank of the manacles jarred in her
head. She spotted the flaming head of McDonald, his
rifle slung over his shoulder. They were very close now,
almost parallel with where she stood.

The voices of the men rose above the creaking and
rumbling. One of them, in the harness, was swearing
foully, and with a musical ring to the words that drew her
unwilling admiration. She closed her eyes, savouring it
as she would memories of innocent childhood. The
sound of hooves spoiled it, and she watched Nick come
galloping after the cart.

'Move it, you bastards!' he said. They had reached the
barn now, and disappeared behind it. Mary Anne
stepped back, in the act of turning, and came up against
a warm chest clothed in harsh cloth.

Someone caught her arms and spun her round. Somewhere in the back of her mind she thought: He must have
come up from the beach, round the waterline, while I

was watching the cart. But even that thought died before his white face, the savagery in his voice.

'What the hell are you up to?'

For a moment she gaped like a lunatic, but anger came to her rescue, rising swiftly, and her voice was icy. 'What the hell is it to you?'

The grey eyes were brilliant with rage, dark as the sea. He took her hurt arm in a grip that drained the colour from her face. She fell against him dizzily, and found his shirt, under the red coat, was wet, clinging to him like skin. His fair hair was wet, too, and darkened by the water. He bit out, 'Unless you want to see a man who's lain in water near a fortnight, you'd best go inside.'

The ache of her arm was forgotten. She stared at him in horror and disbelief. 'But . . . Oh no, not . . . not Toby?'

'I doubt if anyone could tell, now.'

She swallowed abruptly. The ground seemed to heave peculiarly, as if she were back on *Infanta* again, and a blackness rose in her mind. She came to herself a moment later, puzzled, the cool air tingling on her nape. She was sitting on the ground, she discovered, her head pressed uncomfortably in the direction of her knees. Her back ached, and she struggled to straighten up. But someone was holding her, and after a moment she cried in a muffled voice,

'Lieutenant Rowe, let me up!'

He released her. She straightened her neck, and pushed back the strands of hair which, coming unpinned, had fallen about her face. He was crouched beside her on his haunches, with a frown to make anyone's knees weak. She rubbed at her arm, trying to calm her shaken nerves. Seeing it, he brushed her hand aside without a word and rolled up her sleeve.

The arm was a little inflamed where the white bandage had slipped, but otherwise healthy enough. He turned it this way and that, straightening the bandage. 'I'm sorry,' he said abruptly. 'I thought to save you pain, not cause it.'

The apology was unexpected. She let out her breath a little shakily and let him help her to her feet. Her skirt was damp and dirty where she had sat on the wet ground. She twitched at it with distaste, and tried to straighten her hair. He was watching her, grim faced.

'If it's any consolation,' he said, 'the man was stout, and his hair might have been grey.'

Her eyes closed briefly. 'It sounds like the captain.'

'There will probably be more washed up now. The current brings them into the inlet. I suppose we'll have to find a spot to start burying them.'

Her eyes swung up, and she stared at him a moment without breathing. 'My God, how can you be so callous?'

The grey eyes mocked her savagely. 'Callous? I'd call it being practical. I've no time to weep over dead men—it's the living who need my attention.' He half turned away, then remembered something else. 'Last night, I told you it was dangerous here. If you have any sense, you won't take sides.'

'Take sides?' she repeated furiously. 'Any side against you, Lieutenant, would find me a ready convert.'

His smile was grim. 'Go inside, Mary Anne.'

She went, without another word, shaking with reaction and anger.

Bessy was in the sitting-room, and the smile she gave as she looked up turned swiftly to concern. 'Mary Anne?'

'They . . . They found a body. From the ship. It wasn't Toby.'

'Poor child! Sit down here. You didn't see . . .'

'No. The Lieutenant described him to me. I think he must have gone into the water to . . . to . . .'

The thin lips tightened. 'Yes, *he* would.'

The hateful Lieutenant was right. That was the thing

of it. It wasn't practical to weep for dead men. One must look to the living.

But the episode had shaken her, and she was grateful when Bessy found a way to divert her. She had some cloth, purchased from Hobart and never used, and insisted that Mary Anne select some.

'You can hardly go around in the same dress!'

So they set about cutting and stitching the new dresses. These were necessarily simple, and Bessy seemed truly enthusiastic about the project.

Lieutenant Rowe was not at dinner, and sent Hagetty, the smaller of the two soldiers, with apologies. Mary Anne, relieved, enjoyed the meal far more without him. Nick was most attentive, and spoke a great deal of his time in the army. Not that they weren't rotten to the core, Mary Anne reminded herself, but one had to make sacrifices. And, besides, he wasn't in the army now. What did it matter that he thought her a wealthy widow? She liked him, and if he asked her to marry him . . . Well, what was wrong with that? She'd bring him round, once the ceremony was over. The name of Etwall was as good as any to approach Hobart with.

'The Etwalls!' he laughed, when she tentatively approached him about his name and the possible power it held. 'I suppose we do hold a bit of authority. Old Ralph has done what everyone said he couldn't. He's built an empire out of wilderness, if one could call this bitch of a place an "empire".'

She smiled at the slip of the tongue as much as his realisation, look of dismay and profuse apologies. 'I suppose you have a great many friends in Hobart,' she murmured.

The blue eyes warmed. 'Yes. Unfortunately, however, my friends tend to play for stakes I can't match. Hence my stay here in Etwall.'

She laughed. 'You're very honest!'

'Yes.' The blue eyes were a little surprised. 'For some

reason, with you, Mrs Gower, I find it easy to be honest.

Flattering, from someone like Nick Etwall. And promising. They might yet strike a bargain. He would do, and in time perhaps she might even forget Toby, or shape him to be more like Toby. Well, it was something to think on. But the truth was, the more she did think on it, the more she was certain that Nick would be a perfect partner. He was cunning, and if a little gullible, she could temper that with time and training. And he was personable and clever, and completely without scruples. Yes, he would make the perfect partner. They would make a fortune from the citizens of Hobart, and then move on to richer fields. London, perhaps . . .

She was still thinking about it when she said her good nights, and climbed the narrow stairs to the landing outside her door. The more she thought, the more she was certain she was making the right choice.

There was someone waiting for her in the shadows. The swish of skirts. A white hand grasped the banisters. Simone. Her hair was as untidy as ever, her apron as grubby. Her yellow eyes were like hollows in her skull, dark and gleaming. Something about the girl frightened her, and she felt tension tighten in her stomach.

'Madame,' the breathless voice whispered. 'Oh, madame.'

'What is it?'

She stepped closer, into the light that filtered up from the hall. The yellow eyes flickered from side to side, quickly, as though afraid of listeners in the darkness. 'I—I heard a man calling for help. Out in the water. I . . . Please come and see.'

'In the water?' she repeated in amazement. 'Have you told Mr Etwall?'

'Oh no!' This time the eyes looked straight into hers, and shook Mary Anne to the very core. There was terror in them, and grief. The emotions were obscured as quickly, like shifting sand before the tide. 'I couldn't tell them. They don't believe me. They never believe me. They think I'm . . .' There was no need to finish. The eyes drowned with tears, the face went chalky white. She looked so dejected and unhappy. Mary Anne took her cold hand.

'Where is this man, Simone?'

Simone took her hand away, folding it in her apron again. 'I heard him,' she said. 'Beyond the orchard, where it runs down to the water. I was frightened, though, and ran away. I came to you. I know you would understand.'

She should know better. She really should know better than to go with this child. And yet Mary Anne knew she would go. The fear and hope in the girl's eyes beckoned irresistibly, and pity overwhelmed cold good sense.

'I'll come with you,' she said softly.

Outside, it was cold and dark. The fresh wind bit through her clothing, and the sky was cloudy, half covering the pale, distant moon. The sea shone back with the same pale light, the waves moving in shimmering ridges as the water washed at the back rocks further around the bay. The beach was a pale blur, and behind it lights from the Lieutenant's cottage blinked through the trees. Mary Anne's breath was cloudy, and she hugged her shawl closer, trying to still the tremor in her voice. Oh God, what a fool she was even to think it; even to allow that spark of brilliant hope to cloud her judgment.

'Where was this man?'

Simone didn't turn, but stood staring into the bay. After a moment she said, to herself more than to Mary Anne, 'He called my name. Again and again he called.

'Your name?'

'I was afraid, and ran away. I shouldn't have run, should I? Not from him. But I thought . . . They killed him, do you see?'

Mary Anne stood quite still. Her heart was beating

strangely; a muffled, thudding beat. And yet her voice
was oddly calm. 'You knew this voice?'

Simone turned and looked at her. The white face was
blurred, smudged with hollows. She looked like a lost
ghost. 'I knew it. Like my own. I love him so, madame.
Why did I run away?'

'Simone, my poor child.' She stepped forward to
comfort her. But the girl jerked back, tears glittering on
her cheeks.

'They killed him, don't you see?' Hysteria wrenched
her voice. 'Murder!'

Somewhere behind them, a foot scuffed on the pile of
leaves Perkins had raked from under the trees. They
whirled round together. For a moment Mary Anne
thought it was indeed the poor girl's dead lover, returned. There were shadows everywhere, embracing the
trees' silver trunks. Her hand came up in a forgotten
gesture; Simone's aped it, swiftly moving down and
across her breast.

'Simone?'

The sound of the voice dispelled fear. Mary Anne felt
dizzy, and took a gulp of air. It was Luke Rowe, the
bloody redcoat. She had never been so glad of the sound
of the man's voice since he had first pulled her out of the
water. The smell of tobacco caught at her nostrils, and
she saw the red glow of a cigar-tip. His coat buttons
gleamed in the light from the house, and vanished again
as he turned towards them, picking his way between the
trees. 'Simone?'

The girl had lifted her head at the sound of her name,
and now gave a sudden shudder and dropped her face
into her hands. Her untidy hair fell forward to curtain
them.

He had reached them at last. He seemed to know what
had happened, and tossed the cigar on the ground,
pressing the heel of his boot down on top of it.

'She said she heard a man calling, from the water,'

Mary Anne said, breathless, feeling the foolish need of explanations. 'I thought . . .'

'That it was your husband, returned from the dead?' he demanded with quiet sarcasm. The barb found its mark, and stung. She fell silent, watching him place his hands gently on Simone's shoulders. 'Simone? I thought you'd given up on your voices.'

She lifted her face, her eyes gleaming. 'But it was so sharp, Lieutenant! So clear. I thought it must be so . . . I know he will not rest until he is avenged.'

'There's nothing to be avenged. Nothing for you to avenge, my dear. Leave it to me.'

Simone gave a sob, and broke away from him. She caught her skirts up as she ran, light-footed, back towards the lights. Mary Anne let out her breath with a hiss. 'Was there any need to be so brutal?'

'Brutal?'

Somewhere a door slammed. A curlew gave out a mournful cry, and the sound echoed in the dark bulk of trees behind them, rising with the hills. Mary Anne shivered. 'I feel sorry for her. I knew she was . . . I didn't realise.'

'Perhaps you should try thinking before you act.'

She glared back at him. 'It wasn't my fault!'

'If you'd behaved less impetuously . . .'

'She would have run off without me.'

'It's not safe to be out here.'

'Not safe?' she demanded, and laughed. 'Why should I be afraid of the dark, Lieutenant Rowe?'

'Where do you think you are?' He sounded angry, and she was glad. Pompous, stupid man. How dare *he*, of all people, tell her how to behave?

'I think the only harmful thing this darkness holds is you!'

He gave a bark of laughter. 'Do you? Well, maybe you're right. Remember it, next time you decide to come strolling.'

She went to turn away, but stopped as memory jolted her curiosity. 'Simone said something about murder, didn't she?'

He looked at her for an instant. 'I think your imagination is overactive.'

'Overactive!'

'What a temper it has!' he mocked, soft and infuriating, fanning the flames. 'What happened to all that sugary sweetness I saw you dish out to Nick Etwall the other night?'

The realisation that he meant to anger her had the opposite effect. She sobered, and with calm came a further realisation. 'What are you doing here anyway? You said you had work to attend to. What are you doing here?' A pause; she stepped closer. 'Is this your work? Spying?'

His hand came out and fastened on her wrist. She tried to jerk away, but he drew her inescapably closer until she had come up against his chest and stood trembling between rage and fear. The moon whitened his hair, and turned his eyes to silver. His breath warmed her cold forehead.

'You won't be telling anyone else of these wild accusations, will you?' he said. 'Will you?'

Murder, Simone had said. And then she had run. God, it was so easy at this moment to picture that murderer in Luke Rowe. She shook her head from side to side. A pause, and she held her breath. And then he had released her and was bowing, mocking in his formality. 'Good night, then, Mrs Gower.'

She marched back to the house, back as stiff as a ramrod. But she was shaken. The man beat her at every turn. The sooner she got Nick over to her side the better. What did marriage matter, anyway? Anything was preferable to spending any longer under the threat of Lieutenant Rowe.

*　　*　　*

The following morning, again, she spent some time on her sewing. It was hardly what she was used to. Toby had spoiled her—all those silks and satins. Money had spoiled her. As a child, a pretty dress had been as distant from her imaginings as life without fear, and pain. And was it a bad thing? To rise above one's origins? Wrong to want to forget in a welter of beads and lace?

To question was foolish. She escaped her thoughts by wandering into the little walled garden, where Simone was hoeing. The wind plucked at her hair and skirts; the clouds lurched sullenly across a sullen sky. The girl didn't so much as glance at her. The matter, evidently, was to be forgotten. Maybe Simone really didn't remember. But she had said 'murder', and Mary Anne found that rather difficult to forget.

She leaned against the stone wall, her eyes half-closed as she gazed towards the house. The hills framed it on either side, and further away the squalid cottages squatted upon the flats.

'Simone?'

The girl continued to hoe.

'Simone?'

Her arms worked furiously, digging at the soil with a will. A strand of hair fell over her eye, but she ignored it.

Mary Anne sighed. 'There's no need to be afraid of me,' she murmured, in what she hoped to be a conciliatory voice. 'And if it's the Lieutenant you dislike, you should know that . . .'

Simone's head flew up, the yellow eyes scornful. 'Dislike? You are crazy, madame. The Lieutenant is a good man; a *good* man. If you wish for a new husband . . .' The yellow eyes narrowed slyly.

Mary Anne's mouth dropped open, and she started forward in a torrent of fury to deny it. Someone cleared his throat behind her, and she spun about inelegantly.

'I'm sorry, ma'am.'

'McDonald, isn't it?' Her voice shook with anger and embarrassment.

'That's right.' He looked past her, to where Simone had resumed her hoeing. 'The Lieutenant told me the girl was . . . upset last night.'

Mary Anne wondered why the Lieutenant should tell the man anything. Perhaps McDonald saw the animosity in her eyes, because he flushed again and said, 'The Lieutenant knows how I feel, else he wouldn't have told me.'

She scowled. God, what fools men were! Simone nearly mad with grief, and thoughts of revenge, over one of them, and here was another ready to fill his shoes. Well, it wasn't her concern—and if it was, she'd tell the girl to run a mile rather than get involved with the army, so there!

The man, a boy really—he was perhaps twenty-two years, younger than herself—was watching a little uncertainly as her thoughts flitted over her face. She allowed her most dazzling smile to spread across her red mouth and shine into her dark eyes. This time the colour drained from the boy's cheeks, leaving the freckles marooned.

'I wonder your commanding officer has the time to concern himself with servant girls.'

'The Lieutenant? Why, he's . . .' The boy's eyes glowed, this time with admiration. Mary Anne found it a little sickening. She supposed it amused Luke Rowe to play on the boy's sensibilities, to have his devotion, his hero-worship. After all, he wasn't going out of his way for it, was he? A crumb here, a morsel there . . . She had done the same herself when the part called for it. If she put her mind to it, she could probably even wean McDonald away from the redcoat and attach him to her side.

'It's not an easy life,' McDonald was saying. 'The army, I mean. Lieutenant Rowe's a hard man, ma'am, but fair. He's always fair.'

'I'm sure he is,' she said tartly. The boy eyed her a little uncertainly, but she suddenly didn't care. Let him tell his officer anything he wanted to. Let him say that the widow Gower hated his guts. It wouldn't be anything he didn't already know.

'There's no more about the wreck,' she said into the pause.

McDonald shook his head. 'Not yet. I expect there will be, though. When one body comes, generally more follow.' He looked stricken, remembering belatedly who she was. Her own smile wavered a little but remained taut.

When McDonald had gone, Simone looked up, her face almost hard. 'The boy is foolish,' she murmured. 'He cannot see that the other must be finished, before I think of my future. There is no future, until it is over.'

Mary Anne felt suddenly stifled, and turned out of the gate, hurrying across the pasture towards the beach. The sand was wet, and she sank into it as she neared the water's edge. There was little wave, and the few that reached for her skirts she easily avoided. Occasional shells littered the shore higher up, marooned by the earlier high tide. She spent some time examining them, and looking down, was not aware of the approaching figure until he was almost upon her.

The man was making his way along the track above the beach. He was loping, head lowered, like some animal rather than a human being. A big, gambolling animal. He must have felt her watching him, for suddenly he looked up. It was not the soldier, Hagetty. Indeed it was too big for him. A stranger in baggy trousers and a shirt rolled up at the sleeves.

'Mrs Gower?' he said, his voice gruff, a throaty sound to it.

'Yes, I'm Mrs Gower.'

He had thick brows; they all but hid his eyes. His smile

was polite enough, and yet she disliked it. 'I'm Davey,' he said. 'Foreman up at the timber camp. Come down to have a word with Lieutenant Rowe. Know where he is, do you?'

'I do not,' she retorted. 'Have you looked in his cottage?'

'Oh ay, I've done that.' He smiled again, as though it were a habit with him. 'I'll just have to go up to the house, won't I?'

'I doubt he's there.'

He sighed. 'Damn the man then! Begging your pardon, ma'am. But the man's forever snoopin' about the bush.'

'I suppose it's his job—to snoop.' The word pleased her. It described him exactly. Hadn't he been snooping last night, in the orchard, when he threatened her? Davey nodded and walked on, that same shambling stride. She watched him idly, wondering what the timber camp was like.

Davey reached the house. She watched him pause by the walled garden. Simone was still there. The girl's bright head turned, and she fairly flew inside. Even from the beach, Mary Anne thought she could hear the door slam. Simone, then, didn't care for Davey as much as she cared for the Lieutenant! With a sigh, Mary Anne turned back to the sea. Toby would tell her, if he were here, that she judged people too swiftly, and too unbendingly. One needed to be flexible, willing to be persuaded. Mary Anne had never yielded her beliefs easily, once they were fixed in her head. It was like that now. She could see the Lieutenant as nothing other than an enemy. And she had failed to heed his advice about taking sides and firmly aligned herself with those against him.

Nicholas returned in the early afternoon, and strode into the sitting-room, obviously seeking her. 'Mary Anne! You don't mind me calling you Mary Anne?'

She laughed. 'Indeed not. It is my name, after all.'

'Do you ride, Mary Anne?'

'Ride, Mr Etwall?'

'Nick, please.'

'Nick. I don't, and I'm not sure that I want to try.'

'You must at least try.' The blue eyes teased her and challenged her at the same time. Mary Anne could rarely ignore a challenge.

The horse was rather old, and Nick made an apologetic gesture. 'My brother's. Unfortunately we can't waste cash on horseflesh. There are other things more important.'

His voice was mocking, but she smiled at him. 'It's just as well; I'm a mediocre rider.'

The thin mouth smiled in return. 'I don't see you as mediocre in anything, Mrs Gower.'

Flattering! she thought, as he swung her up into the saddle. She had, perforce, to ride astride as a man would. There were no side-saddles at Etwall. They walked for a moment, across the fields beyond the huddle of the cottages. A shutter swung shut, a woman and a child glanced up from a doorway. There were no words of greeting, as might have been expected from employees to employer, false or otherwise. One woman, stooping to collect dung in a basket, turned her back to them.

'I was speaking with one of the soldiers this morning,' Mary Anne said at last. 'Mr McDonald.'

'And did our gallant Lieutenant set him to watch you? I warn you, he watches us all.'

'But why?'

The blue eyes mocked. 'Why not? He's nothing else to occupy his mind. There are none of the amusements of Hobart society, as I well know.'

She smiled. 'Indeed no! But why watch me?'

The black eyebrows lifted. 'Why not? I'd rather watch you, Mary Anne, than anyone else I could name.'

She laughed. *This* was more like it. This was the sort of thing she understood and could control. Nick Etwall grew more promising by the minute!

'When will you return to those amusements?'

He was silent, gazing a moment out over the land to the bay. 'I'd go tomorrow, if it were possible.'

'Poor Nick,' she whispered, mocking. 'He has the right name, but no money to back it up.'

For a moment anger flashed in his eyes, but was gone as swiftly. 'And you have both, ma'am. The world is a most unfair place.'

'Yes.' She looked at her hands, gripping the reins, and relaxed them, finger by finger. 'You should beware of illusions, Nick,' she added, as softly.

'Illusions?'

'Nothing and no one are as they seem. Don't you know that?'

He was puzzled, and examined her face as if for some clue to the answer. But she said no more. Let him think about it, and, with thinking, he would be drawn further into the net.

At dinner, Bessy seemed put out by Nick's spending the afternoon with her, despite her unselfish attitude of earlier, but Mary Anne pretended not to notice. And pretended not to notice, too, the Lieutenant's hard watching eyes. Instead, she smiled at Nick, and laughed at his dry humour, and leaned close to reply to his questions, her hair brushing his cheek, her fingers brushing his sleeve.

He was very like Toby. And, like Toby, he was a fool for a pretty, smiling face. He was already hooked, but she must make sure he was well and truly landed before she released the hook. Once he knew the truth about her, and what game she wanted him to partner her in, he might go cold. And then there would be hell to pay.

When it came time for her to retire, the Lieutenant opened the door. She glanced up at his face as she passed him, and something in his expression startled her so much that her faint smile froze. A look of almost . . . yes, hatred in his eyes, as though he wanted to hurt her. It disturbed her, but she thrust it aside as she prepared for bed. The man was unimportant to her, and her future.

CHAPTER FIVE

MARY ANNE sewed the final stitch in one of her dresses the following morning. It was grey—a rich, dark grey. A compromise between mourning and Toby's opinions on the subject. The colour reminded her of the sea, beyond the entrance to Etwall bay. She was admiring her handiwork when there was a tap on the door and Joan Perkins poked her head in. Her black eyes scanned the room. 'Simone not here, then?'

'Why, no.'

The woman chuckled deep in her throat. 'Sly puss! That young soldier's been hanging round her for weeks. He's finally caught her.'

Mary Anne's eyes widened. 'I'm sure you're wrong.'

'Why's that?' The black eyes mocked now. 'A woman can only grieve for so long, Mrs Gower.'

There was a barb in that, Mary Anne decided. She meant Nick Etwall—Joan would be sure to notice how attentive he had lately become. 'Simone told me so,' she said, setting aside her sewing. 'She said . . .' But Simone had spoken of murder, and she could not repeat that. Instead she said, 'What was her husband like?'

Joan chuckled. 'He was a big man, and quiet. I used to wonder how they came to meet and wed, them both being so peaceful. Luke Rowe was quite partial to him, too, and since he died, Luke's been kind to Simone. I thought, for a time, that him and her . . . But no.' Her gaze returned to Mary Anne, sly, watchful.

'What a paragon he is,' she retorted sharply.

Joan put her hands on her broad hips. 'Now, then, Lieutenant Rowe's not a man to slander!'

'I've no interest in the army or its men,' Mary Anne declared, and yawned.

Joan smiled. There was a pause. 'Nick Etwall likes you, don't he?'

'I hope so.'

'Oh-ho, so that's the way the wind blows, is it? He's got no money, you know. Bane of the Etwall family, he is. Old Ralph always says he'll end up on the gallows.' She laughed. 'But I say he's handsome for all that, eh?' The door closed. Mary Anne rose and went to the window. The woman annoyed her, coming prying like that. What had she wanted to know, anyway? Whether she liked Nick Etwall? Well, she knew now, gossiping busybody! If Bessy had been here, she would never have spoken so, or laughed. Mary Anne sighed. Evidently Joan knew she was no tyrant when it came to servants —perhaps she even saw through her disguise to what she really was. Like was attracted to like, after all.

The sound of boots in the hall broke through her musing. She turned abruptly as the door opened and Ralph Etwall, dirty and rather windblown, came striding in. He stopped, looking in a distracted manner about him before his eyes lit on Mary Anne.

'Where's Bessy?'

'She went to visit Leah Connor.'

He sighed, rubbing his jaw. It grated a little, with stubble. 'Drat that woman! Always ill with something or other.'

'Surely she can be forgiven, Mr Etwall, for this particular illness?'

He frowned, then caught her meaning and gave an involuntary laugh. 'I'm not even so sure about that. Well, you'll just have to do it.'

'Do what?'

'I can't stay long, and Joan refuses to give any help, while Simone, it seems, can't be found. So, it's up to you.' He turned back down the hall and called out,

'Luke!'

More steps in the hall, echoing in the sudden stillness.

Ralph had turned back to her, a little apologetic. 'I insisted he come up here. I feel responsible, in a way. And Bessy usually binds up cuts and wounds . . .'

Lieutenant Rowe appeared in the doorway, his coat unbuttoned; in his flushed face his grey eyes were as hard as ever. She watched him, rather like a wary doe.

'I've found Mary Anne for you, man,' Ralph said, and shifted his feet almost like a nervous schoolboy. Mary Anne had the impression he wanted to get out as quickly as possible, and wondered why. 'She'll fix you up a treat,' he went on. 'No false modesty now,' to Mary Anne, when she opened her mouth in an instinctive protest. He smiled, and brushed past the Lieutenant. The door closed, and the house lay still again.

'Lieutenant,' she said coolly.

'Mrs Gower,' with a brief nod of his head. He was holding one hand in the other, cradling it, almost. Curiosity, one of her worst sins, caught hold of her with sharp, worrying teeth.

'Perhaps you should come and sit down,' she began, trying to sound brisk and medical.

'There's no need,' he said stiffly. 'The wound is in no need of immediate attention. My men can see to it when they get back.'

'Back from where?'

The grey eyes mocked. 'They've gone after my attacker, madam. I was shot at, from the bush round the timber camp.'

'Shot at!' She was shocked, despite herself. Her eyes dipped back to his hand.

'Yes,' his mouth flickered into a smile, 'with a gun.'

'But . . .'

'I think I will sit down,' he added, and did so. He was pale now, and perspiration shone above his lip.

Another tap on the door, and Joan entered, eyes

bright with curiosity. 'I've brought some warm water
and Mrs Etwall's box of tricks.' A chuckle for that, deep
in her throat. She surveyed the Lieutenant, hands on
hips. 'You should know better, boy, than going poking
round that camp.'

'Oh?' He lifted his eyebrows. 'Do you know anything
about it, Joan?'

She chuckled again. 'Me? I cook, that's all I do. I
know naught about nothing.' The door closed on her.
Mary Anne looked down at the Lieutenant's fair bent
head for a moment. Perspiration had dampened the hair
round his brow and temples, where it clung, curling. His
shirt was damp too, and his coat wasn't as spotless as she
was used to, but marked across one shoulder. He
seemed abstracted, for which she could hardly blame
him.

'What happened?' she said at last. He looked up
sharply, frowning. 'Did someone really try to kill you?'

The grey eyes darkened. 'Are you going to do something about this hand, madam, or would you prefer I
bleed to death? No,' she opened her mouth indignantly,
'don't answer that. I fear I already know your answer.'

She moved forward stiffly to open the wooden box
Joan had brought. It was a medicine-chest, full of
potions and bits and pieces. She viewed it with distaste
and some dismay. Nursing was not her forte—blood
made her swoon.

'You'll have to let me see it,' she said, expecting some
minor abrasion she could finish with quickly. Not
serious, Ralph had said. Probably a graze, where the
bullet had glanced.

He seemed to hesitate, and then lifted his hand on to
the table. The improvised bandage was also damp, and
soaked through with blood. Bright, fresh blood. Blood
smeared his sleeve, too, and trickled down his wrist. She
thought, oddly calm, that the bandage looked like a strip
from somebody's shirt, and wondered who had bound it

up. Not everyone at the timber camp, it seemed, hated the military.

She finished unwrapping the bandage—it came off easily enough with the blood still so fresh. The thing was useless now, and she put it aside, out of the way, and turned back briskly to the hand itself. Words quite failed her. She stared at the shattered flesh and blood and grime.

'The bullet passed through,' he said, from somewhere beyond the humming in her head. She blinked, pressing her nails into her palms beneath the cover of the table. She mustn't faint, not before this cold, detestable man.

'You'd better clean it first,' he drawled.

'I know that much!' She took a deep breath and turned to the bowl of water. It was marvellous to take her eyes from that gore. No wonder Joan had refused to play nurse; but then perhaps Joan was more afraid of what the firer of the bullet might say if she became involved. Convicts had a sort of honour system.

'Jesus!'

The exclamation was stifled, and she looked up at him. He had gone even paler, and had his eyes closed. There was a bottle of brandy on the side table, and she poured some, shaking, into a glass. He snatched it and drained it, giving his head a toss.

'You're not going to faint?' she demanded.

He laughed shakily. 'No. I didn't think it was going to look like that. Just a neat little hole.'

The liquor had restored some of his colour, and he waited as she dampened a cloth and began to clean the blood from his wrist and fingers. The bullet had passed through his palm, as he said, but at an angle, ripping flesh as it went. She swallowed, hoping it had not ripped muscle and bone too, and concentrated on the slow job of cleaning. It seemed to take ages, and she bent closer, frowning at her work while the silence grew.

When it was finally done, the table was a mess. The

bowl of water was the colour of blood, and the wound lay bare. She realised, with a horrible, queasy feeling, that she could see bone.

'Pour this in,' he said, close to her ear. He sounded far away, despite being so close, and she found it suddenly difficult to clear her head.

'Shouldn't you have this stitched?'

'Are you going to do it for me?' he mocked.

She did as she was told, her hands surprisingly steady, trying not to notice how the colour was draining from his face.

'Now all you need do is bandage it up,' he went on, his voice turned ragged. 'The edges will mend together like new.'

'Or the flesh will go bad, and you'll have to have the lot off.'

She looked up at him as she said it, noting how bright his grey eyes were. Pain, and probably the beginnings of a fever from the blood loss. 'Unfortunately,' he said softly, 'I've got too much to do to consider dying at present.'

She laughed shakily. 'I suppose that makes it an impossibility, then?'

But she did as he had said, making the bandage as neat as possible and firm without being restricting. When she had done, he stood up carefully, holding the chair back with his good hand. She began to tidy up the bandages, and felt the blood drying on her fingers. The floor bucked and heaved.

'Thank you,' he said. 'I'd do the same for you some day . . . only you're going to Hobart.'

Her eyelids flickered. His face went hard. Hard and cold and dangerous. 'I hardly think . . .'

The lines deepened about his mouth. 'That it's my business?' He leaned closer, his breath stirring the wisps of hair at her temple. 'You'd better not stay here, Mary Anne.'

She drew her breath in sharply, her face hot with

anger. 'You can't tell me what to do!'

The detestable mouth twitched. 'Can't I? I stole you up from the sea, Mary Anne, remember? Some people believe that makes you mine.'

Steps in the hall. She had never in her life been so grateful for anything. Her courage, her quick wit, her mockery had all deserted her under the onslaught of a sudden fear. And something else, something which paralysed her when he came close. The man was positively deranged.

Bessy came in, frowning at the bloody-stained water. Simone peeped out from behind her, yellow eyes big. 'Lieutenant Rowe, what is this I've heard about a shooting?'

'Someone shot at me, Mrs Etwall, when I was at the timber camp. My men went after him, and Mrs Gower was kind enough to attend to my wound.'

'Someone shot at you!'

'Yes.'

Bessy's frown deepened, ageing her. 'I hope we get the culprit, Lieutenant.'

He smiled faintly. 'I shall, Mrs Etwall. I shall.'

When he had gone, Bessy stared abstractedly at the floor while Joan and Simone made haste to tidy the mess. 'I should think shooting at a soldier was nothing unusual,' Mary Anne said at last, into the tense silence.

Bessy looked up, startled, but Simone spoke first. 'Oh no, madame! Not Lieutenant Rowe. He is a good man. People, they do not shoot at him!'

'Well, someone doesn't agree with your opinion of him,' Mary Anne returned smugly. The girl dropped her gaze, fingers twisting in her apron. She knew something, Mary Anne thought suddenly. She had been missing, hadn't she, earlier on? She knew something. Still, after a glance at the other two, it might be better to tackle her alone. And there was plenty of time.

* * *

Nicholas was attentive again that evening, the atmosphere much lighter without the presence of the Lieutenant. He was resting, they were told, and had a slight fever. Bessy offered to take a look at him, but the messenger, Hagetty, said it wasn't necessary. He was a smallish man, dark-haired and a little bow-legged. His eyes, bright and somehow irreverent, went past Bessy to Mary Anne. 'If I might have a private word, madam?'

Mary Anne blinked in surprise, but came nevertheless. The door closed on Bessy's curious and disapproving face, and the little man turned to her with a smile, his eyes gleaming. 'I'm to thank you, ma'am, for your care of our Lieutenant, and to ask you if you'll be so good as to take a look in on him tomorrow.'

'But Mrs Etwall offered . . .'

The eyelids fell, hiding the glow. 'He asked for you, ma'am. I'm only delivering orders.'

'I hardly think it proper.'

'Proper?' he repeated quietly, and met her glance. Irony curled his lip. 'A bit hard to observe society's rules in a place like this, beggin' your pardon ma'am, with only a handful of women to so many men.'

She sighed, feeling foolish, and said impatiently, 'Oh, very well! But tell him I agreed under duress.'

'As you say, ma'am.' He clicked his heels, and as he did so, looked up at her. His eyes shone now with disbelief, and it wasn't until he had turned his back that she realised, with a sting of rage, that he thought her reluctance an act, a pretence. He thought she actually wanted to come, and she was playing the coy maiden for propriety's sake.

'Mary Anne?'

Nick Etwall had come up behind her. Had he heard? She swallowed rage and dismay, turning with a courageous smile. He returned the smile briefly, and took her hand between his two, smoothing her fingers. 'Aren't you chilled out here?'

She laughed, suddenly more than happy at the look in his eyes.

'You're a wicked child,' Toby used to say. 'You enjoy making fools of them, don't you?'

'But of course! All men are fools.'

'All?'

'Except you.'

He had laughed for that, and flicked her cheek. 'Not all, my sweet! Don't get too smug; that's when the game gets dangerous. Even you will meet your match, one day.'

Well, Nicholas Etwall certainly wasn't it!

'What are you thinking about?'

She smiled.

'Your husband?'

She smiled, and taking a breath said, 'Perhaps I should tell you, Nick, that I didn't feel for my husband. Not . . . Not as a wife loves a husband. I had known him for so long you see, and . . .'

His fingers tightened, comforting. 'Why tell me this?'

She smiled. 'To assure you I'm not the grieving widow you think me. And to assure you that you don't have to handle my emotions with kid gloves.'

Some emotion flickered over his face in the dim light, and he laughed softly. His mouth was hard and warm when he kissed her, demanding a response. She responded easily enough. There was no flicker of desire. Only triumph that he should want her as desperately as his mouth was now indicating. She always found it difficult to love men who could be so easily fooled, and difficult to do more than pretend desire when they kissed her. Still, she reminded herself firmly, this was a good start, and boded well for the future. And if she meant to marry the man . . . Well, time enough to worry about feeling more than this pretended affection.

* * *

The garden was quite warm the following morning, and fresh with the scent of the sea. Mary Anne leaned against the wall, watching Simone hoeing in the vegetable patch, her tawny hair bound up in a scarf, her neck somehow pale and vulnerable. The girl seemed nervous of her this morning, and kept glancing at her with big, golden eyes. Perhaps she sensed the purpose in her; the determination which moulded her soft mouth.

Over near the cottages a child crouched, making mud-pies with dirty hands. Mary Anne watched as a woman came out, scolding it, and dragged it back inside. The air, despite the faint warmth, had a bite to it, a sharp tug which reached her flesh through her dress. She put herself, for a moment, in the place of that woman, and shuddered. Etwall was not a place to make one's life.

Bessy's cat had followed her out. A big, ginger animal that butted at her feet until she bent to scratch the rough head. Out on the water, it was still, smooth as glass. It seemed harmless today, pallid under a pallid sky, and she found it difficult to believe that it was the same devil that had smashed the little *Infanta*.

'They say . . .' Mary Anne looked up, startled. Simone had sidled over to her and stood leaning on the hoe, staring intent at the harbour. 'They do say, as when a soul is snatched from the sea, the soul is still marked for death by water.'

Mary Anne felt her skin prickle. Peasant superstition, she thought angrily, and drew herself up. 'Simone.' Her voice was brisk. The girl looked up, surprised, biting her lower lip. 'Simone, I don't wish to frighten you. But you know something, don't you, about the Lieutenant's accident?'

Yellow eyes widened, swallowing the thin, pale face. 'Madame!'

'Come, now!' She smiled, conciliating. 'Do you think it matters to me who shot him?'

Simone bit her lips again, the colour flooding into her

cheeks. 'Madame, I did not mean to. I don't know if I . . .'

Mary Anne caught her arm. 'Did you shoot him? I thought he was your husband's friend.'

'He was, indeed, indeed, he was, madame!' Tears sparkled, were gone. She dropped her chin and mumbled, 'He was kind to my poor William, and to me. I should not keep back what I know. I meant no harm. I, too, hate her.'

'Her?'

'I saw that Belle going along the track to the camp. I saw her, madame, when I was on the beach. She paid me no heed—she never does. She went to the camp, madame. I followed her a little way, but Davey saw me and shooed me away.' She grimaced. 'Like a pest—they think me no more. But they will learn.'

'But . . . Is that all?'

Simone blinked. 'She carried a gun, madame, that Belle. A long gun.'

She had been determined not to be surprised, and yet she was. Belle, by all accounts, had distributed her favours, among others, to Luke Rowe. Had she hated him so much she wanted him dead? Or, like Mary Anne, did she detest the military for other crimes?

Simone was watching her, her fingers white about the handle of the hoe. 'Will you tell 'im, madame?'

Mary Anne considered the girl with narrowed eyes. If Belle was the culprit, it really was an amazing piece of luck. Belle was a rival for Nick Etwall—the only rival here. And Belle herself had handed her the weapon to destroy her. She would tell Lieutenant Rowe and so dispose of her altogether. Her mouth curled up, and Simone stepped back, stumbling over her hem.

'Madame?'

'Yes, Simone, I think he should be told, don't you? But not by me. He would believe it better coming from you.'

'But he . . .' The girl was trembling. Mary Anne took her cold hand fast in her own.

'You must come with me. Yes, you must! It is your duty.'

The girl sighed. 'It is only that Belle is bad, very bad.' She sighed again, and then straightened almost as briskly as Mary Anne. 'Yes, I will come.'

The Lieutenant's cottage was as sparse as the others. It sat on the hillside, built into it almost, sheltered by tall trees. The track leading to it ran on, round the bay. Somewhere above her, Mary Anne could hear the ring of an axe. The door to the cottage was open, and she pulled Simone forward. Her triumph was like a wave, carrying her onward. She rode the crest, straight to the door, and knocked imperiously on the jamb.

Hagetty looked up as they reached the doorway, his sharp eyes narrowing. He glanced at the Lieutenant and cleared his throat. Luke Rowe, who had been sitting with his back to the door, shiny boots propped up on the hearth, now dropped them to the earth floor and turned in his chair. The grey eyes seemed momentarily startled, but he recovered swiftly and smiled his half-smile.

'Mrs Gower! Come in.'

'You said you wanted to see me, Lieutenant.'

'So I did.'

Private Hagetty dropped his gaze. Mary Anne could feel his amusement like a warm tide. Why should he laugh at her! She wished, with a sudden gleam in her own eyes, that she could clout him across the ear and not destroy forever her role as a gentlewoman.

'Is Simone your chaperon?' Lieutenant Rowe murmured, his eyes warming at the sight of the other girl. Simone ducked her head, fingers twisting in her apron.

'Simone has something of importance to tell you.'

His grey eyes moved back to her, and went hard. Mary Anne remained impassive as they scanned her face. 'Has she indeed? You still haven't come inside, ma'am. Hagetty, shut the door behind you.'

'Sir!' The man saluted and went out. With the door shut, the light was severely diminished. Mary Anne could just view her surroundings, such as they were, in the gloom.

The cottage was larger than that of the Connors. It had two rooms; a further doorway led no doubt into a bedroom, at the back. The room they occupied was furnished with a table, two chairs and a heavy-looking trunk against the wall, under the narrow window. The hearth took up a good part of another wall, with fireplace and mantel. A uniform lay folded neatly, a bundle of letters was bound with tape, and a polished box such as a man might keep his shaving gear in all rested on top of the trunk.

Mary Anne allowed her gaze to return to Luke Rowe, who had risen to his feet. He had been smoking a cigar, and now tossed the butt into the ashes. The smell of it clung in the room—she coughed pointedly.

'Well?'

He sounded impatient. Mary Anne drew Simone forward, and the girl darted a quick glance at him before hanging her head again. Mary Anne made an impatient sound. 'It's about your hand.' It was still bandaged, she noted, but other than that he looked as healthy as ever.

'Simone?' he said, almost gently.

The girl clasped her hands firmly. 'Lieutenant, I saw that Belle. She had a gun, and she went to the timber camp. I have never seen her with a gun before. She does not . . . not shoot the game you know.'

There was a pause. Luke Rowe scanned her face briefly, but thoroughly, before turning to Mary Anne. There was something in his eyes she couldn't read. 'Thank you, Simone,' he said softly. 'You can go back to the house now. Don't speak of this to anyone else.'

'Oh no! No, Lieutenant.' The girl hurried out, slamming the door in her haste, as though she were escaping something horrible. Mary Anne turned to follow her, but he stopped her, his soft, cold voice like a blow across the face.

'What a bitch you are.'

She turned to face him, so astounded that she could only stare.

'Do you think me as thick-witted as Etwall?'

'Simone saw . . .'

'Oh yes, she saw. I don't disbelieve her.' His mouth curled in derision. 'We're discussing you, Mary Anne.'

She felt the colour sting her cheeks, the rage mounting two steps at a time, consuming all good sense and logic. 'You are obviously deranged. You don't know what you're saying.'

'Jesus,' he whispered savagely, and struck out at the grate with his boot. 'You're a cheap, conniving little bitch. Is that plain enough for you?'

Astoundingly, tears pricked at her eyes.

'You're using us all for your own gain. You've set your sights, and nothing and no one else counts. You can't even *see* what danger there is here. You're too blindly selfish. You blunder through all those fine threads, snapping them and causing turmoil. Can't you see this place is dangerous?'

'You . . .' But the tears spilled over, and she groped for the door. He was there before her, and before she knew what he was about, scooped her up against him. She struggled furiously, but he held her hands against his chest, and in the end she gave up the struggle.

'Well, isn't that what you are?' he demanded in a quiet, hard voice.

'I hate you!' she spat, shaking with fury and misery. She felt exhausted, too exhausted to do more than glare up at his face. He exhausted her with his very presence, as though he drained the vitality from her flesh. She could feel his heart, beneath the hard muscle of his chest, the rough cloth of his red coat, the shiny buttons . . . It was all unpleasant in the extreme, she thought, and said venomously, 'If there's one thing I hate more than toffee-nosed, arrogant pure merinos, it's military men. Now let me go, at once!'

He laughed, suddenly, and without humour.

'They are full of a black, viscous substance which I will not name, but which stinks as much as their morals.'

The grey eyes narrowed sharply. 'You bitch,' he said deliberately. 'First Belle, and now you. God Almighty, why should I have the misfortune to be lumbered with them?' But he let her go.

She straightened her cuffs with sharp, jerky movements. 'I'm sorry whoever shot you missed a more vital place. I do hope they try again.'

He smiled, without amusement. 'I have no doubt they will. Ma'am!' He bowed briefly and turned his back. Mary Anne went outside, slamming the door resoundingly. Private Hagetty was standing only a few feet from her. He avoided her gaze, but she caught the curve, of his lips and marched away with a furious rustle of her skirts. Damn them all! May they rot in hell! How dared he, how dared he? How could he possibly know the truth about her carefully laid schemes and plans? Had she truly given herself away as easily as that?

Her steps slowed as she reached the orchard. And what now? Was everything to end like this, so unsatisfactorily? Perhaps Luke Rowe would be despatched promptly, erasing all her troubles? And there was always cajoling and perhaps winning him to her side . . . But the thought of playing up to the Lieutenant, without Toby to protect her when things got too serious, made her shudder. Somehow she doubted the man would be content to dangle on a string, awaiting her favours. No, she must just bide her time. Nick wouldn't believe Luke Rowe anyway, if he did decide to spill the beans. She smiled arrogantly to herself, and set off at a brisk pace for the house. No, Nick was too far entangled in her charms already.

A headache kept her from the dinner table that evening. Cowardice, she knew, but it seemed the best policy. She was in no state to face Luke Rowe's sarcasm tonight —the tears had not receded far enough. Instead, she lay in her room, thinking over what he had said. About the danger, and what was going on. It seemed incomprehensible to her that there was anything other than what was plain before everyone's face. The convicts hated the Etwalls and the military. The convicts would take revenge if they had a chance. Obviously one of them had had that chance, and shot at Luke Rowe. That was all. And Belle? Well, she was dangerous, that much was obvious. Perhaps Luke had jilted her, but Belle was the one who had done the jilting, surely? No, it must be a mistake. Simone had seen Belle with a gun, but that was coincidental. The shot had been fired by a convict at the timber camp. She did not think women fired at Luke Rowe. Like Joan, they were more likely to be his champions. She grimaced. Women! They seemed to fawn on the man, God help them. They knew no better. Not so she. She would never, never forgive him. He had called her a bitch. She would never forgive him for that.

She approached Bessy the following morning in some trepidation, expecting the worst. But the woman's greeting was neither strained nor chilly, and she felt a tremendous relief. Lieutenant Rowe hadn't told them, then, in her absence. The relief trickled away beneath a wave of suspicion. What was his game? Perhaps he had believed her protestations? Perhaps he spoke like that to all women? She tried to concentrate on what Bessy was telling her.

'Ralph says we can't expect life to be easy here. To do

one's duty by God is all one can ever hope to do.'

'Indeed,' Mary Anne murmured in what she hoped a pious tone.

Bessy frowned down at her folded hands. 'I find it hard, I must admit. The convicts seem unable to see that the punishment is for their own sakes, their own . . . cleansing. They must be made clean.'

Clean? From what? What did harsh punishments do but make them more like animals, and the more likely to behave so to others? She stared at the window, Bessy's voice fading again. All she ever asked for was a nice, eligible husband, with enough money to buy pretty dresses when she wanted them, and to set her up in a nice little house in a fashionable quarter where she could occasionally catch an admiring glance or two from the class she so scorned. Not too much, surely, to ask? And now Luke Rowe was spoiling it.

Nick Etwall was home early again, and greeted her with his easy smile, his hard eyes warming as he surveyed her. 'Will you come out with me again today?'

After her worrying of the morning, it was wonderful to be able to escape into the stinging air. They rode north, round the beach towards the further rocky headland. Rocks sprang from the sea as the tide washed back and forth, black and deadly. The cliff faces stood stark, where the sea, rolling in from the horizon, struck them with an impatient, ceaseless caress.

Nick stood and gazed at the sight without comment, his harsh features drawn into a frown, his dark hair tosselled by the brisk breeze. There was a pistol tucked into his belt, half hidden by his jacket.

'Are you afraid that whoever shot at Lieutenant Rowe will try again?'

He looked at her a moment, as if weighing her words, or perhaps how best to answer her. And yet she had the impression there was more to it than that—as though he wondered if he could trust her.

'So many people,' she went on after a moment, 'have murder in their hearts for the military.'

The thin lips quirked. 'Just so. I won't dispute that, Mary Anne.'

She debated briefly whether to tell him what Simone had said. It smacked a little of telling tales, and she was loath to tarnish the man's opinion of her. If he must find out about his precious Belle, let Luke Rowe tell him. Perhaps he already had.

'It's a precaution, nothing more,' he said finally, and reaching out, took her hand in his own. It was a soft hand, but strong. A hand more used to gentling a horse and playing cards than any manual labour. She envied him that hand, and yet, incongruously, despised him for it, all at the same time.

'Come on,' he said. 'There's a place I wanted to show you.'

Grass grew tenaciously along the cliff top, sprouting from cracks in the rock. A stunted tree, bent far over by the force of the west wind, clung precariously to a patch of soil near the very edge. A track, steep and narrow, wound down from the cliff top towards the sea in a wedge-shaped area which had been sliced into the rocky face. As though someone had cut a slice of cake.

The tide was out now, and the sand stretched out around the bay. The house and cottages looked tiny at the far end, sheltered by the orchard and the tree-heavy hills. Smoke wound up through the branches at the timber camp, and more smoke drew the eye to the Lieutenant's small white cottage.

They left the horses tethered at the top, and Nick helped her to climb down what was in fact a much less steep track than she had thought from above. Beneath them, where the sea had receded, the water lay trapped in pools and crevices of rock. Further out, where the waves still surged, mats of weed moved and shimmered green beneath the pale sun. They reached the bottom at last, laughing and puffing. Nick held her hand and they picked their way over the rocks, towards the sea.

Well-brought-up young ladies did not walk hand in hand with gentlemen they hardly knew, Mary Anne reminded herself. But she couldn't seem to draw way, couldn't pretend to be something she was not.

It was sheltered here, where buttresses of rock rose and made a sheltering niche. There was a larger pool, too, in close to the rock, shining green in its depths, the water like a mirror.

'It's beautiful,' she said, and Nick laughed.

'Extremely.' He paused, looking up to the face of the cliff, where far above more scrubby bushes dotted the unsafe, almost soil-less ledges. Mary Anne stooped to fan her hand in the water. It felt warm from the sun and the sheltered position, and when she shook her fingers, droplets of water scattered and circled, making patterns.

She smiled up at Nick and asked, 'Do you come here much?'

'Not often, no. I'm so rarely at Etwall, and when I am I don't have the time. It's a special place; my place.'

Her mouth curled wider. 'And mine, now.'

He put his hand on her cheek, tracing the line of her jaw to her chin. 'Tell me about this husband,' he said at last. 'About the man you married.'

She frowned, but his eyes were curious, insistent.

'Where did you meet him?' he murmured, and sat down on a rock, stretching out his long legs.

She smiled. 'At an inn. I met him at an inn. We were staying there, and it so happened we had both reserved the parlour for our supper.'

'And?'

She turned to look at the sea. Why should he want to know? The past should mean nothing to him. Perhaps, after all, he knew the truth. Perhaps Luke had told him. Perhaps he was testing her. With superb control, she turned and smiled a little sadly. 'And we arranged to meet again, and he was kind to me, and gentle, and in time . . .'

'Yes?' The black brows lifted.

'He was wealthy, in a small way, and my father approved of him, and after a time it was settled.'

'Just like that?'

'How else should it be? Unmarried girls have little say in their futures.'

He rose, his solemn mood going as abruptly as it had come. Stooping to her, he brushed his mouth across hers lightly—an affectionate kiss rather than one of passion. 'Come on,' he murmured. 'We'd better get back. My brother will be cursing me; we were supposed to be going over more of his damned books.'

She laughed, as much with relief as amusement. It was all right, then. It had been just curiosity after all. How stupid she had been to think differently!

'Perhaps you should return to Hobart,' she said off-handedly, as they scaled the path to their horses.

'Perhaps I should. And if all goes well, I shall.'

That sounded intriguing, but she bit her tongue on more questions. He would tell her in his own time, no doubt. For a time, at least, she must play it safe and be patient.

'No news about the shot, Lieutenant Rowe?' Ralph Etwall leaned forward over his plate, eyes narrowed. Luke glanced up at him, his smile twisting his mouth.

'Everyone seemed remarkably unhelpful,' he replied smoothly.

Nick frowned. 'What did you expect? Redcoats aren't greatly loved, to my knowledge, by anyone at Etwall. We didn't ask for them, and we neither need them nor want them.'

There was a pause. Mary Anne concentrated on her food. The atmosphere was anything but relaxed. Luke Rowe's fault, of course. Why had he come? Surely he could have rested his damned hand a few days more? She had been uncomfortably aware of her heart quickening from the moment he came into the room. Fear brought her eyes, wider than she meant, to his neat figure. But he had barely glanced at her, and when he did, his eyes were cold and hard. That had infuriated her. What right had he to despise her? If anyone had to be despised, then surely it was he! A disgraced officer sent to the wilds.

'Your hand is healing, Lieutenant?' Bessy murmured, polite without feeling. Her blue eyes were cool. He was, she no doubt thought, beneath her station.

'Thank you, yes.' He smiled a little. He knew he was far from loved in the Etwall stronghold. Perhaps it gave him a perverse pleasure to force their polite acceptance of him.

Mary Anne glanced across the table at Nick, but he was staring at his own plate, abstracted. Simone moved about the outer rim of lamplight, serving the meal and pouring the wine. The girl's presence served to remind her, unpleasantly, of the man sitting beside her, and she flicked him a glance of distaste.

'Have you *any* idea of the culprit?' Ralph asked at last, his worried face a mass of lines, deepened by the soft light.

'I have many ideas, but no proof as yet.' Grey eyes mocked. Nick looked up, and was frowning. The voice beside Mary Anne dropped in tone. 'A guess, nothing more. Time enough to speak of it when there is proof.'

'And until then?' Nick demanded. 'You make it sound as if you suspect one of us, man!'

A silence. Mary Anne could tell by the way Nick was frowning so darkly that the Lieutenant was smiling.

After the meal, Nick excused himself. He paused long enough, however, to take Mary Anne's hand in his. 'Good night,' he murmured, his eyes making the words almost indecent. She felt the colour, foolishly, rush to her cheeks. The door closed behind him, and for a moment she sat near the window, staring into the darkness and listening to the sea. Then Lieutenant Rowe also rose, murmuring good night. Mary Anne met his gaze in the window and found contempt. The door closed on him as well, and the silence was broken only by the ticking of the clock, the sea, and the scratch of Ralph's pen.

A rustle of skirts, and Bessy joined her at the window, smiling. 'My brother-in-law is fond of you,' she said quietly, and patted Mary Anne's hand. But her own was cold, and behind the smile her eyes were bleak.'

'Do you think so?'

'Oh, he is. I've watched him . . . and you.' A pause. 'I suppose it was wrong of me to allow you both to be alone so often, and yet I felt there surely was no harm.' Her eyes went a little hard. 'Women have little choice when it comes to marriage, my dear. A married woman counts, an unmarried one is nothing. She has no standing and no freedoms, she is hemmed in and fenced in, a virtual prisoner. My words, of course, apply to gentlewomen.' She smiled again, stretching her lips. 'My brother-in-law is a good man. A little wild, perhaps, but when he is settled . . .'

Mary Anne arched her eyebrows in surprise. 'You speak as if the matter were already decided, ma'am.'

Bessy glanced away, 'Do I? Perhaps because I hoped it was. I have watched you smile at him, Mary Anne.'

Anger built inside Mary Anne, but she controlled it. Who was Bessy Etwall to speak to her like this? As though she were bestowing Nick on her like some hatbox all tied up with pretty paper and ribbons!

'Well, perhaps I have said enough,' Bessy said quickly, and turned to other matters.

Inside Mary Anne, the rage congealed; set like fat in cold water. Nick was not Bessy's to give. He belonged to Mary Anne. She felt a twinge of pity for the other woman, but shrugged it off. Bessy had a husband, and a house and a station in life. Mary Anne needed all three. And, as Toby had often said, if one wanted something badly enough, one had to take it.

CHAPTER SIX

THE MILDER weather continued. Everyone seemed busy, and with only her sewing to occupy her, Mary Anne spent her time walking in the tiny garden and the bare orchard. Nick had warned her about wandering too far; the gunman was yet to be found. She did not understand why the Lieutenant had not told them it was Belle, and had her arrested. Mary Anne could not imagine he was protecting her, and thought he must be waiting for more information. It made no sense; she didn't bother her head with it.

What would Toby have thought of it all? She tried to conjure him up, with some helpful advice, but all she could see was the contempt in Luke Rowe's eyes, the puzzled surprise in Bessy Etwall's, and the warm glow in Nick's.

With a start, she realised she had walked further than she had intended, and was nearing the track down from the further headland, where Nick and she had ridden that day. She climbed to the cliff tops and wandered to the edge where the narrow path led down. The tide was again out, and the pool was there, as green and glassy as before. She felt the prick of the sun through her clothes, an uncomfortable trickle of perspiration between her shoulderblades. It would be nice to slip into the warm, clear water. Toby had bathed with her once, long ago. He had laughed at her stringy hair, and splashed her until she spluttered for mercy. Strange, but now that she thought of it, he had always treated her like a fellow conspirator, a companion in crime, rather than a woman.

The pool, now she had reached it, really was the same.

The water felt warm. She glanced about her. The place was well sheltered from the bay, facing only the sea, and that was clear to the horizon. Hidden, secret. A breeze, salty and gentle, played on the overhanging greenery of the cliff, but nothing else stirred above the wash of the waves further down the rocky shelf.

She began, slowly, to unfasten her gown.

The loneliness she found soothing to her nerves—strange, that in so isolated a place it was so difficult to be completely alone. Her fingers pulled and twisted hooks and buttons, slipping off the layers of convention. She folded her clothes neatly on a near-by rock and slipped the emerald, which she always wore, among them, hidden from sight.

The soles of her feet curled at the rough warmth of the rock, and she sat down at the edge of the pool to dangle her legs in the water. It was warm on top, so still in the sun, but a foot or so beneath the surface it was cooler, and she shuddered with pleasure. The sun's rays penetrated the water like golden spears, but beyond their length the water was secret, and cloudy. The depths could hide anything . . . For a moment she hesitated, but the water looked too inviting to be denied by foolish fears. She slipped, at last, fully in.

She went down what seemed a long way, and came up as fast, spluttering and laughing, as she scrambled to cling to the rocky edge. Water splashed, glinting in the sun, and the sound was somehow disturbing in the peace of the place. Salty ripples licked at her chin, and she turned over on her back, letting her long, dark hair trail behind her. Above, the sky spiralled beyond the cliff top, far, far away. A bird hovered, gliding back over the land. Insects hummed, the sea splashed. She closed her eyes with a contented sigh.

Where was the genteel, modest Mrs Gower now? She giggled at the thought, remembering with pleasure the performance of the past weeks. The water soothed her, and she floated with eyes closed, pale in the green water. Already she had grown used to the life at Etwall. The uncomfortable dinners and the look in Nick's eyes. She smiled, thinking how clever she had been. After all, her husband was drowned, and all who knew her were supposedly in Sydney Town, too far away to cause questions to be asked. No one in Hobart was to know she did not speak the truth. Who was there to call her bluff, when the time came for Nick to make her his wife?

Her mind wandered pleasantly over this aspect, picturing a rosy future. She was so busy planning and plotting that she heard nothing until a rattle of a rock falling startled her. She jerked up, splashing noisily, and gazing wide-eyed round the little niche. Everything seemed so still and empty, and yet . . . she had heard it. That rattle of a dislodged stone, and the scrape of something against a rocky surface. Her heart beat uncomfortably fast, and she searched the place again, more slowly, clinging fast to the rocky edge of the pool, her legs and feet cool in the depths. But there was nothing. How could there be? Perhaps it was an animal, a creature as frightened as she. A bird, perhaps, had swooped. The idea comforted her and she sighed, and began to relax back into the water. It was all right. Everything was all right. Except . . .

Her breath caught so hard she nearly choked. Her clothes! They had been folded on that rock, and now they were gone. For another moment she stared at the empty space, not quite believing it was so empty. There was a knot of cold dread in her stomach, rolling round and round. Someone had stolen up close, close enough to see her naked in the water, and stood watching. And then they had taken her clothes, and . . . and what? She searched again. The buttress of the cliff that sheltered her from the bay could be climbed round, if one were agile and quick. That was no doubt where they had gone to so swiftly. And with her clothes, and . . .

For a moment her mind refused to work, and then horror overwhelmed dread, numbing her rapidly cooling limbs. The emerald! The beautiful priceless emerald that Toby had given to her, saying so wonderfully,

'Our future!'

Oh God, it had gone with her clothes.

Her mind darted madly. What sneaking, peeping Tom would come here? Whoever knew of it besides Nick? Lieutenant Rowe? But what reason could he have? Or was contempt enough? But why take her clothes; why not just humiliate her? Simone? Why should Simone bother her—and wouldn't she be missed? She must get them back. The emerald. Her future. Without it, she had no choice but Nick, and even with Nick she would have no money to pretend with, nothing to put up as a front, nothing to use if things got tough.

The sun went under a cloud, the air chilled as suddenly, taking her anger with it. How in God's name was she to get back to the house? It might have been ludicrous—Toby would have laughed—only she didn't smile. Her mind darted and turned like a hare trapped before a pack of hounds. How could she walk along the headland stark naked? Or hover in the orchard, waiting to attract attention? How could she stay here, waiting, until darkness, and then make her way back in the deadly dark . . . or indeed, swim, for the tide would be well in by then! And whoever had been watching her might stay, too, and . . . who knew what he might do.

The idea terrified her anew, and she stared round her again, huddling against the side of the pool. Anyone could be hiding there, behind the buttress of sheltering rock. Hiding, and laughing to themselves, waiting. Perhaps it was the same person who had shot at Luke Rowe. Belle?

She shivered, suddenly and violently. Her teeth had begun to chatter. It was colder than before, and without the sun the water was chilling swiftly. She clung on grimly, though her fingers had started to shake, and tried to cover her breasts with her tangled hair.

Simone had said that the sea was never cheated of souls. Perhaps she was right. Perhaps she herself had been meant to die with the others, all along, and now the sea was about to take revenge on her. Oh God, the tide! Her chin jerked up, and she scanned the sea. It was still some way out, but it would start to rise soon enough, and once started, it came in swiftly and treacherously. Nick had warned her about the tides. She could not stay here long. It was either face the humiliation and lurking danger, or remain and drown.

Her toes were numb; she wriggled them in an agony of indecision. Perhaps whoever had taken her clothes was just waiting for her to get out of the pool before taking a shot at her? How much time had passed now? Five minutes? Ten, fifteen? She tightened her grip on the edge, noticing how wrinkled the flesh of her fingers was becoming. She couldn't recall clearly her sojourn in the sea, but she remembered the way her fingers had wrinkled. Her arm began suddenly to ache, in sympathy, the pink scar livid against the white of her flesh. A mindless fear gripped her; a fear of the water cooling about her body, of the slap of the waves and the low roar of the sea. It drowned out the other fears, the fear of the thief and the gun, and the missing emerald. If she did not move, the sea would have her. She contracted her muscles in a move to push herself clear out onto the rocks.

At the same moment, somewhere beyond the out-cropping rock, came a rattle of stones and a low, mono-tonous sound, like whistling. She was so startled that she dropped back into the water, flaying and floundering to regain her hold. The splashing blinded her, and filled her mouth with salt water. Please God, she thought dizzily, not now . . . Don't let me die now!

A shadow fell over her—the sun had come back. She

glimpsed red cloth, and with a cry ducked completely under the water. The green depths stung her eyes, and she held her breath until her ears hummed and her heart threatened to burst, while her blood sang through a million veins and arteries, weeping for air.

She came to the surface with a rush, gasping weakly, breathing and breathing. She was too weak to struggle when he grabbed her hair and, painfully, hauled her over to the edge. The pain of the stone scraping her tender flesh jarred her mind back to reality. The dizziness subsided.

He was crouched beside the pool, a little dampened by splashing, staring down at her as if he could hardly believe his eyes. She gasped, and began to struggle, but his fingers only tightened more painfully in her hair, jerking her head back.

'Mary Anne?' he said, and his eyes narrowed and slid down her white throat to the transparency of the water. She screamed and he shook her, and she screamed again. His hand forced down and she went under. The scream died abruptly.

When he released her, she came up like a cork, spluttering and coughing, her lungs aching for a second time. He caught her arm this time, hurting the hardly healed wound. She felt the rock scrape at her stomach as he lifted her and dragged her out on to the edge, leaving her legs to trail in the water.

His hands pressed down on her back, hurting again. She felt water come up her throat and was, involuntarily, sick. Tears of misery and humiliation poured down her cheeks, burning the cold flesh. She lay limp and still, hardly noticing the rough rock digging into her, or the jabs and jerks from her tangled hair every time she moved.

'Here.' Something warm was pushed at her, and over her, covering her. Hands, warm and gentle, forced her arms awkwardly into the long sleeves. She moaned, and tried weakly to struggle. 'Stop it,' he said sharply and, finishing with her arms, dragged her bodily from the water, setting her down on her knees. Her chin dropped to her chest and more tears trickled down her cheeks. He supported her in the crook of his arm and began, businesslike, to button up the front of his jacket. It was *his* jacket, she realised, shivering in its warmth. The red one. It smelt of tobacco and sweat, and him. Her mother, she felt sure, was even now turning in her shallow grave!

'There!' he said, with satisfaction, and sat back from her, where she knelt before him, dejected and weak with misery. The jacket swallowed her, literally. The cuffs hung down over her hands, the hem reached her knees. After a moment she clasped her shaking fingers, drawing strength. He seemed to be waiting for something—an explanation, perhaps. She still felt ill, but the growing anger was both warming and invigorating. She lifted her head at last, her hair falling back over her shoulders, and glared at him.

He was smiling, laughter lurking like sunlight in his grey eyes. He met her glare blandly, and in the end it was she who, with a sniff, looked away. The pool still rippled from her struggles—she flushed at the memory.

'I could say you were making a habit of this, but I doubt it would be appreciated,' he murmured. She sniffed again, and he rose and held out his hand. She took it ungraciously, and let him pull her to her feet.

For a moment her legs wavered, and she clung to the hand, trying to clear her head. 'Poor Mary Anne,' he said, and tilting her chin suddenly up, closed his mouth on hers. She shivered, too weak to pull away as his warm lips caressed hers. He drew away as suddenly, and pulled her against him, pressing her face to his damp shoulder. She was crying again, stupid weak tears, and tried to jerk away. But he held her easily, and when she twisted her face, straining back from his warmth, he said in a harsh voice,

'Be still, woman, I'm only trying to warm you.'

'Warm me!'

'How was I to know you were here? Ladies generally don't swim naked in broad daylight.'

The words bit. She thrust away from him harder, and this time he let her go. 'Was it you?' she demanded, her voice husky. Her throat ached, and stung with salt.

'Me what?' he seemed puzzled, and amused. His mouth twitched as he surveyed her. She supposed she did look a sight. God, how much she loathed him!

'Who came spying? Who took my clothes?'

'Your clothes?' he gave a bark of laughter. 'Jesus, so that's what the bitch was about!'

'How dare . . . How dare you call me . . .'

Her voice trembled with fury, but he only laughed again. 'Not you, though if the truth be known . . . Belle. I followed her. She probably followed you. She used to come here with Nick Etwall; proper little love-nest it was then. Now he's brought you here. Belle wouldn't like that.'

She stared at him speechlessly, her dark eyes wide with mingled shock and outrage. 'I don't believe it!'

The grey eyes darkened with mockery, his mouth curled. 'You'd do the same, I imagine, if the tables turned. An effective revenge, wouldn't you say? If I hadn't come along . . .' The smile broadened as the connotations of the situation came to him. She lifted a hand to strike him, but he stepped back and she almost lost her balance and fell into the pool. A wave crashed close by. His head came up, and he frowned. 'Tide's coming in.' She followed his gaze, and bit her lip, but he had already turned towards the cliffs, saying in an arrogant, detestable voice, 'Come on.'

For a moment she stood glaring after him, as he disappeared around the outcrop of the rock. But he didn't come back, and the tide *was* coming in more quickly than she liked. Besides, the clouds had returned, and completely covered the pale sun. They were darker out over the sea—brooding. There might be a storm. She had had her fill of storms for a lifetime.

She felt the tears prick again, tears of frustration, and began to hurry after him, wincing as her soles were bruised on the sharp, uneven rocks. The coat was of rough cloth that chafed her tender skin. She felt sticky with drying salt, and the scratches on her stomach were starting to sting painfully. And apart from all that was the humiliation and—oh God!—the loss of the emerald.

He was some yards away by the time she reached the rocky buttress, striding easily over the sharpest stones. She tried to quicken her own steps, but it hurt too much. The waves were much closer, and a particularly large one broke with a roar, the white foam rushing round her ankles. She stood huddled on a relatively flat rock until it had receded, trying to quell her panic.

'All right?' a voice said close to her, making her jump. She glared up at him.

'There's no need to wait.'

The grey eyes mocked. 'Likely you'll be carried out with the tide. Come here!' He bent, and swung her up into his arms. She was too surprised to say anything, but as he began to walk with her she cried out and twisted in his arms. He held her even tighter, and said, 'This gives me even less pleasure than it does you!'

The words stung, and she went still, staring away to the rising bulk of the sea. The clouds were deepening along the horizon, and the air felt thick, unstirring. But at least it was too gloomy for them to be easily seen from across the bay, at the house. She prayed it was so. Besides, he seemed to be keeping to the cliff and its poor shelter, as though he, too, feared being seen by the Etwalls.

'Why don't you do something about Belle?' she said at last in a sulky voice.

'She's best left free,' he said briefly. His voice was cold again; he had remembered his contempt for her, she supposed. Besides, they'd reached the track and he'd begun to climb up to it, breathing quickly. They reached the top soon enough, though she had to force herself not to cry out. But he neither dropped her nor slipped, and she was glad she had stayed silent.

When he set her down, she had to cling to a tree-trunk to regain composure and the shaky use of her body. He wiped a hand across his brow and frowned up at the sky. 'Looks like what fair weather we had is gone. At least for the time.' The frown extended to her. 'There won't be a ship while it lasts.'

She ignored that, and turned back towards Etwall. She felt safe in the shelter of the trees, and could examine the settlement without flinching. The house brooded against its backdrop of pines, and beyond it the cluster of cottages huddled on the edge of the marsh, their smoke pale protection against the threat of the storm. What a fool she had been to come here like this! If only she could learn a little common sense, as Toby had always told her, how much better life would be! Then she would not feel sticky and uncomfortable, with her hair clinging like a weed. Then she would still have the emerald to keep her warm for the future.

There had been a choice. Now there was none.

'You've no choice,' Luke Rowe said, as though reading her thoughts. 'You'll have to come with me.'

She opened her mouth, but he was right. She had no choice. She flicked a glance at him, but he looked as annoyed as she, and she nodded without replying.

The soft earth was kind enough to her tender feet, but as they wound their way further into the bush, it gave way to wiry shrubs and hidden stones and spikes.

Everything seemed to drip with moisture; everything was dark. The silence frightened her.

Branches tore now, and scratched. The bush hemmed them in, the undergrowth hadn't been touched by man in a long time. This was how it must be for those poor devils incarcerated at Macquarie Harbour, only worse. No escape. And even if they reached the interior, what was there to reach? Scarred, rocky escarpments swathed in milky, continuous rain, a luxuriant, deadly forest of green.

He paused ahead of her, to gauge their position. She took the opportunity to rub her calf and twist her hair back over her shoulder. The air was chill, and she huddled the coat closer about her. He started off again almost immediately, and she followed, her feet sinking into damp, mouldering soil. The ground began to slope, after a time, and she knew they were descending again to the bay and the beach. The timber camp was no doubt somewhere to their left—pray God they didn't come upon that!

Lieutenant Rowe turned, pushing his hair back from his eyes. He was sweating, and the white shirt stuck to his chest and sides, stained in patches with earth and sap. 'You can see the bay now,' he said, 'through there.'

She peered, and there was the network of grey water between the leaves. They started down. She tripped once on a root, hurting her toe, but he glanced at her with no more than impatient amusement before hauling her back to her feet. The cottage was immediately below them now, and she could see the roof jutting out of the hillside and smell the slightly stinging smell of the chimney smoke.

'I'll get rid of Hagetty and McDonald,' the Lieutenant said. 'Wait here.' His glance told her there was little else she could do.

She glared, biting her tongue to stop her lips

trembling. He laughed softly and turned away, whistling casually as he descended to the cottage.

Voices. She crouched low in a patch of undergrowth, trying to be invisible. A door closed. The sky was almost black now, making the afternoon more like early night. A low rumble spread across the sea, drawing her eyes. Sheet lightning flickered deadly white, followed by another low rumble. A sudden, brief breeze whispered around her, curling the ends of her drying hair.

She was so intent on the approaching storm that she did not realise he was approaching until she heard the close crunch of earth and undergrowth. 'Mary Anne?'

She got up, and moved swiftly forward. The sooner she was safe at Etwall, the better. The storm frightened her, and there were memories connected with it best put aside. Her foot caught in a vine, and she stumbled, coming down the last of the slope at a run. He caught her with a grunt, and swung her about to stop himself from falling. She opened her mouth to berate him, but he was already drawing her into the warmth of the cottage, and remembering in time what he could still do to her reputation, she stayed silent.

The fire sent out waves of heat, and she sank into a chair beside it and leaned forward. Luke Rowe poured out some brandy and brought it over to her. She sipped it, letting the fire warm her inside as well as out. After a moment, he said, 'I've sent Hagetty to Simone.'

'He doesn't . . .'

'Know you're here? No.' He sat down abruptly opposite her. 'I warned you about the dangers here, didn't I? But you're so self-centred, so busy practising your wiles on Etwall.'

'My wiles!' she returned furiously, the brandy slopping on her hand.

'Perhaps, now, when the ship to Hobart comes, you'll be ready to leave.'

'It's none of your affair,' she said, shaking in the effort

to preserve dignity while her blood burned for her to strike out.

'No?' he mocked, his eyes as hard and angry as hers. 'I think, if you stayed, you might be sorry. Very sorry. I'd see to it personally.'

'It has nothing to do with you! Etwall is not, as yet, under military rule.'

'I still happen to be the military commander here, and as such am in charge of all safety measures.'

'Safety measures! What possible difference can I make to you and your damned safety measures?'

'Look, you stupid, stubborn . . .' He broke off, and rose as abruptly as he had sat down, striding to the window. In the pause, Mary Anne tried to control the urge to rake her nails across his cheek. There was a loud crackle of thunder overhead, mirroring her feelings.

'Simone's coming.' His voice was quiet now, controlled.

There was barely time for Mary Anne to crouch lower in her chair when the girl had reached the door and he had opened it. She came uncertainly into the room, and her eyes bulged at the sight of Mary Anne in the red coat. 'Madame!'

Luke Rowe's mouth twitched, wryly. 'Yes, it is. Madam has met with an accident in the water, Simone. Can you bring a dress and . . . well, whatever you think necessary. A cap, too, perhaps. Her hair is still wet. And hurry! It's going to rain, and I'll be damned if I'll have her trapped here with me until it stops.'

She went, running. He turned back to confront Mary Anne, grey eyes mocking the expected attack. She opened her mouth, but the words that came out weren't the ones she'd prepared. She had seen his hand.

The white bandages were stained red: bright, fresh red. The thunder shook the sky again; a gust of wind set the trees swaying and hissing. 'Your hand is bleeding,' she said conversationally, though her mouth was oddly dry. He glanced down at it with surprise. 'You'd best let me re-bandage it, seeing I'm the one who probably caused it to bleed.'

'You may as well make yourself useful.' He sat down opposite her again. She met the mockery in his eyes coolly.

'You won't make me bite again,' she said blandly, and began to unwind the bandage as carefully as she could. It came easily, and after some mopping, she could examine the wound. It was healing, though parts had split to cause this bleeding. He flinched when she dabbed on the ointment he handed her. 'What is this?'

A shrug. 'Hagetty swears by it. He made it up, out of the bush.'

'Out of the bush? It's a wonder you're not poisoned!'

'And why should I be? If the natives can survive in these surroundings, why can't I?'

There was a clean bandage, and she began to rewind it, frowning. 'I suppose this will stand me in good stead when I take up work for the needy,' she murmured. 'I suppose I will have to. It wasn't only my clothes Belle stole. The emerald . . .'

'The what!'

'The emerald you so admired, remember?' She darted him a mocking glance. He looked quite pale. 'The one my husband gave to me,' she added. 'You *do* remember?'

He pulled his hand away, frowning. 'Oh, I remember. It was considered unlucky, I believe. You're well rid of it.'

'Well rid of it!' she whispered, and tears pricked her eyes. She had not cried so much in her life as she had today, and yet she couldn't seem to help herself. 'Well rid of it? *He* gave it to me, just before *Infanta* went down, saying . . .'

'If you had worn it in Hobart,' he retorted harshly, 'you would have been arrested for thieving. An emerald like that can't be stolen without the newspapers screaming it out to all and sundry.'

'Stolen?' She turned away. 'I don't know what you mean.'

He made an impatient sound, and caught her chin, forcing her face round. 'Don't you indeed! How would you fancy a few years in the Female Factory, hmm? Would you enjoy your little cell, and your prison rations, and your daily session on the treadmill? You'd soon lose your pretty looks then, my girl, and that temper. There'd be nothing left but the lowest emotions; like the rest, you'd be willing to do most things to be allowed to live.'

'Do you know all this from personal experience?' she whispered, harsh in fear.

'But of course!' He leaned closer, and his fingers slid along her jaw. 'I believe when he was in the army, Nick Etwall found a whore in that way. Personally, I find little to excite me in such women . . . I pity them too much.'

'Why should I care what Nick Etwall has done, or what you say?' she retorted. She felt curiously loath to draw away, and when he stooped even closer, let her eyelids flicker and close. His mouth was soft and gentle. She knew then, almost immediately, why she hadn't drawn away. Because she had wanted him to kiss her, because she had known all along that his kiss would not be that same, desperate performance she was used to. Even while she had been hating him, some part of her had claimed him as *the man* for her.

His fingers slid down her throat, and his kiss deepened. She felt her mind begin to cloud—all the determination and warnings, all the fears, fading beneath this feeling growing inside her. She put her arms round his neck, and felt his hand slide under the stiff collar of the coat, warm on her bare shoulder, cupping her breast. She was shaking, and when the thunder cracked so close and so loud, pressed closer to him,

1. How do you rate: _____
   (Please print book TITLE)

   1.6 ☐ excellent   .4 ☐ good   .2 ☐ not so good
   .5 ☐ very good   .3 ☐ fair   .1 ☐ poor

2. How likely are you to purchase another book:
   in this *series*?   by this *author*?

   2.1 ☐ definitely would purchase   3.1 ☐ definitely would purchase
   .2 ☐ probably would purchase   .2 ☐ probably would purchase
   .3 ☐ probably would not purchase   .3 ☐ probably would not purchase
   .4 ☐ definitely would not purchase   .4 ☐ definitely would not purchase

3. How does this book compare with romance books you usually read?

   4.1 ☐ far better than others   .4 ☐ not as good
   .2 ☐ better than others   .5 ☐ definitely not as good
   .3 ☐ about the same

4. Please check the statements you feel best describe this book.

   5 ☐ Realistic conflict   18 ☐ Too many foreign/unfamiliar words
   6 ☐ Too much violence/anger   19 ☐ Couldn't put the book down
   7 ☐ Not enough drama   20 ☐ Liked the setting
   8 ☐ Especially romantic   21 ☐ Made me feel good
   9 ☐ Original plot   22 ☐ Heroine too independent
   10 ☐ Good humor in story   23 ☐ Hero too dominating
   11 ☐ Not enough humor   24 ☐ Unrealistic conflict
   12 ☐ Not enough description of setting   25 ☐ Not enough romance
   13 ☐ Didn't like the subject   26 ☐ Too much description of setting
   14 ☐ Fast paced   27 ☐ Ideal hero
   15 ☐ Too predictable   28 ☐ Slow moving
   16 ☐ Heroine too juvenile/weak/silly   29 ☐ Not enough suspense
   17 ☐ Believable characters   30 ☐ Liked the subject

5. What aspect of the story outline on the back of the cover appealed to you most?

   31 ☐ location   32 ☐ subject
   33 ☐ characters   34 ☐ element of suspense in plot
   35 ☐ description of conflict

6. Did you feel this story was:

   36.1 ☐ too sexy
   .2 ☐ just sexy enough
   .3 ☐ not too sexy

7. Please indicate how many romance paperbacks you read in a month.

   37.1 ☐ 1 to 4   .2 ☐ 5 to 10   .3 ☐ 11 to 15   .4 ☐ more than 15

8. Please indicate your sex and age group.

   38.1 ☐ Male   39.1 ☐ under 18   .3 ☐ 25-34   .5 ☐ 50-64
   .2 ☐ Female   .2 ☐ 18-24   .4 ☐ 35-49   .6 ☐ 65 or older

9. Have you any additional comments about this book?

   (40)_____
   (41)_____
   (42)_____
   (43)_____

SABCDEFGHIJ

Thank you for completing and returning this questionnaire.

PRINTED IN U.S.A.

slipping to her knees on the floor by the fire and his chair. He stroked her face, looking down into it, the misty eyes, the untidy hair streaming down her back, the red of her mouth.

'Mary Anne,' he murmured, his lips brushing hers again. 'I can always send Simone away again.'

Her first thought was: Oh Lord, what would my mother say? To lie abed with a bloody redcoated lieutenant? Her second was: I've never felt like I'd want to lie abed with anyone before, not Toby and not Nick and not any of the other nameless men I've flirted with. I never may again. This is a once-only thing—I know it.

He took her silence, evidently, for assent, for suddenly he was kissing her again, taking away what breath she had left to protest. He was lifting her up off the ground, where she knelt, up against his chest, close between his white-breeched thighs. She felt his tongue slide over her teeth, seeking the sweet secrets of her mouth, even as his hands were finding those of her body. She wanted him to go on; he had lit a fire she had not known was there to light, and which would now never be quenched, except by him.

Her head was spinning. She drew his head closer, feeling the tosselled silkiness of his hair in her fingers. He was kissing her throat, nuzzling the hollow between her breasts, and for a moment she was too dizzy to realise that someone was outside, tapping on the door.

He stood up so suddenly that she fell to one side, gasping. When she was able to comprehend that Simone was there and what he meant to do, her eyes went to the narrow bed in the other room. And she knew it would be a mistake. He would use her and discard her. Why shouldn't he? He cared nothing for her; it would be a waste of her innocence and her emotions. Was not the loss of the emerald—the future—enough for one day?

Legs shaking, she rose to call Simone back, but the girl was already inside, coming to take her arm. She met

Luke's eyes across her head. They were hard, grim. He, too, it seemed, had thought better.

Simone was babbling, flushed and breathless from the run, about the storm, and to hurry. Mary Anne snatched the bundle of clothes with shaking hands. Luke Rowe had taken up a cigar, and as he lit it, turned for the door. 'I'll wait outside, to save your . . . modesty.' The door slammed sharply on the irony. Mary Anne began hastily to dress.

Simone helped her to shrug off the coat and pull on her own clothes. They were warm and dry after her cold experience, and familiar. She felt she was herself again, calm and clear. She found she was shocked, and angry . . . very angry. Thank God Simone had come when she did! It was all a terrible joke, it must be. Why on earth had she become so helpless when faced with her enemy?

The wind was stronger, and spots of rain hit the roof with echoey thuds. Simone opened the door. Luke was standing against the wall, leaning back, the smoke from his cigar a cloud in the air. He looked round without interest when Mary Anne stepped out, and turned away again. Mary Anne thought, with a sense of shocked outrage, that he cared for her no more than he would a harlot.

And why should he care more? She was stupid. Stupid, stupid, stupid! He was a soldier, and therefore he had no morals, no sense of right and wrong, no care for those less fortunate, no love for women beyond physical use. She thanked God again that Simone had come. To be tied to such a man as he must blast her hopes for all eternity. She would end as her mother had, a sodden, abused wreck of a woman.

'You'd better hurry,' he said coolly. The rain was splattering on the ground, raising dust. Simone clutched her hand, pulling her out into the strengthening wind. Luke Rowe ground out the cigar under his heel, the wind tousling his fair hair.

'Don't stay here at Etwall,' he said, without turning. 'Remember what I said. You know how dangerous it is, now.' He did turn then, but she didn't answer, and when Simone tugged her arm gave in to the girl, allowing herself to be pulled after her down the track towards the house.

Rain pelted them, so hard that it hurt, but she lifted her face, welcoming it against her hair and skin. At least here would be an explanation for the damp hair, if one were needed. Besides, she wanted to wash herself free of all contamination by him, and all her own stupidity in thinking him to be different. And if some little voice inside her mocked that she would never be free again if she were drenched a hundred times, she ignored it, and carried on.

CHAPTER SEVEN

THE RAIN started a spate of cold, rainy weather, and Mary Anne had no choice but to remain indoors during the day, while the men, grumbling in Nick's case, had to go out to their work. There was sewing to do, and help to give Bessy in the house and dairy.

The bad weather washed three more bodies up on the beach, and Ralph came to tell her, his tired eyes sympathetic. 'All seamen by the look of their clothes,' he said. 'There's been some wreckage, too. Bits and pieces of timber from the ship itself.'

'Yes.'

'Of course, your husband may never . . . That is, he may be trapped in the wreckage itself, or . . . You needn't worry, Mary Anne,' he put his hand on hers. 'You won't be called upon to identify him now.'

She bowed her head, thanking him softly, and he smiled and went on, 'Strange, how one gets used so quickly to new faces. I can hardly imagine Etwall now without you.'

Her smile was not feigned.

Nicholas had not heard of the episode at the pool. He would never smile at her so, if he knew. 'There are usually ships calling in before the winter really sets in,' he told her, one night at dinner. 'When this bit of a blow-up settles down, Mary Anne, there will be one along for you.'

She nodded. Bessy cleared her throat, glancing at them before starting a rather hectic conversation with Ralph.

'Speed on fair winds,' a voice mocked softly at her side. She turned a cold look on him, but he seemed

unimpressed. He had been sarcastic, and cruel, since the
day of the storm. He hated her, and she him, more than
ever. She had come to dread meeting him here at dinner
every night—elsewhere she had learned to avoid the
places he might happen to be.

Later, at cards, he beat her at every turn until even
Ralph was moved to protest that it was hardly gentle-
manlike. But Mary Anne laughed airily and rose to her
feet, saying, 'My mind, I'm afraid, wanders when I find
something very tedious.'

'You won't find Hobart tedious,' Luke Rowe said,
and glanced up at her from his perusal of the deck.

'Without my friends?' she retorted, and her smile
encompassed Nick and Ralph and Bessy, widening and
making her beautiful.

The Lieutenant, however, seemed unimpressed, and
after viewing her as one might coolly appraise a work of
art, said, 'You'll make new ones, I'm sure. I have quite a
few there myself. I'd be honoured to give you a few
names.'

'Thank you, no!'

He smiled. 'They're rich.'

'Rowe.' Nicholas's voice was quiet and hard. The blue
eyes scanned the other man's face. 'What's your game?
You're being deliberately insulting. Mrs Gower says she
doesn't want to meet your friends. I must say I can only
agree with her good taste!'

The smile remained, but the grey eyes had turned as
hard as granite. 'Good taste is something I've yet to see
from our Mrs Gower.'

The silence was brief and potent. Nick rose slowly to
his feet. But Mary Anne was first, and stepped between
them, as if to shield him, arms outstretched in a gesture
straight from the stage. Nick seemed too surprised, and
touched, to notice the theatrical quality of it. 'Mary
Anne,' he said gently, and put his hands protectively on
her shoulders. 'You needn't fear for me!'

She laughed a little shakily—in truth, she was shaken. The Lieutenant was trying to ruin everything, as well as making her life hell. She was almost eager for the boat. 'I . . . Oh, please don't argue over me!' Tears blinded her, and she dashed them away.

He nodded, but his eyes hardened again as they returned to Luke Rowe. 'You'd better get back to your men, Rowe.'

A chair scraped. Mary Anne heard him crossing the floor, and then the door shut. She let out her breath in sudden, weak relief. What was the man playing at? If he must expose the truth, why could he not do it and be done? She was not up to his waiting game.

Lieutenant Rowe was absent from their table after that, sending his apologies and saying he had things to attend to. They were all relieved, for their various reasons. Mary Anne played her role to the hilt, chattering about Sydney Town, while Bessy cooed and Nick watched her, smiling.

It was perhaps a fortnight after the incident at the pool, on a blustery, rainy afternoon, that Mary Anne went out to the kitchen on an errand from Bessy. The wind blew at her skirts and her hair, and when she reached the kitchen and shut the door she was too breathless, at first, to notice anything but that it was warm and dim, and that Joan was looking at her with profound relief.

'Mrs Gower! You look all wind-blown. Sit down here, by the hearth. I've tea to give you, just made.'

Mary Anne thanked her for the civility, and sat down.

'Ah, but the weather's been terrible, hasn't it? No ship will put out in this. But you wait; wait for a few days more. It'll blow itself out. You'll see.'

'So everyone says.' She took the cup with a smile.

'But you think you won't be on the ship, don't you?'

The voice came from the corner near the sideboard.

The cup shook in Mary Anne's hand, the tea spilling into the saucer. She looked up with wide eyes. A shadow in the shadows. The form moved, red hair caught the firelight, pale eyes glinted like steel. Belle rose with a swish of silk and sauntered across to stand before her. Slowly, Mary Anne put her cup down.

'Don't you?'

Joan clicked her tongue against her teeth. 'You, girl, get out of here!'

'Shut up, you old bag! I'll have my say.'

'Did you hope I would be leaving?' Mary Anne murmured, and met those eyes. Belle was smiling, but there were shadows under her eyes that had nothing to do with the firelight, and the muscles of her throat were tight-drawn.

'You will. You'd better! There's no place here left for you: they're all taken.'

There was a smell of pie in the room, and dishes yet to be scoured lay piled to one side. The firelight glinted off them like winking eyes. Mary Anne blinked to regain her composure. 'Why do you hate me?'

Belle's smile flickered but stayed. Her pale eyes narrowed to slits. 'He shouldn't have taken you there,' she said in a whisper. 'He shouldn't have.'

'*You* don't own him!'

The laugh was soft. Joan crossed herself surreptitiously. 'But I do! I own them all. Nick Etwall and Luke Rowe and . . . and himself. I own them all.'

She laughed again, and went past Mary Anne. The wind chilled her as the door opened, prickling her skin to goose-pimples. Joan ran to shut it, ungainly in stiff-legged fear. Mary Anne felt it in the room, blocking out the warmth. Fear and something else, something evil.

Joan was breathing quickly when she returned; there was a bottle of gin in the cupboard, and she got it out and poured a hefty snifter into her cup. She looked up at

Mary Anne, and poured her one too.

'She must be mad,' Mary Anne said calmly.

Joan gulped down the tea. 'Ay, she's mad! A bad, mad girl is that one.'

'I'm not frightened of her.' It had the sound of child's bravado.

Joan looked at her oddly, the disbelief shining in her black eyes.

'What's wrong?'

Mary Anne paused, her hand on the banister, forcing a smile as she turned back. Nick was looking up at her from the dim hall, frowning. 'Nothing's wrong.'

He smiled back, but shook his head at her. 'Something is wrong. I know it. I feel it.'

'You sound like a soothsayer!'

But he didn't laugh, and started up the stairs after her. Her smile faded. 'No, don't,' she said swiftly, breathlessly. 'I must change. For dinner.' She whirled about and hurried up the last few steps to the landing. With the door closed behind her she could breathe again, and sank down by the window, staring out at the grey sky with blind eyes. 'I own them all,' Belle had said. And Mary Anne was afraid that Belle really believed it was true.

The girl must be mad; or was she just pretending to be? The stealing of her clothes was a practical joke, after all, albeit a malicious one. But no one had actually harmed her, had they? Not yet. She took a deep breath. Well, until they did, she would not be stopped. Nick was as much hers as Belle's, and she meant to have him, destitute as she now was.

The wind dropped during dinner, and Nick insisted she walk with him in the orchard. The scene was bleak, but still, and she let him draw her arm through his. 'The weather will settle now,' he said into the long, companionable silence. The beach lay pale, washed by foamy waves. Mary Anne tried to imagine Toby lying there, beneath the bay, but couldn't. She had already moved on, experienced things that Toby had not experienced, and he had been left behind.

'Mary Anne?' She turned to look at him, his features harsh in the darkness. 'Mary Anne, don't go to Hobart. Stay here with us a while longer, until we can go together. Stay with me.'

'Oh, Nick!'

'I know. I know you're barely a widow, but you didn't love your husband, you told me so. So stay a while longer. The winter would soon go, with you here, and in the spring . . .'

He sounded sincere. She bit her lip. She wanted this. She had prayed for such a man for husband. Someone who would lift her status in society, who would scheme for her as well as Toby had done. It was so overwhelming that she could not speak.

His fingers tightened on her arm. 'Think about it, anyway.' He bent, brushing her lips with his own. 'Sweet, sweet Mary Anne.'

He left her alone, and she watched him stride swiftly back to the house. For a moment she stared into the night, not sure whether to laugh or to cry. Her eyes slid away, round over the black bulk of the hillside and the bush, to the light that glimmered from Luke Rowe's cottage. She felt suddenly trapped, without knowing why, and shivered.

The footfall startled her. She whirled to face it, thinking Belle had come. Red winked, like a single eye, and then the smell of tobacco caught her nostrils. He had been there, in the orchard, all the time. Listening, all the time.

'What do you want?'

Her voice was harsh, angry and frightened. He stopped a few feet from her, leaning almost nonchalantly against the trunk of an apple tree.

'Spying on me, I suppose,' she said, twisting her hands.

'Hardly that.' He sounded uninterested. The cigar winked red again. He flicked the ash to the ground with the same nonchalance. 'You can't accuse me of listening when I was here first.'

'You could have moved away!'

'Why should I?'

'A gentleman would.'

'But I'm not; as by the same token you're certainly no lady.'

'You slanderous, immoral . . .'

'My morals aren't in discussion here, are they?'

She turned to go, but he caught her arm before she had taken a step. 'Do you think it matters to me whether you seduce Nick Etwall or not? Can't you get it through your head that this place has dangers? Dangers that you're only making worse.'

She stared up at him, trying to read his face, failed. 'You mean Belle?'

He laughed. 'Belle? Hell, no! Because of the convicts and the Etwalls. Because one cannot live with the other, not here. Because of things you have no knowledge of, in that selfish little head of yours.'

'I'm not afraid of them!'

'Then you're stupid as well as selfish.'

'I'm not leaving.'

He drew a sharp breath, and gripped her arm. Somewhere across the cove an animal wailed, echoing into silence. A flock of birds scattered up in the darkness, specks against the moon and stars. The cry came again, louder, more terrible, ululating into silence. Mary Anne shuddered.

'A tiger,' Luke Rowe said softly. 'Or so they're called. They're much like wolves, I'm told, but with the stripes of the tiger.'

'I've seen none.'

'They don't care to be seen,' he retorted caustically.

'Why do you so dislike me, Lieutenant Rowe?'

'Dislike you?' he said, and gave a bark of laughter. 'Why do I dislike you?' he repeated, more softly. 'Because, I suppose, from the moment I set eyes on you with the Etwalls, I realised what you were. They wear a certain look, your sort of woman. A calculating look that makes their faces hard. Oh, I grant you, you played it well. But you're a lying cheat, Mary Anne, and I saw it. You've got no feelings in you, nothing to grasp hold of, nothing to hold up as an example to others, nothing fine and untarnished. Everything about you is second-hand.'

'I think you must be as mad as Belle,' she whispered.

'I think I'm remarkably sane. What was I saying? Oh, yes, we were talking about you. I'll never forget the look on Belle's face when I first saw her and she found out I was . . . well connected, shall we say? The smile grew, the eyes shone. She clung like a leech, using all the wiles. The bitch! I saw that look on your face, Mary Anne, when you looked at Nick Etwall across the dining-room table. That same shining, melting look.'

'But the wreck . . .'

'Oh yes, there was a wreck, all right. But a husband? What were you really going to Hobart for, Mary Anne? Perhaps you wanted a change of scenery? Perhaps Hobart offered something more, hmm? There's plenty of room for new faces in Hobart. God, isn't there just! What with the whalers and the sealers, the barracks . . . the place swarms with life like a hive. You'd do well there! You're well rid of the emerald; you'll soon make your fortune again.'

She had slapped his face before she knew she intended to do so. The flesh stung her palm, and she stared at him in horror. He tossed his cigar to the ground; the butt winked and died. The tree shivered as he straightened.

'I'm not going there,' she breathed. 'I won't.'

He smiled, and she realised too late that she should

have repudiated his words. Should have screamed and wept, expounded upon her untarnished innocence. He put his hands on her shoulders, light and yet inescapable. 'What did Etwall call you just now? "Sweet Mary Anne"?'

Tears sparkled in her eyes. Rage, she told herself, but it felt more like pain than anger. It felt like fear.

'Sweet *coated*, all right. Toffee and sugar, all shiny and bright, while beneath it the flesh lies rotten.'

She jerked away from him, her face stinging with blood. 'You can't speak to me like this. Lies, all lies! I never . . .'

'I won't let you marry Nick Etwall.'

Her mouth dropped open.

'I have my reasons, "sweet Mary Anne".'

She raised her hand to slap him again, but he caught her wrist and used it to pull her hard against him. Her eyes blazed back at him, and he smiled faintly, bitterness twisting the lines on his pale face.

'Why not take me, instead? Not marriage, of course. But the exchange is a fair one. I know you, don't I? You wouldn't have to pretend. And just because I'm out here doesn't mean I won't be back in Hobart soon enough, when my particular job is done. I own land, and I've money. It's good land, and I have a house there. I'm not likely to remain in obscurity for ever.'

'How can you think, even imagine, for one moment . . .?'

'But why not?' His breath tickled her cheek. 'I'd find you a fine house, wherever you want it, and you could furnish it as you choose. Live in style, hmm? Don't you want to live in style?' His voice was savage. Cruel and hard, without either liking or love. He had neither for her, only contempt and the sort of desire that led him to make her these insulting proposals despite his dislike.

'I hate you,' she breathed.

He smothered her voice with his mouth, bruising her

lips. The kiss was one of cruel determination. She suffered it, struggling in his hold, trying not to remember that other kiss, when she had almost weakened. It was as if he read her mind.

'I know you want me,' he whispered, his breath warm on her cheek. 'I felt that want. Give in to yourself, Mary Anne. Give in to me.' His mouth claimed hers again, coaxing, forcing a response. She felt her body sag against his, felt his arms tighten, the tremor of triumph in him. Despite all the wicked things he had said, she couldn't seem to get close enough to him; her blood turned to warm syrup in her veins. When at last his kiss was done, he rested his chin on the crown of her head, breathing raggedly.

'Dear God!' he said. 'Have you any idea how much I've wanted you, since that first moment? And I'll have you, Mary Anne, body and soul!'

It was too much. She wrenched herself out of his grip, much as she longed to stay, and ran blindly back towards the house. Her tears burned her cheeks, but she didn't stop. She had betrayed herself, she was as lost as any soul in hell. Down the hall she ran, and up the stairs to her room. Simone was there, and rose at her entrance, making little sounds of distress. Mary Anne went into her arms, sobbing bitterly, and the arms, after a moment, closed about her. There was comfort, of a sort, for them both.

Mary Anne woke shadowy-eyed after a restless night, longing for Toby as she hadn't done for weeks. Toby had kept her safe from the evils of their work, and the world at large, standing over her as an elder brother his little sister. And now Toby had gone, and Luke Rowe thought her a harlot.

'What's wrong, love?' he'd ask, head cocked enquiringly, the laughter dancing in his bright blue eyes. 'The man's an animal in his passions, to be sure, but . . .

Did you encourage him, in any way? No? Are you sure now?'

'No!' She started up in her bed, and then with a sigh lay back again. Had she encouraged him? She hadn't even thought of him, only of Nick Etwall. She had actually disliked him, and shown it. Hadn't she? She squirmed a little inside. What about his carrying her from the pool, and seeing her all naked? What about his kissing her by the fire, and her response, wild as it had been? Was that not encouragement? The man already thought of her as an adventuress, and she had merely confirmed his suspicions.

'Oh, Toby!' she whispered. 'What shall I do?'

What had that detestable man said? 'I won't let you marry Nick Etwall.' He wouldn't let her! He! What was *he*, after all? An immoral, monstrous . . . The adjectives were endless. God, did he mean to lock her up? The thought brought her to her feet, and she stood by the bed, staring at the square of watery sun staining the curtains.

'Stay clear of the military, my girl, they'll lock you up.'

Who had said that? Toby, or her mother. Her mother had spoken often of men, her voice weary and bitter with living and being treated as of no more consequence than dirt. Poor men treated their women harshly, degraded men degraded their women. Why should he care a damn for her, the bloody-coated lobster? He didn't love her, didn't even like her. He felt only what an animal might feel. He *was* an animal!

She went to the window and looked out into the garden. The grass sparkled with dampness, the ground lay sodden and muddy in places, beyond it the sea was a sullen, swollen mass, brooding on fresh ways to assault the land.

'Now, then,' Toby would say. 'Look at this objectively, Mary Anne.'

'Objectively,' she muttered between her teeth. All

right, then, Nick Etwall was attractive and amusing and liked her enough to ask her to marry him. The idea of herself as a wealthy widow had something to do with it, too. He could offer her security and a home and the sort of life she was used to with Toby. And the other figure in this tragedy? He offered a position—short-lived, no doubt—as his harlot, a house in Hobart, money, no security, life with fear.

'Fear?' Toby mocked. 'Fear of him? Or fear of being tossed aside as your mother had been tossed aside?'

'Men,' her mother had said often enough, the dark eyes hard with memories. 'Selfish and careless. Don't trust them, not one of them. Take what you can get, Mary Anne, and when you've taken everything, don't feel pity. They never do.'

'Ah, but that's harsh, Mary Anne,' Toby whispered, laughing. 'I was a man, after all, and what has all that to do with me? No, Mary Anne, look carefully. Be objective.'

Mary Anne closed her eyes. 'But what's the use of being objective when the choice is no longer a free one,' she said in a dully, weary voice. 'He said he wouldn't let me marry Nick. And he can do it.'

CHAPTER EIGHT

'ARE YOU all right, my dear?' Bessy's eyes were worried as they scanned Mary Anne's face.

She forced a smile. 'I didn't sleep well.'

'I'm off to visit Leah Connor. Do you wish to come?'

She didn't, but the need to get out of the house was great. They took their time, strolling across to the cluster of cottages. The door was open, and as they entered, a man rose from the side of the bed. He was small and strong, with broad shoulders and an unshaven, deeply tanned face. Bessy seemed surprised. 'Connor? Shouldn't you be up at the camp?'

The man's eyes flickered away. 'I'm sick.'

Bessy frowned at his tone. 'Sick?'

Leah sat up behind him, catching his hand. 'My husband's sick, Mrs Etwall. Really he is.'

A silence, and then Bessy shrugged. 'I've brought some things for you, Leah.'

Connor glanced at Mary Anne, and she saw the hostility in his eyes. 'You play the lady of the manor,' he seemed to be saying, 'but one day . . .' She said something of the sort to Bessy on the way back to the house, but she laughed.

'Connor? He wouldn't dare. None of them would. They're convicts, after all.' She pronounced it much in the same way she would have pronounced slugs. 'Felons, Mary Anne. We find them useful, but they're not like us.'

'More like horses,' Mary Anne murmured, but the sarcasm was lost on Bessy Etwall.

Simone was in the hall, and smiled at Mary Anne. 'Madame, you are better now?'

'Much, thank you.' Mary Anne looked at her fingers, paused, and then mentally shook her head. Simone could not help. It was up to herself.

'You have seen the Lieutenant?' Simone asked her softly, when she went to pass. 'He is nice?'

Mary Anne bit her lip on hysterical laughter. Simone thought that she was love-sick then, over the bloody lobster!

'He likes you,' Simone said, nodding her head wisely. 'I know.'

The following day was cloudy, but dry. Nick insisted she come up and see the camp that morning. She dressed warmly, with a cloak, and laughed with Nick when Bessy expressed uncertainties. 'You forget the Lieutenant was fired upon.'

Nick cocked an eyebrow, 'I'd shoot at him myself, Bessy, if I thought to get away with it. The man's a fool.'

Mary Anne smiled at him warmly as they rode down the track through the orchard. 'Would you really?' she asked, dark eyes glinting.

'Really what?'

'Shoot him.'

He laughed. 'Yes, indeed! The man's an intolerable nuisance. Good God, do you know he had the impertinence, when he first came, to insist upon an increase in the convicts' rations? I was tempted then to shoot him.'

Mary Anne swallowed, in what he took to be indignation, and Nick nodded his head vigorously. 'Perhaps he will return to Hobart soon,' she suggested.

'If he can, he will,' he retorted sarcastically. 'He has friends to pull strings. Would that we all did'—with bitterness.

They rode on in silence. As they approached the track to the camp, Hagetty came out of the trees, and looked up with a startled expression as they passed. Mary Anne glanced back at him, and saw that he was staring after her, frowning. He would tell Luke Rowe, of course.

'Mary Anne?' Nick's hand closed over hers on the reins. 'Have you thought about my question?'

'Yes, I have. A great deal. But it's one that requires a little more time.'

His fingers tightened a moment. She saw vexation on his face; a tremor of impatience hardened his features and was gone. He shrugged. 'As much as you wish.'

The ground was saturated, and the watery sun barely penetrated the trees. Below to their left the beach lay white and unmarked by human feet. The tide had washed it pure again, apart from the tidemark of weed and flotsam. Nick pointed out a secondary, narrower track leading up through the ravaged stumps to the camp.

As they drew closer, Mary Anne could hear men's voices and the crackle of wood, and smell a fire burning. They rounded a corner of scrub and came upon a clearing. The tents were to one side, also a solid construction of timber in which sat several men in brown jackets and trousers. Half a dozen were bent to a log further across, moving perforce in unison. Their wrists and ankles, she saw, were manacled, a longer chain stringing them together.

She felt a stirring in the pit of her stomach, a squeezing that made her shift uncomfortably. Nick was pointing out where the tree had come from, explaining this and that. She hardly heard him. One of the men from the hut had risen, tossing out the contents of the mug he held in his hand. He looked sullen, and unshaven. There was a scar on his forehead, near his eye, puckering the skin. She recognised Davey.

'Don't mind Davey,' Nick said, seeing her look. 'Davey's the overseer. Aren't you, man?'

'I am that, Mr Etwall.' But the mouth was smirking, and Mary Anne avoided his hands as she jumped down. Davey turned to shout over his shoulder to the others by the fire. 'Hey, one of you, come and fetch Mr Etwall's mare!'

There was a laugh. A voice piped, 'Which one, Davey?'

Nick's face went puce. Davey hissed out breath between his teeth, and pushed the reins into Mary Anne's hands as she stood staring. But Nick was already striding forward to the group. The others had scattered. But the one who had spoken was still sitting, staring at Nick in shocked stillness at the enormity of what he had done. Nick grabbed his jacket and jerked him to his feet. Mary Anne could see his white face from where she stood, and then Davey went running up, shielding them for a moment. Nick threw the boy—he was no more than a boy—down on to the ground. Davey was shaking his head, saying something low.

Nick shouted, 'God's blood, man! Do as I say.' The clearing rang with his voice. Mary Anne took a stumbling step forward, still holding the horse's reins. Davey had dragged the boy to his feet, and was beckoning across two other men. The convicts had stopped work and were watching, using the diversion to rest on their log. The boy was taken to a tree; a young tree which had as yet been spared and now stood a little apart from the rest of the thinned forest of the clearing. They forced him to embrace it, like a lover, and Davey was lashing his hands together on the further side. Nick went up to him and took the scruff of his jacket in his hand. Mary Anne heard the wrenching sound as it tore and was jerked aside. The boy's back was pale. She could see the line of his vertebrae standing up under the milky flesh. Davey had taken up a length of rope in his hand.

She moved then, hardly knowing what she did, only thinking that such punishment was, for her, too much, too excessive. The boy had spoken in haste, a joke. A quick wit, an unwatched tongue. Should he be flogged for such a thing?

'Nick, please! No! Nick!'

He spun around, his hard face grim as death. The lines made him older, drawing down his mouth, his eyes. He jerked a hand impatiently at her, and turned away.

'Nick!'

Davey came over to her, wiping his palms on his jacket. 'You'd best go away now, ma'am. Can't be stopped. Mr Etwall wants the lad punished, and punished he will be.'

'But it was me he said it to; surely I can stop it?'

He met her eyes, as though startled at her venom, and then looked again at the ground. 'You can't stop him. The slight was to him, not you. Proud as the devil, is Mr Etwall.'

She twisted her head round, seeking help, but all attention was on the boy. Nick had the rope doubled over his hand. He tested it, jerking the length a moment before stepping back a judged distance. He lifted his arm back and then brought it forward. The rope hissed, the boy jolted as it struck, and cried out. An animal sound of pain. Mary Anne could see the red stripe on his pale flesh, and then another, as the rope struck again. Davey had hold of her arm, but she started forward despite him. 'Stop it!'

For a moment she thought the voice was her own, but then someone strode past her. Nick's arm was caught as it went back, the rope jarred from his surprised fingers. Luke Rowe brushed him aside as if he were of no more account than a mosquito. The boy was sagging; his legs had buckled. Two men came running forward to cut him down. Davey swore, but kept by Mary Anne. Perhaps he felt it safer to stay away.

'What the bloody hell!' Nick swore furiously, spinning round to the soldier. As Luke turned, Mary Anne saw his white face, and almost flinched.

'What's he done?'

'Insulted the lady, sir!' Davey called out. Luke didn't even look at him.

'The boy will be on half rations for a week.'

'Rowe! What right . . .'

'It is my job to dole out punishments here, Etwall, not yours. I've told you before. This time will be the last.'

'I'll see you flogged, Rowe! God help me, I will!'

But Luke had turned away. The boy was laid down on the ground. Mary Anne dragged her arm from Davey's hand, and picking up her skirts brushed past the gathering circle of men. The boy was conscious, his face white with pain, a trickle of blood on his lips where he had bitten them. Her hem brushed his cheek. He looked up into her face with eyes clear and blue as a summer sky.

'There's no need for there to be any punishment,' she said shakily.

'Mary Anne!' Nick's voice was raw with rage and humiliation. The boy closed his eyes.

'Davey.' Luke turned to look at her. The overseer came shuffling forward. 'Take this . . . *lady* away.' The grey eyes were deadly. She cowered under them, but stood her ground.

'I want to see if anything can be done.'

The glance flickered across her face, burning contempt. 'Haven't you done enough, *ma'am*, for one day?'

Tears welled, and she turned, blindly, so that he could not disdain her further. Her shoes slipped on the sodden earth, but she kept on, down the narrow track towards the sea. The sun had gone, and the wind held more rain. She hardly knew where she was going, hardly knew why. Her mind was numb from what she had witnessed, and felt, and what he had said. As if she were no better . . . no better than Nick Etwall. She understood suddenly, savagely, what he had meant about danger. She had smelt it, like some acrid profanity, burning her nostrils.

It had emanated from those men; their hatred for Nicholas Etwall.

The beach lay before her, smooth, and she clambered over rocks, tearing her skirt and bruising her leg, to the pale sand. The weed smelt, and there was a tangled heap of sailcloth half buried. The waves lapped gently. She thought, then, it might be nice to walk into them. The water washed her hem, where it had touched the boy's smooth, beardless cheek. She closed her eyes, and it was not until the hand closed on her arm she realised she was not alone.

'Leave me alone!' she cried, and spinning, shook herself free. Surprised, he stood away. The cold water soaked into her shoes, but she ignored it; her rage kept her warm.

Nick was pale beneath his sallow flesh, his eyes puzzled. 'Mary Anne? My dear, dear girl.'

'I am not your dear girl, nor ever shall be!'

'I understand,' he went on, almost smiling. 'I forgive you. You were shocked by what he said, but it's over now. Rowe has had his way this time, but next time . . .' His hands closed on her shoulders, but she shook him off, backing away.

'There will be no next time, ever.'

He shook his head gently, as though she were some truculent baby refusing her porridge. 'Come now, Mary Anne. Calm down.'

'I will not calm down. No, stay away. Don't come near me!'

'Mary Anne, you are distraught.'

'Am I?' she demanded. 'I am angry, yes, and shocked, yes. Does that mean I am distraught, too? I have seen a man treated as an animal. A man? No, a boy! I feel outraged it should be so. I feel sick that I, and you, should be the cause of it.'

His face darkened. He opened his mouth to speak, thought better of it, and spun round on his heel, making

his way back up the beach. Mary Anne watched him go,
her breathing gradually slowing. He had gone—angry,
humiliated by what he had thought to be his champion-
ing of her honour and good name. And she would not
have him back, even if he forgave her. Even security
would be a betrayal—not that she would get much of
that with Nick!—of Toby and her mother. The water
splashed up her calves, and almost absently she stepped
back on the dry sand. It must be Hobart, then, after
all.

'Ah, gay Hobart, Mary Anne,' Toby had said, teasing. 'You'll have them swooning for you. Swooning in
the streets.'

'And that's where I'll probably be,' she murmured in
weary despair. 'In the streets.'

Her head ached abominably that afternoon, and she
slept through dinner. Bessy brought her some hot soup,
and Simone tucked her in with murmured concern. The
girl was an ally, a friend—she forced a smile. But, alone
again, she lay in limbo, trying to think. To think of some
way in which to come out on top. To fight her way from
that interminable maze. But each time she thought she
had discovered a path to freedom, it twisted back again
to the one thing she dared not even consider. Nick
Etwall or Luke Rowe, each as obnoxious and cruel and
despicable as the other.

'Poor child,' Bessy murmured. 'Such a pity!'

Mary Anne made a valiant effort to smile.

'Perhaps Nicholas will forgive you?'

She didn't reply, and after a moment Bessy squeezed
her fingers. 'That horrible man!'

'Yes, that horrible man.'

Bessy seemed a little startled by the look in her eyes,
but she lowered them swiftly, and the moment passed.

Simone perhaps understood better. She came to fuss
about the curtains, and when Mary Anne didn't seem to

notice her, bent over to dab her temples with lavender water. 'Madame, does your head ache still?'

'No.'

Simone bit her lip. 'Private McDonald wishes to see you, madame. He is outside.'

Mary Anne frowned. 'See me about what?'

Simone shrugged, but curiosity brought Mary Anne out of the bed to be dressed and tidied. The soldier entered nervously, glancing at Simone and as swiftly away. 'Mrs Gower, I've a letter for you.'

'A letter?' She held out her hand. The boy searched in his coat and brought out the crisply folded sheet.

'From the Lieutenant, ma'am.'

Her fingers tensed. 'What possible reason could he have for writing to me?'

The boy coloured. 'Ma'am, I hardly know.'

She ripped the paper across once. McDonald's eyes widened, and grew wider as she ripped it across again and again, until only tiny pieces remained. She held them out to the boy, and after hesitating an instant, he took them. She turned her back on him and went to the window. She heard Simone whispering, and then the door closed. Bloody lobster! Let him rot in hell. She'd see no more of him. Let the ship to Hobart make speed; Etwall held nothing more for her.

'They' had all heard about the scene at the timber camp. Joan watched her with sly black eyes; at the cottages they whispered as she paused. Perkins avoided her. Nick spoke the merest civilities to her, Ralph was sadly kind, and Bessy sympathetic but inwardly, no doubt, relieved. It scraped her nerves raw. And when Hagetty came up to her in the orchard, she almost slapped his face.

'Mrs Gower, sorry to disturb you but I've a message for you.'

'Another?' she demanded with sarcasm.

'Verbal this time, ma'am,' with a smirk. His eyes

laughed, and something about him cooled her rage.
'Lieutenant Rowe wants to see you. Important.'

'Tell Lieutenant Rowe I don't want to see him, ever.'

'Ma'am!' He caught her arm as she went to turn away.
She looked down at his fingers but he didn't let her go.
She met his eyes again. The laughter was gone, and he
smiled apologetically. 'I'm sorry, ma'am, but orders.'

She struggled a moment with her rage, but controlled
it. It would hardly be dignified to do battle with the
man. Lifting her chin high, she marched before him in
silence.

The door was closed. Hagetty knocked and opened it,
standing aside for Mary Anne to enter. She did so with a
savage swish of skirts. Luke Rowe was sitting at the table
and he rose abruptly, his face frowning. 'Mrs Gower, sit
down, please.'

'Thank you, no.'

The frown grew. 'Shut the door, Hagetty.' The door
closed. 'Mary Anne, sit down.'

'I have no intention of sitting down!'

'Davey told me about what happened,' he said
abruptly. 'I wronged you.'

The apology was ungracious, to say the least, and she
looked at him with distaste. 'It doesn't matter to me
what you did or thought. You won, didn't you, in the
end? I'm going to Hobart. I have no choice.'

He had taken out one of his thin cigars, but paused
to look at her. 'You've friends there? You'll find
employment?'

She turned her face away, staring at the window.
There was a pause. He slammed the box down on the
table, making her jump.

'Damn you, woman! What do you want me to do?'

She didn't reply. He strode to the fireplace and back
again. It gave her a certain pleasure to cause such a pang
to his conscience, and she schooled her face to sacrifice.
He stopped suddenly, and had jerked up her chin before

she realised it. Hard grey eyes scanned hers, and his mouth curled contemptuously.

'You're enjoying this, aren't you, you bitch? Why should I give a damn what happens to you?' After a moment he dropped her chin again and lit the cigar. There was a silence; he drummed his fingers on the table. 'Etwall is about to bring his own downfall. Surely you can see that now?'

'Nick Etwall can do what he likes.'

'And so you're going?'

'I'm going.' She looked at him. 'Is the offer still open then? The fine house?' The words bit, and she thought he coloured faintly.

'Mary Anne . . .'

'No?' She rose to her feet. 'Goodbye then, Lieutenant. I doubt we'll meet again. We'll hardly be moving in the same "circles", will we?'

She had opened the door when he spoke. 'It's still open.'

Her fingers went white on the latch. God, oh God, what now? To turn and spit in his face, to slap him and let out all this rage and humiliation and hurt. She hated him, hated him!

He had come up behind her and closed the door. His hands rested lightly on her waist, and he turned her round. 'The offer is open,' he said without expression. 'The ship to Hobart will be here any day. You'll be on it either way.'

'And you?' she whispered, her breath unsteady.

His mouth smiled, mocking. 'Unfortunately, no. I have orders to remain at Etwall. I cannot leave my post, even for you, my dear.'

'But you'll come back?'

'I shall. When I finish what I came to do. Unless they finish me first . . .' His hands tightened on her wrist. 'But that won't matter to you, will it?'

'No, it won't.'

'At least you're honest, for once.'

This time her eyes flashed before she could veil them.

'I'll write a letter to my solicitors. They will find you suitable lodgings, and supply you with pin-money. They will also keep an eye on you until I come. Is that understood? If you double-cross me, I will hunt you down, Mary Anne. Remember that.'

She glared. I will escape him, she thought. I'll get away long before he sets foot in Hobart.

'Never mind,' he said sarcastically. 'It's better than the streets.' He dropped his hands and turned away. For a moment she stood dizzily, but he didn't speak again and she opened the door. The fresh air struck her like a blow, and she hovered on the edge of freedom.

'Then it's a bargain,' she said, some wickedness forcing the words, forcing him to speak them.

'I've told you so,' he repeated sharply. She shut the door. The harbour tossed in white crests before the freshening wind. The sky was cloudy, but they were white clouds rather than grey. The ship would come, and she would go, leaving Etwall behind her. Hobart. It had a solemn ring. Would Toby approve? Would her mother? She had a feeling that they would not.

Simone was back at the room, was looking down into the walled garden, and seemed startled at Mary Anne's entry.

'What is it?'

Simone flushed. 'That Belle,' she muttered. 'She is bad, that one.'

Mary Anne went across to the window and peered out. Belle was leaning again the wall; her head tossed as she laughed. On the other side Davey leaned close to her. He seemed nervous, glancing about as though afraid he would be seen.

'Are they lovers?' Mary Anne enquired in a cool, brittle voice.

Simone flicked a look under long lashes. 'Perhaps.

That Belle is a bad one. She goes off at night. Into the bush. The others in the cottages, they are frightened, and lock themselves in when the darkness comes. But Belle, she goes into the bush.'

Mary Anne was puzzled. Luke Rowe was right. There were things happening here of which she knew nothing, or at most a mere surface scratch.

Davey looked up. The eyes under their heavy brows narrowed. He looked at Mary Anne. For some reason he frightened her, and she stepped back, her heart beating hot and hard. After a moment she heard Belle's laughter, and clenched her fists.

'I shall not be sorry to leave this place!' she cried.

Simone frowned. 'You are not to stay then, with Nick Etwall?'

A sigh. Mary Anne shook her head. 'I fear he has done with me.'

It was to be Luke Rowe, after all. Unless she could somehow get the emerald back without arousing suspicion—assuming she could find it. Would Belle give it to her for a bribe—for she was certain that Belle had taken it.

With the emerald again in her possession, she could cock her nose at them all, including Luke Rowe. The thought occupied her mind, and she hardly noticed the Etwalls' coolness during the next few days.

Eventually she extracted the direction of Belle's cottage from Simone, and one cool afternoon, made her way there. It was set apart from the others, as though solitary as the woman herself. The door stood ajar, and when there was no answer to her gentle tapping, Mary Anne pushed it to and peered inside.

The single room was in a shambles. Dust and grime collected on sills and floor and the few pieces of furniture. It was a surprising room. Rough mingled with fine—a poorly-made clothes chest and atop it a finely-made, engraved wooden box. There were two cheap

vases on the mantel, and between them a fine, dainty
figure. Rich gowns lay across the tiny window seat,
mixed among rags of a different order.

So fascinated with it all was Mary Anne that she did
not hear Belle come up behind her until her voice stirred
the hair at her nape, and made her jump.

'What do you want here, Mrs High-and-Mighty?
Snooping around where you ain't got no business.'

The pale eyes were hard in the pale face. Belle pushed
past her into the room, and turned, hands on hips, skirts
rustling.

'I was merely passing, and . . .' Mary Anne began
nervously.

But Jezebel laughed outright. 'Passing? Here? Have
you come calling maybe cause you think I've stolen Nick
from you? Well, it was your own act that sent him off,
and none of mine, so there. And if ye think I'm a witch,
as can give you a potion to bring him back to you, you're
wrong. And them as tells you so are fools!'

'I did not come about Nick,' Mary Anne said, and
took a breath, refusing to allow the creature to frighten
her. 'May I come in? What I have to say is private.'

Belle eyed her with hostility a moment more, and then
the pink lips curled back on a smile. 'Come in then,
ma'am.'

The door closed behind her. Belle threw herself down
on a rickety chair, skirts rucked up to disclose red
stockings and rather grubby white knickers. 'Well?'

'I won't pretend you're a fool, Belle. We both know
what I'm here about. What I should have come about
long ago. You have something of mine, something we
both know to be of value to me. I want it returned. I will
pay for it.'

Belle eyed her, swinging one foot. 'Or else?'

'Or else I will send Lieutenant Rowe and his men to
search your hut.'

She laughed, throwing back her head. 'You? You

fool! No one searches my hut. No one dares. You think you'll frighten me?' She rose up, suddenly gripping Mary Anne's shoulders. 'I'd kill you, if I wanted. There's plenty'd do it for me, but I'd have pleasure in doing it meself. You stupid cow! Luke Rowe would spit in your face. He wants you gone, just as I do.'

'Give me my property, or I'll inform the Etwalls.'

'"Inform the Etwalls",' she mimicked. 'If you want to do that, you'd have told 'em straight out. Why wait so long? No, you've no power here, *Mrs* Gower. Go back to Hobart before I do kill you.'

Her eyes gleamed, and Mary Anne was suddenly struck chill. The woman was evil, and meant what she said. And yet the emerald meant the difference between a life of security, alone, and the fear of Luke Rowe hanging over her head . . .

'What if I were to tell Davey?' she said suddenly.

Belle's eyes narrowed to slits. 'Davey? What do you know of Davey? He would laugh in your face. I have no secrets from Davey.'

The hope she had believed in slipped away. Mary Anne turned, suddenly defeated. Belle would never return the emerald, and she could not make her. And if she were to tell the Etwalls, even assuming they would look for it for her, Luke Rowe would put a stop to a search.

Outside, voices were suddenly raised. Mary Anne heard the high-pitched excitement of children, the murmur of women. Belle frowned, and went to the window.

When she came back, she was smiling. A cat after cream. 'They are saying a sail has been sighted at sea. It is your ship come, Mrs Gower, to take you to Hobart.' And Mary Anne knew by the glow in her eyes that her dismay and despair showed all too plainly.

Bessy met her at the door of the house, babbling with excitement. She, too, would be glad to see her gone. She would have Nick's entire attention once more—unless he decided to share it again with Belle.

Simone met her in her room. She, at least, seemed sad to see Mary Anne leave. She dressed silently for dinner, and went down with low spirits. The captain was there, dour and straight-backed. He offered sympathy when told the now overtold tale, and was prompt in offering a passage to Hobart. Nick looked hard and distant—Mary Anne knew she would never pierce his pride again. Bessy bubbled uncharacteristically, and with her flushed cheeks was almost attractive. Ralph was his usual earnest, quiet self. Mary Anne was relieved to find Luke Rowe not there, and thought he must not be dining.

However, halfway through the meal he entered before Simone, a little flushed himself, the gleam of news in his eyes. 'Forgive me,' he began, his slight smile belying the apology of his words. 'I had a packet off the good captain here to study.'

'Indeed?' Bessy at her coolest.

'Anything of importance?' Ralph asked, setting down knife and fork.

'Well, yes. I am ordered back to Hobart at once. Hagetty will be in charge here while I am gone, and of course is a competent and trustworthy man.'

No one spoke. Mary Anne felt the room swaying before her eyes. 'No, it could not be!' But she had not spoken aloud, as she feared, and the room steadied.

'You are leaving for good?' Bessy breathed.

Luke's gleaming eyes met hers—he knew exactly how she longed to be rid of him. 'Fortunately, no. I return after I have received direct further orders.'

'Perhaps my contacts in the army have paid off at last,' Nick said quietly.

There was an uneasy silence.

'So you will have a friend to accompany you on your voyage,' the captain said solemnly to Mary Anne. 'Someone to assist you in an unfamiliar city.'

'Indeed,' Mary Anne croaked, and with shaking hands clasped beneath the table, smiled with trembling lips.

Luke Rowe caught her eyes across the oppressive atmosphere of the room, and the unholy glee in them turned her pink cheeks to white.

He had her in his power, and there was no escape.

CHAPTER NINE

HOBART TOWN throbbed with life. Mary Anne, despite herself, was impressed with the place, and the setting. Even Luke Rowe's mocking, drawling voice could not spoil it completely, as he pointed out the sights from the rail of the ship.

Mount Wellington sprawled above the calm waters of the harbour, slopes thick with bush, buttresses chequered with light and shadow. Beneath, the raw capital of Van Diemen's Land bustled, teeming in both harbour and town. The docks were alive with men, cargoes coming and going, the warehouses behind both prosperous and stolid. Chain-gangs carried barrels of rum and bales of wool. The red-coated overseer sat smoking on his haunches.

Mary Anne breathed deeply of the fresh, clean air, and felt her spirit soar. There, Luke said, was the white spire of St David's Church, at the top of Macquarie Street, and there lay the Governor's residence, and there the battery. The houses of the rich had a smug air, and yet the poorer quarters were as crowded and jostling as those in Sydney Town. It felt more like home, more so than the isolated wilderness of Etwall. She felt safe here.

Etwall. A shudder for that. The parting had been a tearing affair. What could she say? Never the truth. She had merely made her farewells, babbling about lots of friends and contacts in Hobart Town, and left. They were glad enough of it, she supposed. Nick hated her, Ralph was uncomfortable for his brother's sake, Bessy pretended to pity her. Simone alone would really miss her. The only thought that gave her pleasure now was that if they had been glad to see the back of her, they had been ecstatic to see the back of Lieutenant Luke Rowe, no matter how brief the parting.

The voyage had been smooth enough, and she had overcome her fears. She had expected Luke Rowe to visit her. He had not. In fact, he had spent the entire voyage with the captain and first mate, while she ate her meals alone and remained in her cabin. There had been the orders for him, come from Hobart. He had not shown her the sealed letter—she would never expect him to. But, reading them, he smiled.

At night, the timbers of the ship had creaked, and the waves dashed against the hull, splashing up to her porthole. She lay often wakeful and wide-eyed, afraid to sleep. She dreamed of *Infanta* and Toby, and her dreams were vivid and frightening, and she knew, despite everything, that she had no wish to join them. No wish at all to die. Life had promise, and she could be optimistic when the mood took her. It was the dark depressions she found hard to bear, the thought of being alone and unwanted. The thought of being another like her poor mother.

Hobart saw her haggard, pale, with shadowed eyes. In contrast, she thought Luke Rowe seemed more alive than ever, with colour in his cheeks and his grey eyes alight with mockery and triumph. She distrusted the spring in his step, his ready laugh. He acted as though he had been the victor in some unnamed fight.

'Regrets?' he murmured beside her, at the rail.

The anchor had been dropped, with a splash of clear, cold water, and they were getting ready to lower the boats which would take them and their baggage ashore. Mary Anne shrugged, and ignored him, continuing to gaze out at the town.

'I'm to report to the barracks as soon as I'm ashore,' he went on. 'I'll find you a room first. You can rest.'

'Thank you.' Her voice was cold and stilted. Her head still ached, although there was this new hope inside her, at the sight of the place. She wished he would go away and leave her to enjoy it in peace. She had forgotten how taxing it was to meet those hateful, mocking eyes.

'My pleasure,' he murmured, smooth as butter, and turning his shoulder began to chat with the captain, who had come to join them.

The ache in her head had grown worse by the time they reached the wharves, and she was helped up on to dry ground. She clung to Luke Rowe's arm perforce, and he took advantage of it to whisper into her ear, 'Did you have such little faith in the the captain, sweetheart? You look positively ill with terror.'

'I do not like the sea.'

He pulled a mocking face. 'I would have comforted you, only I feared you would not welcome me. Would you?'

Some of the old coquetry returned with the mounting confidence, and she let a smile twitch her lips, looking at him under her lashes. 'That you will never know, Lieutenant. Not now.'

He laughed, and squeezed her elbow, before turning again to the captain. Mary Anne let her eyes devour the scene. The hustle and bustle. The shouts of working men, the curses of the convicts. She took a deep breath, and smiled. Home, or near enough to make no matter. Lord, let the ladies pine for their soirées and their feather mattresses! Give her a swarming dockside and a narrow tavern-infested street any day of the year. Rough, ragged men and hard, lined faces. Women with scarlet smiles and biting tongues, the smell of gin and damp. Home and childhood.

One of the seamen had found them a hackney, and in a moment they were turning into the hilly, narrow, cobbled streets of the capital. Mary Anne leaned forward to peer from the window, scanning the shop and tavern fronts, the fine clothes and ragged poor. A boy called his wares, a government chain-gang clanked to their work or back to their prison, a servant-girl hurried with a pail of milk, a farmer's cart lumbered slowly, laden with supplies. She was so lost in the place that she jumped when the hackney came to a stop, and turning with wide eyes, found Luke Rowe watching her.

'This is the place.'

Grey stone, an inn-sign hung low. A boy came hurrying out, sharp faced, demanding their business. 'The lady's luggage,' Luke called, and stepping down to the cobbles, held out his hand to assist her. She climbed down, straightening her skirts. The cloth was harsh and poor. First thing, she must buy herself something fine. At the thought she looked at the Lieutenant, but he was already leading her towards the doorway.

It seemed dark inside. She hung back, but he tugged her impatiently, saying, 'What do you think it is, Mary Anne? A house of ill-repute? I have business to attend to, and until I have time to find something more comfortable, you'll stay here.'

'Indeed.' She looked at him with dislike as they passed through the doorway.

'I think you have no choice.'

There were voices coming from an open room to their left, but ahead were polished stairs and the peaceful gloom of a landing. A man bustled out, subservient. Luke took him aside, bending his fair head. Mary Anne saw the gleam of gold pass from one palm to the other, and turned sharply away. The place seemed well enough, but a little shabby. There were voices from the taproom, and laughter. Her heart ached towards it, but he was already back at her side, his hand brushing her arm.

'I'll leave you now.' The grey eyes teased. 'The Governor awaits.'

He went out of the door, and the hackney clattered away. With a sigh she turned, and allowed the boy to lead her upstairs to her room. It was small and cosy, with

a back view over the sprawl of houses and gardens. She
slept through the afternoon, and after taking supper on a
tray in her room, slept again. She felt much refreshed
when she woke, about midnight, and lay listening to
the muted sounds from the taproom, the occasional
whinney of a horse outside. Otherwise, there was little
to disturb her—apart from her thoughts. *He* would be
busy enough tonight and tomorrow. But the next day
. . . The future stretched out into infinity, and uncertainty. She squirmed a little in the trap, and turned her face
into the pillow, sighing for Toby.

'What now, my girl?' he would ask her, his eyes
dancing. 'You've turned the corner and taken your road.
Why not go through with it? Take everything you can
get, and more. You can do it, if you want to. You always
did have a way with men. You'll have the Lieutenant by
the nose soon enough.'

That thought made her squirm even more.

'Survival is the thing, my girl,' Toby whispered
furiously, determinedly. 'Survival is what this world is
about, for our kind. Nothing more. There's no miracles
and no pity. You take and grab your way up that ladder,
girl, or I'll know why!'

'Yes,' she murmured obediently, and yet the hope
remained. An alternative might yet introduce itself,
might yet shed light into the night of her future. And,
thinking so, she slept.

She visited the shops the following morning, and wandered through roomy warehouses, choosing what she
would buy, if she had the money. In the afternoon she
returned to the inn, tired but happy with the expedition,
and changed into one of the Etwall-sewn gowns. The
shadows under her eyes had faded, and colour stained
her pale cheeks. Her looks had returned, she thought,
preening before the glass, and smiled, remembering
several flattering glances.

He came at about four, when she had been certain he would not. He looked tired now, and was frowning when she opened the door to him. Her greeting was brushed aside, and he strode in and said without preamble, 'I've found a house.'

'Indeed?'

'In Harrington Street, just off Murray. Not a fashionable quarter, I'm afraid, but quiet enough. It's a place of clerks and lawyers and the like. I thought you'd prefer anonymity.'

She mocked him with her eyes. 'Why should I? Why can't I strut in satin and silk and proclaim my status to the world?'

He laughed abruptly. He seemed restless with energy, everything about him jumping with life. 'Why can't you, indeed! Governor Arthur would enjoy the sight, I'm sure! And make your name known to the colony. He has a cruel, cold tongue, ma'am.'

So he was pretending to protect her name. She resisted the urge to laugh, and said instead, 'Are you still in disgrace?'

'Disgrace?' he frowned, and then smiled. A warm, amused smile that made her frown in turn. 'The opposite, my dear! I have done very well indeed. I am in high favour at the moment.'

Mary Anne slanted a look at him. 'Favour? I don't understand? Bessy said . . . That is, you were sent to Etwall because . . . well . . .'

He laughed, softly, teasingly. 'Bessy believed what I wanted her to believe, sweetheart. Doesn't it please you to be the mistress of a success rather than a failure?'

'You make me sound cheap,' she said quietly. 'I assure you I am not.'

He laughed again, and took a lock of her hair between his fingers. She felt uneasy, and searched to distract him, disturbed by his hints at secrecy. 'And this house you spoke of?'

'"This house", as you so charmingly put it, my love, is in Harrington Street, quiet and neat, with furnishings I feel sure you'll find . . . appropriate. It was pointed out to me by a brother officer who had the luck to use it only recently, but unfortunately his wife discovered the fact.' He shrugged. 'His wife is a sharp-tongued lady. So now the house is empty, and merely awaits a . . . mistress.'

She avoided his eyes. His fingers brushed her cheek, his breath tickled her ear. When she rose abruptly, the chair rocked and all but fell. He caught it, laughing aloud. He had done it on purpose, she thought furiously. Playing with her like a puppet.

'Are you packed?' he was saying now, looking about the room. 'But I see you are. Then we'll waste no more time. Come!' He held out his hand and she glared at it and him, and stalked past without a word. His laughter followed her down the stairs, where the little man was waiting with his ingratiating smile.

The house was, as he'd said, tidy and neat. It was built of tawny stone, shadowed now in the late afternoon with the bulk of Mount Wellington blocking out the sunset behind it. There was a small garden, rather overgrown, behind a white fence. Harrington Street lay narrow, twisting away down a hill, the occupiers showing no signs of themselves. Prisoners, she supposed, of their class. Luke Rowe helped her down from the gig, and she swept, white-faced, through the doorway. A woman was waiting, a pretty, plump girl with blonde curls, who bobbed a curtsy.

'Clara,' he mocked, 'comes with the house.'

The hall was airy, the rooms fine enough. The place spoke of simplicity, of quiet, peaceful lives. She stripped off her gloves with jerky pulls, while, in the hall, Luke directed the luggage up the stairs. There were three rooms in all, with a kitchen at the back. She swept a finger along the mantel and frowned at the dust, while Clara watched with curious eyes.

'The last lady was out most days,' she offered, stepping hastily back as Mary Anne bustled into the next room. 'Always out, she was. She didn't care much for the house.'

'Indeed.'

'Too quiet it was, for her.'

'Oh?'

'Mary Anne!'

She bit her lip, and turned as he came in. He jerked his head, and Clara scuttled out with a twist of her full lips. They faced each other across the carpet; the plush, polished furniture looked on.

'It hardly looks the den of iniquity you suggested,' she said at last.

He laughed. 'Wait until you see upstairs.' A pause. 'I have to go out again. I'll be back for dinner.'

She didn't reply, and he went out of the room. She heard the murmur of his voice in the hall, Clara's giggle, and then the horse's hooves moving away. The quiet descended on her like a shroud. No voices, no life, not even despair. She hated it—she feared it.

The windows faced the street, and she lifted aside the heavy curtain. It was empty, and silent. She was reflected in the pane, stony-faced, her eyes betraying her fear. Behind her, Clara peeped in at the doorway and went away again. Clara knew what was expected of her; probably she hoped one day to occupy a like position.

Mary Anne did some unpacking, and chose one of her dark, plain gowns, smiling sarcastically. Clara dressed her hair in ringlets, so that she looked reasonably elegant. The bedroom, as he had warned her, was tawdry. There were brocade hangings above the bed, and pink, cupid-sprinkled wallpaper. The furniture was delicate, if a little too embellished with gilt and curls. It looked like a high-class bordello, and she winced every time she looked about her. The view from the window was charming, however. A vista over the garden at the back across to Mount Wellington against the black, starred sky.

'Will you come to the parlour, ma'am, before dinner?' Clara asked her with a knowing look, making her long for Simone. Clara was an assigned servant, a felon. It needed little imagination to guess the crime.

'I'll come down when I'm ready.'

A bob of a curtsy. Mary Anne followed her to the door, stiffening her spine and lifting her chin. The fan clicked open in her hand—she had found it in one of the drawers. Let them all go to damnation—the lot of them! She meant to drag herself up that ladder, as Toby had said. It was herself that mattered, after all.

Clara's dinner was simple, but well enough cooked. The girl served it silently, while Luke poured himself some claret and spoke of generalities. Mary Anne drank, too, half a glass at first, and then another. The wine calmed her, and she hardly noticed when the last dish was removed and Clara withdrew silently into the kitchen for her own occupations.

The house was as still at night as during the day. Outside, the breeze had dropped and mist crept down into the hollows and alleys, reminding her of Etwall. Mary Anne rose and went to the window, pressing her brow against the cool pane. Luke was smoking near the hearth, watching her across the room. Watching without speaking. She swallowed more of the wine, and stared blindly back at her reflection.

'Mary Anne,' he said, quiet and harsh. She turned, despite herself, and found his eyes deep and unreadable in the lamplight. 'Are you afraid of me?'

'No!'

But there was something frightening her, something in his eyes matching something in herself that the wine had set free. Her legs felt weak, the muscles turned wobbly. He had risen and was coming towards her. She closed her eyes and his fingers burned the flesh of her wrist. His lips brushed her cheek, her eyelids.

'Sweet Mary Anne.'

He lifted her up, and she lay against his chest. She couldn't seem to help herself; the inevitability of it drew resistance like poison from a wound, and left only blind, unreasoning obedience. Up the stairs, one, two, three, four . . . to the landing, into that terrible bedroom. It flickered about her, bright colours muted. Clara had left candles.

Oh God, oh God! she thought. He had set her down, and she slumped there, watching him taking off his red coat. 'The view . . .' she said, stumbling over the words. 'The view is most charming.' Somehow she regained her feet and went to lift the curtain. Lights shone from houses all about; lives being lived out, people happy and sad. Oh God, oh God, he was taking off his shirt, and his body glowed gold in the candlelight, strong and smooth. Toby had never been so strong. Toby was pale, gold freckled when he had swum with her that day. Toby had never caused her heart to leap so in her throat when he came near her.

She felt him rest his hands on her shoulders, firm, yet light. Was she indeed a mare, to be kept on a light rein? He bent to kiss her nape, nuzzling the tendrils of hair that had escaped Clara's pins.

'Perhaps you wish to see the other rooms?'

He laughed softly, and turned her round.

'There aren't many, and you *are* paying . . .'

'That claret seems to have loosened your tongue,' he mocked. He kissed her lightly, brushing his lips against the corners of her mouth.

'I can hold my liquor as well as any man!'

But she couldn't, and gulped in horror at the realisation that the courage-giving wine had made her helpless. Her mind refused to obey orders to slap and scratch and bite. He kissed her again, and began to remove the pins from her hair.

'Luke . . . Oh, Luke!'

He didn't seem to notice the catch in her voice. Her hair came tumbling down her back and shoulders, rich and dark and scented with rosewater. He covered her mouth with his in a deepening kiss, his tongue invading the wine-sweetness.

She tried to twist away, but he laughed at her, grey eyes darkening. The little hooks at her bodice offered no problems; he undid them with ease. Practice, she thought. The bloody lobster! She tried to say it, failed to get her tongue around the insult. He was kissing her throat, and she arched it despite herself. Her heart was thudding wildly.

'I . . . I wish you wouldn't.'

He had reached the hollow between her breasts, and looked up suddenly. 'Don't tell me any more lies, Mary Anne. You want me as much as I want you! I know. Don't lie, not now.'

'But I don't,' she thought. 'I don't!' While her body trembled under his touch.

He pushed his fingers up through her hair, drawing her mouth down to his, and her arms came up and held him. She drowned in the kiss so completely that she was not aware that he had carried her to the bed until she felt the sheets cool on her bare shoulders and arms. The mattress sank under their weight. He was pulling off her chemise now, haste, hurrying . . . The colours of the bed-hangings befuddled her mind, and suddenly he blocked them out altogether, kissing her so that she could no longer catch her breath or twist her face away, so she did not want to.

Her body ached under his hand, hot and sweet as honey. Please, she thought. Please stop; please make him stop! His breath burned her face and throat; he whispered things that made no sense. His back was

broad and muscled, and her fingers clung there, sliding
up to twist in his damp hair. His strong, hard legs seemed
tangled with hers, and she felt his male body tremble a
little with impatient desire. She had no resistance now
—he had won the battle through means and ways she
could not fight. There was a voice crying out, mingled
pain and pleasure, and Mary Anne knew with a sense of
despair that it was her own.

Everything was so still, afterwards. The storm of their
passion had come and gone, and even when he realised
she was innocent, and tried to check himself, it was far
too late. And, to her shame, she had not wanted him to
stop, and her kisses and hands had grown more urgent.
She could hear his breathing slowing; she hardly dared
to breathe at all. There were no tears. She had pulled the
sheet over her body, and lay gazing away at the window,
watching the play of light and shadow on the plush velvet
of the curtains.

The scent of his tobacco was on her flesh, in her mouth
and her body. He had invaded her with that as surely as
with himself. He was mingled in her blood and her mind.
She could never be free of him again.

'Why did you do it?' His voice seemed hard, indiffer-
ent; such a contrast to the other, warm, passionate
whisper.

'We made a bargain.' Her own was as stiff and cold,
and brittle as a dry twig.

'You know what I mean. You were a virgin. Why
didn't you tell me?'

'You thought me a whore—how could I make you
believe otherwise? Would you have believed me? You
despised me. You still do. I know I still hate you!' Her
voice caught and broke, and she swallowed desperately.

'Jesus, woman! If you'd told me you were innocent,
I'd never . . .'

'Liar!' She sounded hysterical. The alternative didn't
bear thinking about. 'All the same, all of you, lying.

Twisting things with lies, and . . . and hurting us. I hate you all.' The voice was her mother's, and frightened her even more.

He grabbed her as she tried to rise, and she struggled against him. But he enfolded her in his arms and seemed quite impervious to blows. 'Be still!'

'Go to hell!'

He gripped her nape, forcing her face to his bare shoulder. He smelt of her own rosewater. 'My immortal soul is not in question!'

'Bloody lobster,' she hiccupped.

'I know. Rotten to the core.'

'All of them. Liars and cheats.'

'Perhaps the ones you associated with were.'

She laughed shrilly.

His eyes burned a moment, and then he rose and began to dress.

'When I was hungry,' she bit out, sitting up to glare at him, 'when I was cold and alone, a man took me in and fed me and clothed me, and warmed me before his fire. And he asked for nothing from me. *He* was a good man.'

He turned on her, holding his shirt, and his mouth twitched up. 'Perhaps he was incapable of asking anything from you,' he drawled, and left her spluttering. The door closed on him. Bloody lobster, she thought, as the room grew silent and she lay spent. The room drummed with his presence, or lack of it. The bed was warm where he had been. She tried to convince herself he would not be back.

CHAPTER TEN

THE FOLLOWING day seemed to confirm her belief. Clara's eyes followed her with a glimmer of interest, or perhaps fear. Her livelihood depended on Mary Anne, after all, and if Mary Anne were to be turned out into the street . . .

She was neither sorry nor glad she had spoken as she had. It seemed not to matter either way. The thing was done. It was, therefore, with great surprise that she heard his step in the hall the following morning. He opened the door to the sitting-room, where she was sitting by the window trying to concentrate on the *Hobart Town Gazette*.

'Here you are, ma'am!' His face was as cold as ever, but his eyes slid over her almost . . . yes, possessively. She disliked it.

'What do you want?'

The eyebrows lifted. 'Hardly a greeting.'

'What sort of greeting did you expect?' She, too, could be cold.

He smiled mockingly. 'A kiss, perhaps. Are you capable of real affection, Mary Anne, or only pretending it? God Almighty, you showed enough to Nick Etwall, dimpling and smiling and fluttering your eyelashes. I'd seen nothing to compare, even on stage.'

'What do you want?'

'What a contemptible bitch you are.'

She felt her face whiten under the sting. He strode to the window, circling her, observing her like a ringmaster. 'I think you should leave,' she managed at last.

'Why? The house is mine. We had our bargain, remember? I actually pitied you, left high and dry at

174

Etwall. I over-rode good sense for pity. Next time, I'll know better.'

'I hope not. I hope you never learn anything, and your life is a misery.'

He laughed harshly.

She stood up, her voice shaking. 'I'll pack now. I'll be gone in an hour.'

'You'd like that, wouldn't you? Have me curse myself for what I've done. Look out at me with those eyes of yours from every girl on every street corner.'

She went out into the hall, but he followed her.

'Damn those eyes of yours!'

She had reached the landing, before she replied. 'In an hour, you need never look at them again, Lieutenant Rowe.' Her voice was shaking as if she had an ague, and she felt a constriction like a band about her chest. Oh Toby, had she really come to this! He was right, always right. Without him, she was like a bedraggled kitten.

'Oh yes, you'd like that too!' the hateful voice shouted back.

She spun round in the doorway, face white with rage. 'Go away! Go on, go! I can't help what you've done. You're not the victim in the end, are you? Your sort never are!'

He, too, was white, the grey eyes glittering. She had never seen him so drawn; something about that frightened her even more. Her tongue ran away, tumbling over insults that grew worse and worse, dripping and oozing with the language of the Sydney Rocks and its gutters. In the end, as much to shut herself up as to shut out his white features, she slammed her door. There was a silence; she leaned her cheek against the panelling, and swallowed.

'Have you finished?' he said, cool as ice. 'If you have, I'll tell you why I've come. Yesterday I sent a note to a friend of mine. He's expecting to see you this afternoon.

We have to start now, if we're to reach him. He lives in the country, you see.'

Oh God, did he mean, then, to transfer her? Like a deed or a mortgage? Her flesh crawled.

'You should perhaps know that he is a minister of religion. He's going to marry us.'

She was silent for so long he evidently thought she hadn't heard.

'I mean it. Unfortunately for us both, I've a conscience. I find I have no choice.'

She opened the door and stared at him with huge dark eyes. 'Marry me?' Her voice was a croak.

He laughed abruptly. 'Are you going to faint? You're as white as a sheet.'

'But . . . But you . . . I mean, your sort don't marry! My mother . . . she . . . I don't understand it.' Some elaborate practical joke, it must be!

He frowned and grasped her arms. She stumbled a little, her eyes filling with tears. His chest was warm, oddly safe, against her cheek. She could hear his heart beating, strong and sure. It would surely never stop, or so it seemed at that moment. Luke Rowe would go on for ever. She had been wrong. She had thought he was the same as the rest, but he wasn't. She remembered suddenly how angry he had been, at the camp site, when the convict boy had been whipped. How white and angry and indignant.

'Hell, women! Mumble a few words over them and chime some bells, and they turn meek as lambs.'

He had succeeded in stinging her feelings again, and she realised suddenly how close she was, how his arms fitted about her, how his breath tickled her ear. It felt—why mince words?—it felt nice. Too nice. He couldn't be trusted. Besides, he was marrying her only to suit himself, not from any real wish to do so. As he had said, his conscience demanded it of him, nothing more.

She pulled away, colour flooding her cheeks. 'Take your marriage, and . . .'

'Enough!' he said, and yet his eyes were laughing at her. 'I've heard myself called enough names these past days to last a lifetime. No more, Mary Anne, or I'll have to gag you.'

'It's a mistake,' she said. 'Conscience is no reason for marriage. You know I hate you!'

He turned away indifferently. 'Change your dress and come downstairs. It's late as it is. I'll tell Clara to pack some clothing for overnight.'

There seemed to be no argument. The choice had already been made; or lack of it. As she turned back to her bedroom, however, she felt oddly lighthearted. All her worries had been removed—removed? Lord, they had only just begun!

The wine shone like blood in the sunlight from the window. Mary Anne stared into her glass, head bent as she stood against the light in her plain green dress. Behind her, Luke and the Reverend Mr Eggins were laughing. They seemed immoderately amused about something. Mrs Eggins, a plain, worried woman, stood twisting her hands near the pianoforte.

'My husband was in the army many years ago,' she said, as if to explain the laughter. 'He was a friend of Lieutenant Rowe's father, of course. We were neighbours for a time. But then my husband decided to buy land closer to Hobart, and so . . .'

Mary Anne smiled vaguely.

'Lieutenant Rowe was often home on leave, and we would see him then. He was a dutiful son. Have you visited the house at New Norfolk yet?'

'No, I . . .'

'Of course, there's plenty of time. Although I believe he is to return to Etwall soon?'

'Mary Anne?' Luke had come up unheard.

Mrs Eggins turned with a broad smile. 'We were just speaking of you, Luke. When are you to return to Etwall?'

'There's time enough for Mary Anne to get settled to the idea of being my wife,' he said, but his eyes were cool. Then, with a warmer smile, 'Thank you for this. We've put you to a lot of trouble, but it seemed better to be married without any fuss.'

'Better indeed!' thought Mary Anne, turning away to hide her expression.

'But now we'd best be getting back to Hobart. There are things to be done in the morning, and I've only the one day's leave from the town.'

The farewells were hastily done, but it was getting late as they turned down the drive on to the road. The sunlight streaked through the thick bush on either side, and Luke glanced nervously about until they reached a small but peaceful-looking town. And a neat little inn.

Mary Anne went up to their room while Luke stayed in the taproom with the proprietor, evidently an acquaintance of some years. A horse passed by on the otherwise deserted street. Mary Anne watched it from the window. And then his footsteps were on the stairs and the door closed. She heard him pour himself a drink from the jug of water. The dying sun from the window gleamed on the golden ring that bound her finger, and her life.

'Perhaps it's the time now for some truths,' he said.

'Truths?'

'About you, Mary Anne. You were never married; you were never a widow. Your mother seems to have been mentioned somewhere along the line . . . Oh yes, she was the one who told you about soldiers being such a charming lot of fellows.'

She bit her lip.

'What else do I know about you? You were alone and hungry and cold. You lie for a living. You tell lies all the time, in fact. But you won't be lying to me any more.'

'Oh?'

He had come up behind her, and now his fingers bit into her shoulders until she winced. 'One thing I can't abide is a liar.'

'Then you married the wrong woman,' she retorted.

'Perhaps.'

'And what now? What's expected of me? Playing hostess to the officers' wives, playing at married bliss for your promotions? Presenting an heir regularly every year? Visiting the sick and helping with the annual ball? Tatting and sewing and arranging flowers?'

'You could try holding your tongue for a start. No, on second thoughts, don't. I like hearing you talk. I've never heard any woman say the things you do with such an impeccable accent.'

His hands had moved upward to her nape, caressing it with a lover's touch. The change in his tactics put her off balance, and for a moment she stood still, thinking of the past. The words seemed to come without volition, and she didn't try to analyse or stop them.

'I'm twenty-two,' she said in a clipped voice. 'My mother died when I was twelve—she . . . over-imbided. My father I never knew the name of; my mother never spoke of him, and I doubt they were married at the time. When she died, a man took me in. I learned my trade from him. He's dead now.'

'On the ship?'

'It's enough that he's dead.'

'For the moment.'

'And you?' She faced him, and he had perforce to let her go. 'What of you?'

He shrugged. 'I joined the army when I was eighteen. My father owned land near New Norfolk. He died ten years ago, when I was twenty-one and about to come into the inheritance anyway.'

'And your disgrace?'

He smiled faintly. 'My concern and none of yours.'

She glared. 'Why should I speak the truth, when you don't?'

'But this isn't a lie, this is just a withholding of information.' He set down his glass. 'Fetch your bonnet. I feel like stretching my legs before supper.'

She stared at him suspiciously.

'And when we get back to Hobart, remind me to see about some new clothes for you.'

'Surely you'd be wasting your money, when you're soon to be abandoning me? You *are* returning to Etwall, aren't you?'

He held out his hand. 'I won't abandon you for ever, Mary Anne. Come!'

His eyes compelled, the gesture touched at a hope suddenly sprung to life in her breast. She gave him her hand, and felt his fingers curl round hers. She wished, suddenly, that she understood him. She wished she could trust him.

The darkness was drawing shadows into the wide street, and the candles and lamps shone in the cottages and houses set back in their neat gardens. There was a bridge over the river, and they paused there to watch the reflections, silent in companionship. A man on a horse, six or so convicts in chains ambling behind him, went past and tipped his hat. The convicts stared without expression, the shadows making their features grotesque.

'Man's inhumanity to man,' Luke Rowe murmured, and shrugged. 'What's to be done? Crime must be punished, or it would take over.'

'There are surely better ways of punishing?'

He said nothing, and after a moment they walked back to the inn. Over the private table, the candlelight shone in his eyes, matching the glint of mockery. 'I'll be the envy of Hobart.'

'You're a bloody bastard!'

He smiled. 'But that's your station in life, sweetheart!'

The tears blinded her, and she rose clumsily and had reached the room before she knew. The bed sank beneath her weight, and she wept wretchedly into the pillow until her eyes were too dry to weep any more. So he had married her, after all, to taunt her. It pleased him to amuse himself by hurting her. And, like a fool, she had given him the ammunition.

'So it was the truth.' She buried her face further into the pillows. He sat down beside her and, after a moment, slid his arm under her and drew her almost briskly into his arms. Her hair shielded her, tangled and unbound as it was. He pulled her against him so that she lay half sprawled across his lap, her face to his chest, his arm round her shoulders, leaving his other hand free to unravel the dark cloud hiding her face.

'You lie so much. I thought . . .'

'I hate you! I hate being married to you!'

'What a sight,' he mocked, finally exposing her pink, tear-stained face. 'Accept my sincerest apologies for doubting you.'

She gaped. He kissed her, his heart suddenly quickening against her palm. Her lips opened to protest, but the words were stifled against his mouth. He drew her closer and began, casually, to unlace her bodice. 'You look like a sulky little girl,' he said.

'Luke?'

'What?' He had finished what he was doing, and started to drag the gown over her head.

Her voice came muffled. 'Did you mean it, what you said?'

He untied the ribbons of her chemise. His hand went out, paused, and he looked at her with dark eyes. 'What I said?'

'About not abandoning me, not ever?'

He frowned. It seemed to her that he was considering

the question with irritation. She moved back, away from him, and pressed against the pillows. The lace of her chemise hardly covered her bosom, and she knew it well enough. And she knew that the way in which her hair had fallen about her shoulders was attractive. She began slowly to ease down her stockings, stretching out one leg at a time, slowly, seductive. He was watching her with flattering attention.

'Mary Anne,' he breathed. The grey eyes with, it seemed, an effort, rose to meet hers. Their question was clear.

She half smiled. 'Would you abandon me, Luke?' She leaned forward to undo the buttons of his shirt. His hands came up to grip hers in a hurtful clasp.

'What a tease you are! No, I won't abandon you. I've said I won't. I don't promise anything lightly, Mary Anne.'

Her fingers trembled and were still. Frowning, he tilted her chin and scanned her pale features. The smile glowed in his eyes. 'What an actress you are! You're terrified, and yet you can pretend you're as cool as ice.' He kissed her mouth softly, and rose. She closed her eyes as he undressed, wondering what had possessed her to draw such a promise from him. But now, at this moment, the question had seemed the most important one in the world. Her mother had been abandoned, had given way to her feelings and loved too much, and been hurt. She had died from it, in the end. There was no way Mary Anne meant to be abandoned too.

He lay down beside her, drawing her against his warm, naked body, and her mind fled from thoughts, except those of him. This time, he took her more slowly through the dance of love. His hands and lips excited her until she cried out for release, and the grey eyes gleamed down at her, his hot breath stirring the damp wisps of her hair.

'I told you once,' he whispered. 'I saved you from the

sea, and that makes you mine.'

His finger slid down her throat, circling the pink tip of one breast, down over the curve of her belly until she quivered and slipped her arms about his waist and drew him to her, lifting her body to mould to his, drinking from his lips. The mindless joy of desire overtook them, and nothing else seemed to matter until it was satisfied. That he was her enemy, and was doing more at Etwall than he would tell her, and that she was bound to him now with more than words and a promise, were lost in the sweetness of their love, and in the gradual cooling of their bodies as they lay clasped together in the soft haven of the bed.

But then, when it was done, everything came spiralling back again, and she wondered with a prickle of fear if her mother had not asked for and been given the same promise. A promise was not hard, after all, to break.

'What schemes are you planning now?'

She looked up and found him watching her from one propped elbow. The look on her face, perhaps, was amusing. He smiled, and reaching out, stroked her temple. The look in his eyes made her catch her breath. And she knew, with sudden blinding amazement, that at this precise moment, as he looked at her, he loved her. He might never love her again—in a second he might feel contempt. But in that second he loved her. And she hardly dared move, in case the spell was broken.

The next week went so quickly that she had hardly time to breathe. He had leave, it seemed. He didn't talk about the army, and she saw the barracks only from a distance. The rest of the time was spent with Luke. He took her around Hobart with a pleasure she found surprising and a little discomforting. But perhaps it wasn't pleasure after all, that gleaming in his grey eyes when he smiled at her. Not that he had changed, she reminded herself, just because she was his wife. He was as cool and assessing as ever.

He seemed ridiculously generous. One gown, she might have understood. Even Toby had bought her clothes to suit the occasion they found themselves in. But a dozen! He mocked her surprise and her suspicion, informing the seamstress she was a pinch-penny. The woman smirked, her eyes sliding over him. Could the woman actually envy her Luke Rowe? Mary Anne thought. It seemed preposterous! And yet . . . he was a handsome man. She was further amazed by the hats and shoes and the intimacies of underwear. He knew too much, and found it amusing to deck her out like a fashion doll. Why did he do it?

A dozen hats were tipped to him in the street, a dozen ladies smiled from gigs and carriages. A dozen acquaintances turned curiously to Mary Anne, and were introduced. Her face ached with smiling and nodding, and remembering names. It amused him, she thought with a glare, to taunt her this way. To force her to act so unnaturally, to pretend at being his loving wife. The grey eyes mocked her even while she felt herself slipping comfortably into the role expected of her. She smiled, dimpled and fluttered her lashes, but beneath it all anger and confusion mingled red hot.

'So accomplished,' he would mock, when her parcels were deposited. 'I'm the envy of Hobart. "That sweet Mrs Rowe", they call you. "So sweet and shy and unassuming".'

They were invited to many assemblies and suppers, but avoided them.

'Boring as hell,' he informed her. 'Time enough for them afterwards. At the moment, there's no time to play at conventions.'

'After what?'

The eyes mocked. 'When I sell out of the army.'

She stared. 'But you were going back to Etwall!'

'Yes. And when that's finished, I have the Governor's promise I'll be free.'

A candle flickered on the table. The curtains were drawn, making the room into a little world of its own. The scent of flowers filled the air. 'What is it you have to finish?'

'My business.'

'Luke?'

'Mary Anne?'

She shot him a look of distaste, and he laughed. Another pause, while she played with the fringe of her shawl. 'When do you have to go?'

'The ship sails at the beginning of next month.'

'Less than three weeks!' What of *her*? She dared not ask, though she knew by the way in which he was smiling that he was waiting for the question. He thought she cared for nothing but her own comfort. Perhaps he was right. 'Look to yourself and to hell with the rest,' her mother had said. It was a good enough motto. Damn Luke Rowe! She looked up at him, but he was staring into his glass and his face had become grim.

'And when you sell out?' she murmured softly.

He looked up with a smile. 'I would prefer the quiet life. Farming. Local dances and dinner with friends. Visits to Hobart a few times a year, maybe. But I doubt that would suit you, would it, my love? I picture you here, holding court over a dozen love-struck young men, decked out with diamonds.' He shrugged. 'But there's time enough to decide on that when I come back from Etwall.'

It happened in Harrington Street. The thing that was to be the turning-point. She had paused to look back down at the harbour, as they reached the corner of Macquarie Street. And as she did so, she glimpsed a face in the crowd. Only a glimpse, but she knew that face as well as her own. Toby.

She must have cried out, but when Luke shot a question at her, she just shook her head and kept shaking it. He was angry with her, and it didn't seem to matter. Toby was alive! He must be . . . Yet, how could he be?

It was so foolish, she told herself over and over. But something in her would not give in and would not rest. She could not think or speak; she didn't hear what Luke said; her mind wandered when he kissed her or touched her.

He became angry with her, his touch almost cruel. 'I realise you loathe me,' he said at last. 'But you could at least give me some of your precious attention. After all, my future concerns you as much as me.' The grey eyes were hard and angry. 'You act as if you're in love,' he said, cold as ice. 'Are you?'

Impulsively she reached out, but he had already risen to go to the door, where he paused, 'As it is obviously not with me, I prefer the question to remain unanswered.' The door slammed. She heard him going down the stairs. But even before he had reached the hall, her mind had returned to the question of Toby.

Things deteriorated after that. Luke looked at her with mockery and contempt. A brooding look that she avoided as much as possible. He filled his days now without her, but she found things to do. A stroll in the garden or the park. A walk through the bustle of Hobart. There were people who knew her and spoke, but she refused all invitations. Clara had accompanied her at first, but lately had made excuses to remain in the house. She had seen Luke looking at the girl, too. A look she fancied showed interest. For some reason the thought of him lavishing his mouth and body on Clara drove her wild with anger.

It was easy enough to trap them. She went out, ostensibly to the shops, but she had gone only minutes when she returned. She had forgotten her gloves, if

Clara should ask. It was easy enough to slip into the hall
and creep down towards the kitchen stairs.

Voices. Clara's loud laughter. Her fingers clenched on
each other like knives. God damn him! Why Clara?
Tears sparkled and stung, but she held them back. She'd
tear him to pieces, she'd rend his flesh with her bare
hands, she'd . . . she'd . . .

'Mind your hands!' Clara shrieked. Mary Anne threw
open the door. It crashed back against a crockery cupboard, smashing a milk-jug to smithereens.

'You bloody lobster, Luke Rowe!'

Clara leapt up from her lover's knee with a shriek of
terror. Her bosom, most of it exposed, was heaving.
'Ma'am, I . . . Ma'am, you . . .'

Mary Anne hardly heard. Her mouth had dropped.
For a moment she thought she would faint. But she
didn't.

''Tis . . . 'Tis only Toby O'Reilly, ma'am. He's looking for work, he says, and I thought . . . seein' as the
Lieutenant hasn't got a man to see to his clothes and the
like, I thought . . .'

The man rose and came up to her. The auburn hair
curled over his head, the blue eyes sparkled. He put his
finger under her chin and gently closed her mouth. 'Ay,'
he said, in a rich Irish brogue. 'It's the truth an' all, what
she says. I'm lookin' for work.'

'Ma'am, please! I'm so sorry. I didn't think . . .'

'I know what you didn't think!' she retorted, her voice
hard and sharp with emotion. She swallowed. She felt
like fainting, and yet even at such a moment as this she
mustn't fail him. 'I'll speak with you later, Clara.'

The girl hesitated, scowled, and then vanished out
into the hall. The door closed reluctantly. Toby smiled,
and held out his arms.

CHAPTER ELEVEN

'I THOUGHT for certain, Toby, this time . . .'

He laughed, cradling her in his arms. 'The devil takes care of his own, Mary Anne! Don't weep, my girl. It really is me.'

She sniffed and smiled. 'How?'

'I saw you in the street, and followed you. Clara's been *most* co-operative.'

'I'll bet!'

He laughed again. 'And talkative! My God, Lieutenant Rowe this and that. The goings-on in this house! I warn you, I know every sordid detail.'

She hugged him tighter. 'If only I'd found you sooner, there would have been no need for Luke Rowe.'

'The "bloody lobster"?'

She could not help laughing. 'Yes; my husband.' The word annoyed her, and she glanced at Toby. He was watching her a little sadly. 'Oh, Toby, if only . . .'

'Enough of "if onlys", my girl. We have plans to make, hmm?'

'Yes.'

'How did you survive, Mary Anne?'

She told him, swiftly and simply, about the wreckage and Luke Rowe and the stay at Etwall. He listened with interest. 'I felt there were rich pickings there,' she ventured. 'But without you, I bungled everything.'

He tousled her hair, but his smile was abstracted. 'Well, we may yet get another chance at them. Do you know how I escaped? The captain had a boat over. Took off before anyone knew. That's when I tied you to that wood, for safety. I lost you after that, and floated. Thought I was dead for sure. Then I came across the captain's boat again—empty. Don't know what happened to him, unless he and the mate had a fight and disposed of each other! There was a sail. I made for the coast. God, that coastline! There's absolutely nothing, and rugged . . . I zig-zagged close in, going south. A whaler found me and pulled me aboard.'

'And so you came here.'

'I did. I've been working in one of the theatres.' He pulled a face. 'I throw out anyone who becomes a bit vocal. But that'll change now. Do you think Rowe will give me a job?'

She bit her lip. 'I don't know.'

'Can't you use your wiles on him, girl?'

'Toby, he won't give a damn!'

Toby laughed a little mockingly. 'Mary Anne, dear girl, the man, by all accounts, can't keep his hands off you.'

She went scarlet. 'That isn't so? He's not come near me for . . . for . . .'

'Then you must see that he does.'

She glanced at him mischievously. 'You're not jealous?'

The blue eyes dipped, but when they lifted they were gentle. 'Minx!'

'It won't be easy, but . . . Oh, to have you with me, near me!'

'And me you, girl, and me you.'

A pause, and he frowned. 'The emerald, Mary Anne. Where is it?'

The emerald! He saw the distress in her eyes, and covered her twisting fingers with his own. 'Tell me.'

The story came out, briefly. He sighed and shook his head. 'It's clear you *can't* manage alone. Well, we must have it, girl. It's our insurance for the future. I'll just have to get a job with your soldier-boy, and he'll just have to take me back to Etwall! See to it, Mary Anne.'

It wasn't easy. Luke had been drinking. He slouched

in his chair, watching her with that hateful, sardonic
gleam in his eyes, and when she tried polite conversation, drawled monosyllables in answer. 'Luke, please,
must you stare so?'

He raised his eyebrows with infinite slowness. 'Was I
staring, sweetheart? I was comparing you with the little
beauty I was with this afternoon. Raven hair, like yours,
and dark eyed. Not so shapely, perhaps, and not such a
way with her as you, Mary Anne. Still, I enjoyed her.'

Mary Anne stared at him in silence. Did he mean it? A
curious sensation was playing in her stomach, and she
clenched her fingers under the cover of the table.

'Don't you believe me?' he said, and laughed. Like
the devil he was, she thought, and felt the colour rise in
her face as anger bubbled inside her.

'Do what you like,' she said sharply. 'We can both
play at that game.'

The mouth laughed again, the laughter subtly
changed. She smelt danger. 'Do you want me to tell you
what we did?' he said.

Her heart began to thump, and she carefully refolded
her napkin.

'The room was full of red taffeta. Yards of it! The bed,
too. Especially the bed. She unpinned her hair then. It
fell to her waist, like silk. She said she'd been a whore in
London and knew all the tricks.'

Mary Anne stood up, her legs like wood. 'How dare
you?' she whispered in an unrecognisable voice.

'Oh, I dare.' He, too, stood up. 'Come back here! Or
are you afraid to?'

Mary Anne fled up the stairs, aware of Toby in the
kitchen, probably listening to this charade. But he came
after her—he always did. Why couldn't he leave her in
peace?

'Why?' she burst out, turning on him. 'Why did you
marry me if you only want to hurt me?'

He threw back his head and laughed loud and long.

Furious, she threw her shawl at him, and when he took
no notice, picked up a vase. He had caught her wrist
before she could throw it, and lazily replaced it. 'Hurt
you?' he repeated, and his mouth was thin and bitter.
She stared up at him, all anger suddenly going. 'I haven't
finished my story,' he said at last. His fingers hurt her
shoulders, but she made no protest and stood waiting.
He smiled faintly. 'No protests? Perhaps you already
know, hmm? Where was I? Oh yes, the red taffeta, and
her hair like silk. And she began to take off her clothes.'

'Luke,' she said, and her hands clutched at his shirt
front. He bent his head suddenly and kissed her.

'Jesus, woman, she took off every stitch and I sat there
and looked and felt like ice.' He kissed her again. 'Not a
flicker! I kept thinking of you. You!'

She met his mouth hungrily. 'Oh Luke, I didn't mean
. . . It was not you. I . . .' Her arms slid round him of
their own volition. 'It's been so horrible!' She buried her
face in his shoulder, but he put her away and, with a kind
of reverence, undressed her. She opened her arms to
him, saying, 'You don't need anyone but me, Luke
Rowe.' He kissed her and laughed, grey eyes bright. She
stroked his cheek, her lashes shadowing her eyes, aware
of the desire raging through him, barely under control.
'Luke, I was such a fool. I thought you and Clara were
. . . you know.' He stared in disbelief. 'Don't deny
you've looked at her; I've seen you! I burst into the
kitchen today and found her with some Irishman!'

He laughed, burying his face in her hair. But he was
pleased, and she smiled. Smug devil! And yet her smile
was tender, and her voice gentle when she added, 'He
had the gall to ask for employment!'

'Did you give it to him?'

'I said that was up to you, being the master of the
house. I felt foolish, you see, and thought I owed him
something.'

'Mmm.' He smoothed her cheek. 'I'll see him

tomorrow, and decide then. At the moment I've other things on my mind.'

'Luke,' she said, putting her finger on his lips. 'Luke, I want to go with you, back to Etwall.'

The grey eyes hardened. She felt his withdrawal. 'No.'

'I want to come with you!'

'Why?' His look was suspicious, gone the tender light. 'Are you pining for Nick Etwall?'

Mary Anne sniffed disdainfully. '*That* bore!' She walked to the bed and drew her silken dressing-gown about her. 'No. But you promised not to abandon me.'

'God Almighty!' His shout startled her, but she didn't turn. 'You are in the middle of Hobart, woman! If you wish, you can go to my property at New Norfolk. I'll be back soon enough. How can you be abandoned?'

'I want to come,' she pouted, twisting her fingers in the smooth stuff of her gown. She heard his hiss of impatient breath, and then his hands on her shoulders.

'It's too dangerous,' he said quietly, the edge of his voice hinting at the effort he was making to be patient with her woman's quibbles. 'You could be hurt. Besides, it's business, not pleasure. I have work to do there that will be in no way pleasant. That is all I can say, Mary Anne.'

He turned her round and, a finger under her chin, lifted her face to kiss her. Gently at first, and then with deepening passion. A possessive kiss. She was his, the kiss said, and he meant to take full advantage of her. The anger and the gap between them, which had been growing over the past few days, since Toby came back into her mind, shortened and was bridged. Mary Anne let herself drown in the passion which was, if she could accept it, a sort of love. Perhaps even love enough to keep them together for many years to come. But . . . as she moved restlessly in his embrace, she wanted more. There was more. She saw it sometimes in his eyes, lurking behind the mockery and the passion. A something which matched something in her very soul, and which was almost beyond her comprehension. Peace and warmth and happiness, and the knowledge that she meant more to someone than life itself.

But the battle to go to Etwall was by no means over. If Toby went, she would go, too. Luke must just come to accept that, whatever clever games he was involved in.

Toby was waiting in the hall the following morning, cap in hand, looking as subservient as it was possible for him to look. Only his eyes betrayed him, sparkling with laughter as Mary Anne came downstairs. Clara was hovering about, but made a hasty exit.

'Well?' he said, and cocked his head to one side.

Mary Anne, still cocooned in the warmth of a night in Luke's embrace, had forcibly to shake off the gentleness that seemed to have sapped her spirit and was totally foreign to her usual nature. It was Toby, *Toby!* Her fingers itched to touch his cheek, his curly auburn hair. Toby, alive. How could she ever have thought him dead?

'He says he'll see you,' she murmured. 'I can't promise anything. I asked him about Etwall. He says he won't take me. But he will.'

Toby laughed softly and pulled out of the curls that lay on her shoulder. 'Ah, Mary Anne, still up to the old tricks. You could always wind them round your little finger!'

She smiled, but her eyes were uncertain. 'Toby, I don't know about this one. He frightens me. He's warm one minute and cold the next.'

'You frightened of a man?' Toby mocked. 'He's married you, girl, when he could have turned you out so easily.'

'He did it for himself, not me. He has a conscience.'

She said it with distaste, as one spoke of a slug.

Steps above on the landing. 'Is this the bridegroom

himself, then?' Toby breathed. 'The lucky, lucky man!'

'Toby, you fool!' she breathed back, and tried to reduce her colour by coughing into her handkerchief and hiding her face.

Luke came down the stiars. He was not wearing his uniform, but dark trousers and jacket over a shirt and waistcoat, all impeccable. Only his fair hair was a little tousled still. Mary Anne felt her cheeks reddening even more, remembering the night.

But he was looking at Toby, who had resumed his subservient pose and was now shifting nervously from one foot to the other. 'I mean no trouble, ma'am,' he said to Mary Anne in his Irish brogue. 'Only Clara said as . . . Well, she said . . .'

Mary Anne cleared her throat firmly. 'Nonsense. Luke, this is the man I told you about.'

Luke lifted his eyebrows in amusement. 'Oh, yes.' His smile mocked her for what she had told him. 'Your name, man?'

Toby sent him a glance before lowering his eyes again. 'Toby O'Reilly, sir.'

'O'Reilly. What are you doing in Hobart?'

'I'm looking for work, sir.'

'You didn't abscond from anywhere?'

'No, sir, that I didn't. I'm a free man now.'

Mary Anne was watching them, amazed as always by Toby's abilities as a performer, trying to determine what Luke Rowe thought. He seemed amused, but beneath that . . . She never knew what he thought!

'I'm in the army, O'Reilly, as you probably know. I need a good man to take with me to my post at Etwall. After that, if we still suit, you can stay; if not, you're free to leave my employ.'

'Sir! Thank you, sir.'

Luke looked at Mary Anne with a shrug. She smiled, but determined to tell Toby not to overdo the sub-

servience. Luke preferred men to stand up to him than
to grovel.

'Go and get your things, then, and bring them here.
No doubt Clara will see to a bed.'

Toby laughed involuntarily, and turned away. Luke
took Mary Anne's arm firmly in his and said, painfully
audibly, 'Jesus, I half expected him to be at my boots!'

He had someone to see, he said, and so Mary Anne
was alone when Toby returned, and made a point of
sending for him. Clara looked sulky, but fetched him.
Toby came to embrace her. 'It's worked out fine! He
thinks I'm a fool, and I'm to go to Etwall. And Clara
believes you fancy me.'

'No!'

'Jealous little piece, is Clara.'

She laughed.

'Where's your esteemed spouse?'

'Out on business, he says, and won't tell me what. He
never tells me anything!' She sounded like a cosseted
wife, pouting at being kept from the business affairs of
her husband. Toby laughed, flicking her cheek.

'Then we have some time. I want you to tell me about
Etwall, Mary Anne, and everyone there.'

'But I will be coming!'

The blue eyes went dull. 'I wouldn't count on it. Our
Lieutenant Rowe is no fool, or weakling. He might have
a soft spot down yonder for you, my girl, but his mind is
clear and cold as glass.'

'I will go!'

'Perhaps.' But she could see he didn't believe her. 'Is
that claret I see? Do you think I might sample a wee
glass?'

She poured him a large one, and sat watching him as
he sipped it, smiled, and drank it down. She drank him
with her eyes as he drank the red wine. 'Oh, Toby!' she
burst out. 'I was so lost without you! I kept thinking,
"What would Toby have done", but it never turned out

right. I bungled everything. I set my sights on Nicholas Etwall and paid no heed to any of the others; and, most stupid of all, I considered Luke Rowe as of no account.'

Toby leaned forward to grasp her cold hands. 'Poor Mary Anne, and he was the most accountable of the lot. Could you not see it, girl, in his eyes? Men with hard, cold eyes are to be taken account of in any situation. Men like that know what they want and go for it, and generally they get it.'

She sighed, and after a moment smiled. 'Yes, you're right. I'll know next time.'

He choked a little. 'And how do you propose to have another chance? Are we to run off together?'

She seemed surprised. 'But what else?'

'Mary Anne, the man has wed you! He is rich and has land, he buys you things and treats you moderately well. Isn't that what you want?'

She frowned. 'No, I . . . I don't know. But you're here now, Toby! I want to be with you!'

'Do you?' he mocked. 'Well, never mind that for the present. Tell me about Etwall, girl, and quick smart. We don't want to be caught in here, do we?'

She told him. Bessy and Ralph, Nick and Belle, the servants, the timber camp, the emerald. He listened with rapt attention, and when she was finished, sighed. 'So that's it. And our Lieutenant returns on his . . . mission. For what reason?'

'He's in disgrace.'

Toby looked sceptical. 'For what? Lord, it would need to be murder at least to be disgraced from Hobart barracks! And even then . . .'

'But—' her eyes narrowed '—he said that the Governor had promised him his freedom when he'd been to Etwall again. He said he was selling out.'

'Selling out? Etwall, then, has some importance to the Governor. I wonder what it could be?'

She sighed. 'He won't tell me.'

Toby laughed. 'Then there are some men who can resist those eyes of yours, you minx!' He frowned. 'And the army are laying on a ship for his return?'

'I suppose so. I don't know. Only a few ships would travel to Etwall in the winter, bringing supplies and so on. The weather isn't the best.'

'Then we must assume it is so. What is his mission, Mary Anne? And can we make something from it, in hard cash?'

'I don't know. I hadn't thought.'

But he didn't hear her. The blue eyes were dreamy; she knew the signs. Outwardly he might be relaxed, dozing even, but underneath his brain was alive with plans and counter-plans. The look made her more than ever determined to go to Etwall too. Toby and she had been together on every one of their plans, and this time would be no different. How dared Luke Rowe keep her away? What right had he to determine her comings and goings? By the time he came home for supper, she had worked herself into a fine rage, and was waiting, drumming her fingers on the desk.

Unfortunately, he wasn't alone. 'Mary Anne, these are some friends. John and Therese Williams.' She turned. She had never in her life felt less like play-acting, but she had been playing her parts too long to fail now, and summoning up the sweet smile, came forward to welcome the polite and curious Williams couple.

John, it seemed, was a merchant. He owned a number of ships and traded with the mainland, as well as much further afield. 'China is a gold-mine for the trader,' he said. 'Silks and spices, objects of value to the art lover.'

'White slaves?' Luke murmured, lifting an eyebrow. Therese laughed immoderately, and tapped his hand with her fan.

'Luke, how can you talk so? Look how you have shocked your little wife!'

Mary Anne, far from being shocked, was viewing him

with a vacant smile. White slaves, indeed! Well, if anyone knew about them, it would be Luke Rowe.

'No, really?' Luke retorted. John Williams squeezed her arm, and said, 'Take no notice of them, Mary Anne. Luke always did have a wicked tongue.'

Therese laughed again, displaying her long throat. She wore diamonds in her ears and a necklace rested on the curve of her breasts. The gown was low and her figure buxom, to say the least. Mary Anne found her distasteful and vulgar; it was one thing to be fashionable, quite another to be *fast*! She, at least, had always been tasteful in her approach, and certainly never vulgar. There was a line—fine perhaps, but still a line—between the two. Therese, she felt, had crossed it.

The meal was endless, and afterwards they played cards, while Clara served wine, nuts and fruit. Luke won mostly, until Therese said, 'You are no gentleman, Luke! This is the fifth time you've trumped my ace!'

He mocked her with a lift of his eyebrows. Mary Anne remembered suddenly him doing the same to her, at Etwall. A tingle went through her. Perhaps that was his signal of interest in a woman, trumping her aces? Perhaps he was interested in Therese. She watched him from under her lashes, while her mouth smiled and quipped with John. Did he look at her over-long? Or smile with more warmth than was necessary? Did he brush her hand by accident? Or by design?

They were leaving at last. Therese embraced him, offering Mary Anne merely a peck on the cheek. John patted her hand almost fatherly. Luke went out with them. After a moment, Mary Anne sat down by the remains of their repast. Luke returned, shutting the door and going to the hearth. He lit a cigar from the coals before standing and leaning back lazily against the mantel. The candles caught fire in his eyes, and she couldn't read his expression beyond the brilliance. He, it seemed, had no such problems.

'You didn't like them, did you?'

Her mouth sneered. 'Should I? Is that a necessity when you take your mistresses?'

'What are you talking about?'

'Why, Therese. As if you didn't know!'

He laughed and approached her with a confidence she found suddenly infuriating. 'Sweet Mary Anne, your imagination runs away with you. Therese is John's wife, and if he chooses to marry an ex-actress, among other things, that is entirely his affair.'

'An ex . . .'

'Exactly.'

What a fool she was! And yet, he might be lying. She stared at him for a long moment, while he stared back, his mouth curving. 'And your verdict?' he mocked softly. 'Guilty or innocent?'

'Why should I believe you? Your morals are non-existent. There was Belle first, wasn't there? And then you trap me into becoming your wife. Why should Therese be any different?'

His grey eyes lost their warm light, his mouth thinned. 'I see. Perhaps it would help my case if I were to explain that Belle was business, not pleasure, and Therese is my friend's wife, which means more to me than you evidently conceive, and that you would have been far worse off now had I left you to fend for yourself.'

She stood up abruptly, her fingers pressed to his chest, her head thrown back so that she could look into his eyes. He viewed her with cold interest, and she despaired of ever winning that control over him that she had won over so many men.

'What is it you want, Mary Anne?' he said, almost gently.

She took a breath. 'I want to go back to Etwall with you.'

'Oh? Is it the loss of your emerald which causes you such concern? I told you you were better off without it.

But, if you insist, I will make enquiries for you . . .'

'No, it's not that. Well, not wholly. Can't you see why I want to go with you?'

He scanned her upturned face; the parted lips and velvet eyes. All the unspoken longing and passion vibrating through her.

'Luke, I don't want to be alone here, while you go. I want to be with you. Please, don't abandon me.'

'Presumably you mean you love me, or what passes for it with you.'

He sounded cruel. There was bitterness in his eyes, and the smile on his mouth wasn't kind. 'If you leave me,' she said softly, 'If you abandon me as my mother was abandoned, Luke, you will never find me again. I'll not be here with you come back.'

His eyes searched hers, and then he asked mockingly, 'Won't I? Are you threatening me?'

'Yes! I won't stay waiting. I'll run.'

'And what makes you think I would care so much, you bitch? I could find someone prettier than you, and more accommodating. You're not unique.'

That hurt, more than she dared show. She dropped her hands to her sides, and bowed her head. Tears swam in her vision. 'Then do so,' she breathed. 'I won't be here, Luke.' There was truth in her voice. The silence lengthened, and she heard him breathe deeply.

'If I thought it would do any good, I'd strangle you. But I suppose then I'd be left with the memory of you without any way of satisfying myself. If I thought, for one moment, that you did love me, I'd take you to New Norfolk myself and lock you up until my return. But you don't, so what have I to lose? Come if you wish. Why you want to, I don't know, unless it's to embarrass the Etwalls with your presence. Perhaps, in time, your schemes will reveal themselves to me. But if you get in my way, woman, I'll break your back.'

She looked up at him, a smile of triumph beginning. It

died as quickly before his grim, angry face. He turned for the door, then, but paused to look back. 'We leave in three days. Don't expect me back until then.'

Luke, she thought, but bit her tongue on the words. She was going! That was all that mattered. Shouldn't she be happy? She would be with Toby again, like old times! What else mattered? Luke Rowe could think and say what he wished. It didn't matter to her, did it? Or did it? She stood up, smoothing her skirt with shaking hands. 'If I thought that you did love me . . .' he had said. Why in God's name should she ever do a foolish thing like that? Mary Anne sank on to a chair, listening with a heavy heart to Luke's footsteps fading down the hall, and the slam of the front door.

CHAPTER TWELVE

TOBY WAS pleased when she told him, but apprehensive too. 'So you've done the damage, girl? The mar wouldn't have given in unless you hit a sore spot. Wha did you tell him?'

She shook her head, not wanting to repeat it all. Toby squeezed her against his chest. 'Can't you tell me any more? Your very best friend, hmm?'

A laugh shook her, despite herself. 'I can. It's just . . Well, I said I'd run off while he was gone, and he said i he thought I loved him truly he would lock me up here but as I don't, I can come. Or some such nonsense, anc then he said he was going in three days and to be ready.'

'Nonsense indeed.' He squeezed her again. 'Are you sure you want to come after all?'

'Of course I do. And I *will* come.'

'Good!'

Luke arranged for luggage to be collected and taken down to the docks for loading. The ship was a schooner, small and swift, hired for the occasion. The house in Harrington Street was to be closed temporarily. Mary Anne actually felt a pang at leaving it, and found herself being so foolish as to stroke the furniture. Totally alien to her nature, the feelings startled her into hurrying out into the street and into the carriage without more than a nod to Clara.

The girl had been weeping, and Toby chucked her under the chin with a laugh. He was a good-for-nothing scoundrel, of course, Mary Anne decided with a frown. Why was it she loved him so? And why did he love her? The bond was strong. He had been everything to her, he had turned her into a person capable of feeling more than hatred and bitterness at the world. They had been her mother's legacy. All else was his.

Luke was already on board. He greeted her briefly and coolly, and turned at once to Toby. 'O'Reilly, take your things down to your cabin. I'll give you your orders when you're done. The mate will direct you.'

Mary Anne went to follow, but the boat rocked and she was forced instead to cling to the rail. He glanced at her with mockery. 'The wind is coming up. It doesn't promise to be a very pleasant voyage.'

In more ways than one, she decided, but said only, 'Which is my cabin?'

'You are conveniently next to me, isn't that so, captain?'

The captain, a florid-faced man, beamed. 'That's so, Lieutenant. I hope you have sea-legs, Mrs Rowe? The weather promises to be pretty foul.'

'My wife was the one survivor from *Infanta*, captain.'

The man's eyes widened. 'Is that so? But surely . . . Surely, sir, there was another?'

Luke raised his eyebrows; Mary Anne felt her cheeks pale. 'Another?' she whispered.

The captain cleared his throat. 'Well, I'm not sure, but it seems to be I've heard of another. In Hobart itself. Picked up by some vessel or other in an open boat. I didn't pay much mind to it. God knows wrecks are not uncommon in these waters!'

Mary Anne swallowed. 'Perhaps it is so. We must discover more, when we return.'

'Indeed, yes.' Luke was watching her, a frown in his eyes. She breathed out only when he had turned back to the captain, and was grateful to slip away to her own cabin. By the time they returned, things might have changed radically, or he might have forgotten. However, she admitted, the latter was unlikely. Besides, Toby would save her, whatever the outcome!

The weather was not too bad at first, and she was able

to appear at the captain's table with Luke and the first mate. The captain and Luke spoke about matters in general, while the mate—a youngish man with a romantic turn of phrase—gazed at her and spoke of her fortuitous escape from death, so that she felt herself obliged to make the event seem even more exciting than it had been.

But as the meal progressed, the sea grew more choppy and the schooner pitched uncomfortably. Mary Anne felt her stomach quivering, and thought it prudent to rise and excuse herself. Luke came too.

'Another conquest?' he murmured in her ear as they went down the companionway.

She ignored him, concentrating on keeping her stomach in the region where it belonged. Poor Toby! He was probably already groaning in his bunk. Perhaps this plan was not such a good one, after all. What if it was to end as *Infanta*? The thought jolted her abruptly, and she clung weakly to her door.

'There's no need to pretend *mal-de-mer* for me, Mary Anne,' he mocked. 'I'm weary of your . . . charms.'

'Pretend!' she burst out, turning furiously on him. 'Why should I bother to pretend anything?'

Her face was white, tinted green. He laughed faintly. 'Why, indeed? Come and lie down.' He opened the door and she stumbled in and flung herself on the bed, turning her shoulder on him. When she dared to look again, he was gone.

The weather worsened. She no longer rose at all, but lay in an agony of nausea. No food stayed down; she had given up trying to eat. Surely death was preferable to this? Even a visit by Toby had failed to cheer her.

He had come in darkness, green-faced as she, and clinging weakly to the edge of the bed, gasped out a few words before stumbling away. They were only hours out from Etwall harbour. Luke had told him to carry a gun.

'A gun?' Mary Anne repeated. But Toby had already retreated to his own cabin and his own agony.

She woke to stillness, and lay a long time trying to remember where she was. She felt weak and dizzy, but the tearing nausea had gone. Experimentally, she rose. The cabin smelt of vomit and salt water, and she changed hastily and, running a brush through her hair, went out. The fresh breeze struck her as she started up the gangway. She stood swaying a moment, breathing deeply. Her limbs tingled with renewed life, and she walked more firmly as she reached the hatchway and stepped out on the deck.

No wonder it was so calm! They were at Etwall, lying on the smooth grey waters of the harbour. She gazed out upon the place with an almost affectionate wonder. The yellow sand of the beach, where a boat was drawn up. The house rising dark against the skyline, and behind it the clutter of cottages looking a little like dice thrown carelessly upon the ground. Seabirds circled overhead, smoke drifted from the trees where the timber camp lay. Etwall had not changed—only she had changed.

'Mrs Rowe!' The mate had come up with a smile. 'Your husband and his man have already gone ashore. He asked me to let you sleep.'

'How kind.' He meant to leave her here for as long as possible!

'The boat will be back shortly, and you can go ashore. I'll have your luggage brought up.'

'Brought up,' she murmured. 'What a dreadful expression!'

He laughed, and her eyes danced mischievously. God, she had forgotten how it was to have a man hot for her. Luke Rowe was such a bloody cold lobster. It was a good feeling, and she added, 'You're very kind. Tell me, has my husband spoken to the Etwalls yet?'

The mate flushed. 'I believe he has. They came to meet the boat. At least . . . one man on a horse.'

So they knew. With luck, Luke had told them about her, and so saved her the embarrassment. She hadn't thought about that until Luke threw it at her in Hobart. The embarrassment. She had thought only of being with Toby and discovering what Luke was up to, and getting back the emerald from the lovely, evil Belle.

'Tell me,' she began, turning again to the mate. 'This ship was hired especially for my husband?'

The man looked at her and away, then shook his head. 'I know nothing of these matters, Mrs Rowe. My apologies, but I must fetch your luggage . . .'

She sighed, and turned back towards the beach. The boat came quite soon, and she was helped down into it, with her few pieces of luggage. The air was cold and invigorating, the water like grey ice as they glided through it, back to the beach, until the keel grated on gravelly sand. One of the seamen helped her out on to the beach. She lifted her hem and picked her way up to the track. She was so busy avoiding the line of seaweed that she did not see the woman until it was too late. She was standing in the shelter of the trees, and stepped out boldly as Mary Anne approached.

The red hair was fanned a little by the breeze, the blue eyes paler than ever. 'So you've come back.'

There was little to say to that.

'Even after you'd lost Nick, you still managed to get Luke Rowe.' The pink lips parted, and Mary Anne watched, fascinated, as soft laughter floated out. 'I never thought you'd get Luke Rowe, Mrs High-and-Mighty.'

'I hardly know what you mean.'

'You know.' She laughed again. 'I underestimated you, didn't I?'

'Did you get good use out of the clothes you stole from me?'

'I threw them into the sea, didn't I? Where *you* ought to be. You'll be sorry you came back.' And now the eyes narrowed in threat.

'Will I?' Her heart was pounding, but outwardly she remained cool and calm. 'I can't see it's any business of yours what my husband and I do, Belle. Now, if you'll excuse me . . .'

Belle's eyes went hard. 'When the time comes, I'll kill you myself. And Luke, of course.'

Mary Anne watched her go, feeling rather weak. The woman was mad. How on earth did Toby mean to get the emerald from her clutches?

The remainder of the track was deserted, and it was only as she approached the cottage Luke had occupied that she heard voices. The door was open and she paused a moment beyond it, listening.

'You understand, then?' Luke's voice, hard and commanding. 'One of you will be guarding the place at all times.'

'But, Lieutenant—' Hagetty's voice '—if he hasn't shown himself so far, why should he now?'

'I made some arrangements in Hobart. That's why I went, man! There was a spy on the ship today. He'll know soon that I've returned, and then he'll act. He has no choice. The spy will let him know we're on to him.'

'And then, sir?'

Mary Anne held her breath, straining forward to hear. When the hand touched her shoulder, she almost fell. The fingers steadied her, and Nick Etwall's dark, hard face bent over her.

'Mary Anne, how delightful! Or, should I say, Mrs Rowe.' He looked anything but delighted. She swallowed, clutching her throat.

'Nick, you frightened me! I was about to go in and . . .'

He lifted an eyebrow. 'Were you? I've been watching you for some minutes. You certainly took your time about it.'

'Etwall?' Luke had come to the door now. Mary Anne felt her face colouring guiltily. God, why should it? She had listened at a hundred doors . . . and windows. Why should Luke Rowe's be any different?

'I was congratulating your wife,' Nick said. The two men eyed each other with the hostility of two fighting-cocks. Mary Anne had forgotten how the air could crackle between them. She had forgotten a lot of things. Their mutual dislike might even have fermented to hatred by now. Nick would never forgive the humiliation he had suffered, at the timber camp, over the insult to Mary Anne. And now that she had actually married the cause of that humiliation . . .

'How is Bessy?' she burst out, to stop her own thoughts.

'Well enough. You must come to dinner.'

'Thank you.'

He smiled briefly and turned away, striding towards the beach. Luke watched him go. 'I thought it best if you stayed up at the house.'

'But I'm staying here.'

'You'd be better at the house.'

'Better for you!'

He met her eyes. 'Exactly.'

'I've already told them to bring my things here.'

'It's safer at the house.'

'Safer?'

He held up his hand. For a moment she didn't understand, and then she saw the scar on his palm, where the bullet had gone. She had forgotten that, too, in the trauma of Hobart. Someone was trying to kill him. Jezebel.

'Luke,' she said, meaning to tell him what Belle had said, but stopped herself in time. That would only convince him of the right of sending her to the house. 'I heard you say something about spies,' she continued at last.

'Did you, now?' The grey eyes scanned her with interest.

'You don't think it's me?'

He laughed in genuine amusement. 'You? Certainly not.' The laughter died. 'Don't repeat what you eavesdropped, Mary Anne.'

'Eavesdropped!'

'Weren't you?'

She spluttered a moment, then fell silent as Hagetty approached them. Luke nodded and he stopped, waiting. 'I'll agree to your staying here, but only because I can keep an eye on you.'

He turned away without waiting for a reply, and she had to be satisfied.

Toby found time to speak with her later in the afternoon. 'The man runs me off me feet,' he complained, wiping his brow. The weather was even cooler, but he was perspiring.

'You wanted the job.'

'Yes,' he sighed, and winked at her. Mary Anne told him what she had overheard, and he nodded. 'Oh yes, I've had my orders, too! I have the midnight-to-dawn watch! I'll freeze, girl!'

'Poor Toby,' she murmured, eyes brimming with laughter.

'Yes. We're to watch the house, Mary Anne. If anyone leaves it, we're to follow.'

'The house!'

'Evidently our gallant Lieutenant knows what he's doing.'

'Yes,' she murmured, grim. 'They've already tried to kill him once.'

Toby's blue eyes widened. 'Indeed?' And when she had told him, 'I wish you'd mentioned this before, Mary Anne.'

'I forgot it, until now when he . . .'

'I don't like danger,' he said. 'And yet, I smell money here somewhere, and you know what a nose I've got for it!'

*   *   *

Bessy seemed genuinely pleased to see her. Simone smiled broadly, and seemed tongued-tied, as usual. Ralph was kind. Nick was cold. The captain and mate were also there, and the latter greeted Mary Anne with every sign of pleasure. If he had had a tail, she thought smugly, he would have wagged it.

'A surprise, of course,' Bessy said, 'when I heard about you and Lieutenant Rowe.'

'Yes, I suppose it was. But if you had seen how extremely well we . . . we hit it off together in Hobart, you wouldn't have been surprised at all.'

Bessy smiled a little uncertainly. 'I can hardly wait for you to tell me about Hobart. It seems an age since I was there.'

'It cannot be the same,' the mate put in, 'with Mrs Rowe not there?'

He had obviously been waiting for a place in which to insert a compliment. Mary Anne laughed with delight. Bessy looked disapproving. Nick scowled, perhaps remembering his own flirting with her and regretting it. Luke paid no heed at all, and turned his full attention to Ralph and the captain.

After the meal, Bessy drew her aside into the sitting-room. 'I wonder you wanted to come back to this lonely place after Hobart,' she said. 'Surely the Lieutenant will soon be returning there for good?'

Mary Anne opened her mouth to answer and met his eyes across the room. The men had followed them into the sitting-room. Bessy was waiting, and yet something about the studied expression on her face made Mary Anne wonder if she wasn't being pumped for information. 'Luke does what he likes,' she said, loud enough for him to hear. 'He takes no notice of me.'

'I'm sure that's not so,' Bessy protested, and bent to her sewing. She didn't, Mary Anne noticed, take a stitch, but merely played with the cotton and needle for a moment. When she lifted her head again, her face was drawn. 'I'm almost glad you did come back,' she murmured, smiling faintly. 'It's a burden, being alone, and it's impossible to talk with the servants.'

'You can talk to me.'

'Yes.' But her eyes were wary, and Mary Anne knew she wouldn't take her into her confidence. At least, not yet.

McDonald was outside when at last they left, Simone hovering in the shadows. The girl came forward to bob a curtsy. 'I knew,' she said, yellow eyes bright. 'I knew how it could be, madame.'

McDonald saluted, and Luke spoke to him in low tones before taking Mary Anne's arm. Simone was still smiling, and he said, 'How are things at Etwall, Simone? Are they quiet?'

The girl's eyes darted. 'They are . . . Mostly, they are quiet, Lieutenant. I think people are afraid. That Belle, she is not. She is glad of their fear.'

'I can see she would be. Go inside now.'

'I will.' She smiled again at Mary Anne, and turned away. Luke began to walk through the orchard, forcing Mary Anne to go with him.

'You won't tell me, then?' she said at last.

'Tell you what?'

She glowered at him without replying.

'Be satisfied with what you know,' he said at last.

'I'm sure I don't care if you're shot at!' she burst out, and he laughed, as if her anger were a caress. A light was burning in the cottage. Hagetty, by the door, saluted. Toby rose from the table inside, eyes bleary with sleep.

Luke's mouth twitched at the unpretty sight of him, but he turned back to Mary Anne with a slight, cool bow. 'Good night, my dear.'

She could do nothing but leave them. The bedroom was small and cramped, with one window. The luggage sat by the narrow bed. A single curtain revealed a hanging closet. She sighed, remembering the Hobart house with regret. She was exhausted from the sea-sickness and the uncomfortable dinner at the Etwalls', so perhaps she would sleep after all, despite the worry of Luke and Belle and Toby.

She did sleep, and it was very late when she woke. She blinked into the darkness, trying to remember where she was. 'Mary Anne?' a voice whispered beside her. Toby. She sat up, trying to make him out against the light that showed through the crack under the door.

'I thought you should know. Hagetty's just come back and fetched your husband. They've gone out.'

'Where?' She saw him now—a shadow close to the bed.

'I don't know. He told me to stay here with you until they came back.'

'Stay with me?' Her heart was pounding, suffocating her.

He shook her impatiently. 'Yes. They're following someone.'

'Perhaps you should follow them.'

'There wasn't time.' He was silent a moment, think-ing, and she slipped on her gown, leaving her hair loose down her back and shoulders.

'Come out into the light,' she said. He went out through the door, and she followed. The water was simmering over the fire and she made tea, setting out two mugs. He watched her abstractedly, running his fingers over his stubbly chin.

'There's more, isn't there?' she said, setting his mug down before him. He looked up at her, blue eyes catching laughter.

'You know me too well, Mary Anne girl. Yes, there's more. When I was on the ship one day I overheard your husband speaking of money. Oh, not a few coins, but *money*!'

'I see,' she said softly, and when he frowned, quickly told him what she had overheard about a spy.

'If we could get our hands on the money . . .' Toby murmured.

'Yes?'

He looked at her almost measuringly. 'We've been together a long time, Mary Anne.'

'A long time.' She grasped his hand. He smiled at her fingers. A step outside startled them, and they jumped apart. The door opened and Luke came in, frowning. When he saw them, both so tousled with sleep, he frowned even more. His cool eyes moved speculatively from one to the other.

'Lieutenant, were you wanting me?' Toby was on his feet at once.

'Yes. Go and relieve Hagetty.'

'Sir.' He went out brisk as a soldier himself, closing the door. Mary Anne bit her lip. Trust Toby to escape as soon as possible! Had he no sense of responsibility? No ounce of courage?

Luke had gone to the mantel and, fetching down a rifle, started to check the barrel. 'What are you doing up?'

'I thought you must be here, but it was O'Reilly.'

'What were you talking about?'

'He said you and Hagetty had gone out. I made him some tea . . . Sir!'

The grey eyes flicked to her and away. He took down a cloth and a tin and placed them carefully on the table. 'The weather's taken another turn for the worse,' he said. 'Snow probably in a day or two. When it comes . . .' He began to dismantle the gun. 'I've a feeling we'll soon be back in Hobart.'

'The ship is staying, then, waiting for us?'

'Yes.' He began to polish the parts, almost lovingly, she thought with fascination. She had never seen a killer before, and thought with a dry throat that might be just what Luke Rowe was.

'Go back to bed,' he said quietly.

'Can't you tell me?' she burst out, her fingers clenched white round the mug of tea. It was going cold. 'I could help you or something. I could!' when he looked up at her sceptically. For a long moment he scanned her face, before turning back to the gun.

'I doubt, Mary Anne, you could help anyone but yourself. I certainly have no wish to place my life in your hands!'

She had reached the bedroom before she knew it, and stood staring ahead of her in the darkness. She wouldn't cry. She wouldn't. He was a fool, and she wouldn't cry. Why should she care, anyway? She had Toby, and Toby was worth a dozen of Luke Rowe.

CHAPTER THIRTEEN

THE WEATHER was cooler the next morning, and she shivered before the fire, while Hagetty huddled in the corner, sleeping. There had been no more sign of Toby or Luke, though Simone had brought fresh baked bread and an invitation from Joan to visit. In the end, from sheer boredom, she was forced to do so, and found the woman as cheery as her warm kitchen, and seemingly glad to see her.

'And so you married the man after all your hard words, eh? I thought you would. Does he keep you well?' The black eyes were impudent, but Mary Anne couldn't help but smile. They drank tea with gin, and Simone peeled the inevitable potatoes in the corner. 'Things is not good here,' Joan said at last, staring into her cup. She stirred it a moment, carefully, as though seeking something in the pale liquid. 'Your husband would be better away, but then I suppose he knows what he's up to.' Another pause. 'The weather's getting worse, too. When the snow comes, the men'll have to come down from the timber camp. There's always trouble, with men locked up and nothing to do. Nick Etwall'll have a tired arm come spring.'

So he flogged them regularly. Somehow the thought didn't even surprise her. She saw well enough what Nick was. No wonder Luke had mocked at her choice.

They had their dinner again at the house. She wondered why they were invited, but decided that perhaps they preferred Luke under their eye than out of it. Whatever the Etwalls had to hide, they were worried. She wished Toby was about. Perhaps he knew, by now, if the secret were worth all their trouble.

Nick was abstracted throughout the meal, and Bessy

had to call him twice before he would answer her questions about the weather. Ralph teased Mary Anne about never seeing snow before, and the first mate gazed at her in rapture, so that she felt forced to flirt back outrageously. It was afterwards, when they went into the other room, that it happened. Bessy, shivering, asked Mary Anne to find Simone and send her to fetch her shawl. The girl was in the parlour, and Mary Anne was returning from the errand when a hand caught her from a doorway in the gloom of the hall. She thought it was Toby, and turned without struggling, actually smiling. But it was not.

The flushed face of the first mate faced her from the shadows. 'Mary Anne, I had to speak to you alone.'

'What on earth!'

He sighed. 'I'm sorry to have frightened you. I didn't think. I just had to see you.'

'But about what?'

He made an impatient sound, his eyes gleaming. She knew then what about, and her body stiffened. 'I really think you're the most beautiful woman I've ever met,' he said softly.

'Oh no, I'm not beautiful at all!'

'You are, you are.' His fingers caressed her wrist.

'I think you should know,' she murmured, 'that my husband won't be at all pleased about this.'

'He's jealous, is he?'

'Why, yes.'

But the eyes mocked her. 'I should perhaps tell you that I've been watching you both, and I think he doesn't give a damn about you or you him. You hardly speak to each other, and look less. When you were sea-sick he didn't go near you, and spent his time closeted with the captain.'

She had nothing to say to that. The boy's eyes softened a little. 'I'm sorry to hurt you. I just wanted you to know that *I* care, even if he doesn't. Mary

Anne . . .' Before she knew what he was about, he had bent, kissing her hard on the mouth, bruising her lips with his passion.

She jerked away, breathing shakily, the tears flooding her eyes. 'Please, don't . . .'

He sighed, cupping her face. 'Just as long as you know how I feel.' A smile. 'Soon,' he whispered, 'you need not put up with him at all.' And he had gone. The door closed. She stayed in the shadows, tidying her skirts and hair with trembling hands. It took an amount of courage to open the door to the sitting-room.

All eyes, to her morbid imagination, fixed on her. She flushed. It might have been a court of law, pronouncing sentence. But it was Luke's eyes that frightened her the most. She had never in her life seen such a blaze of anger on any man's face, especially a man as outwardly cool as he. The sight caused her, momentarily, to lose her wits, and she stared back at him like a cornered deer.

She knew he knew. And then he had looked away, and she was left, weak and trembling, to make her way to Bessy and pretend nothing had happened. Damnation, to be forced into such a fix! A witless, love-sick idiot! Didn't he know how dangerous Luke was? And what did he mean? About Luke not being there any more? Did he think she would agree to run away with him or something?

She dreaded their walk home, but it had to come. At least she was prepared. Perhaps, she thought hopefully, he wouldn't speak to her at all, perhaps she had imagined that look.

They were hardly out of the door into the chill night before he said, in a cold, biting voice, 'If you let him touch you again, woman, I'll kill you.'

'Touch me? I don't know what you're talking about.'

He looked at her with such contempt that she was afraid, and gazed towards the cottages, telling herself he was a fool.

'I suppose I can hardly blame you for your unfor
tunate upbringing.'

'My, that's generous! What about you? Do you think
like being married to you?'

He laughed softly. 'Too late now, for regrets. You
are, and that's an end to it.'

Once inside, she lit the lamp with unsteady hands
Luke was watching her from the hearth, a frown in hi
eyes, and she forced herself to scowl at him. The frown
lightened.

'I meant it, Mary Anne. I'll have no cheats.'

'And what would you do?'

He lifted his eyebrows. 'I wouldn't know that until the
moment arose. Some women just can't help themselves
Like drink, they get a taste.'

'What charming company you associate with,' she said
with real anger, and turned her back.

His hand brushed her cheek, sliding to her nape. She
felt the light, caressing hold tighten, but she did not turn
'I wonder,' he said musingly, 'if you're redeemable after
all? I thought so, but you can't seem to help yourself
Take tonight, for example.'

'Yes, tonight,' she gasped. 'He hid in the corridor and
kissed me. Perhaps I was at fault, for . . . for leading him
on, but you hate me so and . . .'

He turned her round slowly, as if reluctant to meet her
eyes. She returned the familiar scanning look. 'Hate
you?' he said dispassionately. His mouth brushed hers
and she clung fast, hurting her chest on his coat buttons

'Oh, Luke,' she whispered. 'I don't want you to be
hurt!'

He gripped her chin, his grey eyes brilliant with some
unknown emotion. 'God Almighty, if only I could
trust you! You're such a liar, Mary Anne. Such a bloody
liar.'

She opened her mouth on a cry of protest, closed it
again. How could she even say it, when with every

breath she was lying to him? About Toby, her reasons or being here, everything?

He smiled bitterly. 'Yes. Exactly.' He kissed her again, briefly. 'Go to bed, sweetheart. Much as it pains me, I have to leave you again tonight. Duty.' A shrug.

She gripped his shoulders a moment longer. 'I want to live at New Norfolk,' she said softly, eyes brimming. 'I would even tat and sew, and arrange flowers, if you wanted me to.'

He laughed dutifully, as if she'd made a joke, and released himself. 'Go to bed, sweet liar.'

With a sigh, she went. What more could she say? He wouldn't believe her.

Simone was on the rocky promontory the following morning, and Mary Anne climbed down to join her. The girl was prising mussels from the rocks at the low-tide mark and putting them into a basket. She smiled when Mary Anne came up.

'It will be too cold, soon, to stand in the water. I thought I should do it now.'

The sky was grey, and the wind biting. Mary Anne wondered how she could stand ankle deep in the splashing waves, and drew her own hem back from the white foam. The ship rode out on the bay, at anchor.

'Your husband, he is at the camp again?'

The yellow eyes seemed brilliant with intelligence. Mary Anne nodded.

'He is a determined man, your husband. He will seek until he finds, yes?'

'Yes. Simone, what is going on round here?'

But Simone bent to the mussels. Mary Anne caught her arm, forgetting caution and the cold water. Her shoes were instantly soaked.

'Madame! You will catch a chill.'

'Simone, you must tell me. What is going on?'

The girl frowned. 'There is danger in knowing too much at Etwall,' she said at last.

'Danger, indeed.'

They spun round so sharply that they almost fell. Belle was standing close behind them, pale mouth smiling. 'So your husband hasn't thought fit to tell you?' The pale eyes mocked savagely.

'What is it you want?' Simone burst out, clutching the basket to her. Belle's eyes narrowed.

'Do you dare to speak to me like that, you little bitch? I'll scratch your eyes out.'

Mary Anne felt her cheeks flame. 'You'll shut your mouth and go back to whatever puddle you crawled out of! What we were saying is none of your business. We don't associate with whores.'

She spoke so quickly, so angrily, she was hardly aware of it until Belle began to laugh, the long throat arched back. The sound of it was light and almost beautiful. If was choked off suddenly. Hagetty, too, could walk quietly. He had come up, and slipping a hand about her throat, fastened on the windpipe. He released her as suddenly, and she stooped, rasping and choking.

'Get away!' he said, lifting his hand threateningly. As if she were in fact the mad dog she portrayed.

Belle stared up at him through streaming eyes and the tangle of her red hair. Mary Anne had never seen a look so malevolent, so full of hatred.

Hagetty seemed not to care, and when she had gone, he laughed, saying, 'Take no notice of what she says, little Simone.'

Simone was frowning again, and Mary Anne grasped her arm. Hagetty turned his eyes to her. 'And take no notice of what she says about the Lieutenant, ma'am. I happen to know he is a very cautious man. Not a man to take things lightly, the Lieutenant.'

'No. Thank you.'

He smiled and turned away back to the beach following in Belle's footsteps.

*　　*　　*

They were halfway through dinner that evening when McDonald came, with some seamen behind him. A cry had been heard on the beach, and Hagetty was nowhere to be found. Luke rose without a word and went out, leaving Nick to follow and Mary Anne to sit wondering what to say or do. In the end she went home, and it was from Toby that she heard the news. Hagetty's body had been found floating in the harbour, knifed, and they were searching for Belle. As yet, they had not been able to find her.

The cottage was silent, and she sat and waited. Waited for his step to sound, waited for the door to open. Toby had lit the lamp, and now sat by the light staring at his fingers. She felt his tension as if it were a part of her own. A man was dead, murdered, and suddenly their game seemed a game no more.

'Perhaps we should tell him about the emerald,' he said at last, and looked across at her.

She half smiled. 'Perhaps.'

'Only I've no mind to end up like Hagetty; and the Lieutenant seems to know what he's about.'

'Belle threatened me today.'

They were silent again. Voices, coming closer. She thought she heard the creak of the cart, and shuddered. The cart was one with death. Someone spoke closer, and then receded. Boots scraped beyond the door, and it opened.

They both looked up, wide-eyed in the lamplight. Luke seemed startled to see them, and then turned slowly to shut the door. His hair was damp, she saw, plastered to his nape and shirt collar, while his sleeves were rolled up and he carried his coat over his arm. He looked tired when at last he came to the table, his face drained and drawn. Something inside her twisted, and she stood up without knowing she'd done so.

'You found her?'

He had bent to the fire, holding out his hands, shiver ing. Toby jerked his head to the whisky bottle in th corner, and she poured a mug out and handed it to him At first he seemed not to see her, but sat staring into th flames. The light changed his features, blurring th strong contours. His eyes were hollows touched wit silver. She rested her hand lightly on his shoulder an found it frozen, sopping damp.

'Luke, you're soaked! You'll freeze. Here, chang your shirt, and drink this while I find another. Come on take it off.' She stamped impatiently, and he stare at her in a bemused way as he at last obeyed. In th end she fetched a blanket from the bed, and knelt t wrap it round him. He set his mug down carefully on th hearth.

'Aren't you going to drink it?'

He looked at her, their eyes level. 'I pulled him out the water. I thought it was the least I could do. It was m fault he died.'

'He was a soldier! He expected to face death. It wa his job.'

He shook his head. 'I should have locked the bitch up after what she did to me. I knew what she was. I kept he free for my own reasons.'

'Good ones, I'm sure.'

The grey eyes showed some of their old mockery. 'Ar you trying to make me feel better?'

'No! I'm trying to make you see the truth, as it i You're blaming yourself for something that needs n blame.' She handed him back the mug. 'Drink you whisky.'

He half smiled, and then laughed, a choking sound. ' thought you might be disappointed it wasn't me.'

She dropped her eyes, her lashes making long, spik shadows across her cheeks. A tear slid down an splashed on the hearth, sizzling a little in the warmth.

'Mary Anne!' His voice was sharp, his hands hurt he

shoulders. 'My God, if this is another of your lies, I'll never forgive you.'

But though his voice was harsh, his arms were gentle, drawing her against him. She clung to him, her tears damping his shoulder. 'Oh, Luke,' she whispered, 'don't be sad. You make me sad, too.'

He kissed her cheek. 'Do I? It'll soon be over now. Tomorrow night, I promise. We can go back to Hobart then. Will you like that?'

She laughed unsteadily. 'Very much.'

'Until then, we must take especial care. This isn't a game any more.'

She felt his anger, and drew back unwillingly. Toby had gone; she hoped he had not heard too much. Luke rose, drinking down the whisky with a shudder. 'Come to bed,' he said. 'I've set McDonald on guard outside, and O'Reilly is on duty at the camp.'

She stiffened. 'He'll . . . they'll be all right?'

'They're armed. Yes, I think they'll stay awake tonight.'

Please God it was so! She couldn't lose Toby when she had only just regained him from death. Luke had unpinned her hair, and now kissed her mouth, lifting the silky tresses in his fingers. 'Mary Anne,' he whispered against her lips. 'When I've rid myself of this bloody uniform, we'll go to New Norfolk. I've a mind to refurnish the house there, build on it, perhaps.'

'You wouldn't miss the army?' she murmured.

'That was my father's idea.'

'But, surely . . .'

'Surely?' He looked down at her, mocking. 'Doesn't the idea appeal to you? There's plenty to be done on the land, especially neglected land. And danger enough for any fool.'

It did appeal to her. So much so that she was astounded, and for a moment could say nothing at all. His eyes cooled. He twisted a strand of her hair round his finger and pulled it almost cruelly.

'No? I grant you, there'd be no lying and no cheating, no thoughtless flirting with strangers, but why should you miss that? Unless you actually enjoy living on your greasy knife-edge? There'd still be dances to go to —God knows the place is alive with assemblies and balls. No one could say New Norfolk folk were boring!'

'I know,' she managed. 'I know.'

'But not enough? What is your idea of a rosy future then, sweet Mary Anne? Travelling, perhaps? Do you want to travel? Maybe I could sell the land.' His eyebrows rose mockingly. 'We could go to England; I've cousins there somewhere who'd not say no to some of my colonial money.'

Was he teasing her? She couldn't read the truth in his eyes, and said at last with a sigh, 'I want nothing you're not prepared to give.'

His fingers tightened on her hair, jerking her eyes back to meet his. He scanned them before he let her go. 'Go to bed,' he said at last. 'I'll sit by the fire.'

He didn't believe her, let alone trust her. Her hand snaked out and caught his. 'Luke!'

He turned to look at her and something in her face must have touched if not reassured, him, for he put his arms about her and followed her through the door. The bedroom was dark; beyond the window was still silence. The air was so cold their breath hung white, suspended. How gentle he was, as though he bound his passion with chains and kept it restrained. What was he afraid of showing, or perhaps not showing? Had he meant it, about doing what she wanted? Or had he merely been mocking her again?

It was freezing, and she huddled under the blankets as he undressed. 'Are you glad I came now?' she whispered, the teasing light dancing in her eyes.

'No.' His reply was unflattering and uncompromising

I regretted agreeing as soon as I had spoken. You've no business here. This is my business, and bloody dangerous it is.'

Still, he held her close for someone who was sorry to see her.

'You're here,' she whispered softly. 'Surely that's reason enough for me to be here.'

He laughed softly. 'If I believed you, Mary Anne, I'd be as blinkered as a horse. Luckily for us both, I'm aware of your inability to speak the truth.'

She protested, but he covered her mouth with his, and the words were lost. She'd learned rather more than mockery from him, if she ever wanted to use it. The thought startled her, unpleasantly. She couldn't imagine anyone but Luke holding her so intimately, loving her. The idea was unbearable. She clung even closer, feeling his hard-muscled back against her palms, and kissed him in return, almost savage in her need of him.

'I've come to a conclusion,' he said, when they lay quiet again.

'A conclusion?' she whispered, listening to the steadying beat of his heart.

His arm came round to hold her closer, and his chin rested on her head. 'If you ever get tired of being my wife, or I your husband, then we'll end it. I don't want you to stay because you feel bound to. Do you understand?'

He meant he could leave her when he was tired of her. Toss her aside like an old shoe. She sat up abruptly, dark eyes angry. 'I don't much like your decisions,' she retorted.

He laughed. 'Nevertheless, you may come to thank God for it, in time.'

Was he tired of her already? He didn't seem to be. What was wrong with the man! He put her head in a whirl.

*   *   *

The next morning, the snow had come. She woke to frozen toes and fingers. Luke was already dressed; she could hear his voice in the other room, and when she rose at last, he had long eaten and was engrossed in what looked like a map, spread on the table. McDonald was by him, while Toby sprawled in the chair opposite. They all looked up at her entrance, McDonald colouring. Toby's blue eyes danced.

'Mrs Rowe, it's a mite chilly this morning.'

'Indeed it is,' she murmured, and flicked a glance at Luke. He was frowning at the map, and didn't even seem to notice her. There was hot water over the fire and she made herself some of the strong, coarse tea and sat by the hearth sipping at it, watching the three of them.

'The captain'll be waiting here. Half his men with him, half with you, McDonald.'

McDonald peered at the map and nodded his red head. 'Yes, sir. And you?'

'I've my own plans on that score. Don't worry, lad. This time the bastard's in the net good and proper. There's been a watch on the camp, remember.'

The mug burned Mary Anne's hands. Her eyes turned involuntarily to Toby's, and he winked.

'You know the times?' Luke said sharply. Toby nodded.

'Ay, sir. I remember every word you've spoken, that I do.'

McDonald nodded also. Luke folded the map briskly and stuffed it inside his coat. He stood up with a grating of his chair, and Toby also leapt to his feet.

'Hagetty's to be buried this morning,' he said to no one in particular, and Mary Anne also rose.

'I'll fetch my cloak, then.'

'There's no need for you to come if you don't wish to.'

She looked at him uncertainly; he sounded so cold and uninterested. Toby met her eyes again, and nodded imperceptibly. She hurried to fetch the cloak, wrapping it round her in the hope of keeping out the chill. McDonald had gone when she returned, and only Luke and Toby waited.

The former opened the door for her, and once outside took her arm in his. She clung to it, looking in dismay at the half-melting, sloppy snow that lay everywhere.

'It's not cold enough to keep it firm yet,' he said, as they walked along the muddy track, and Mary Anne lifted her hem. 'There's more to come, though, in an hour or two.' The clouds were dark, glowering with their burden.

'Will the snow matter, tonight?'

He glanced at her. 'Tonight I doubt anything would make a difference. The trap's set and soon to be sprung.'

'Is it very dangerous?'

The orchard lay stark before them, and beyond that the house. Toby, walking behind, smothered a curse as he sank into mud. There were men gathering to one side, where the victims of *Infanta* had been laid to rest. Mary Anne spotted Nick's tall form, and Bessy. So they'd all turned out. She half expected to see Jezebel there too. She shivered, remembering that evil beauty, and gripped Luke's arm hard. 'There's no need to answer, only . . . take care.'

'Tonight, and it's finished,' he replied almost gently.

'Finished,' she agreed.

They had reached the place. The wooden coffin lay on the snow; McDonald saluted as Luke came up. He glanced about the faces, a scanning, piercing look. Ralph cleared his throat.

'I've the book here, Lieutenant Rowe.'

'Thank you, Mr Etwall.' He took the Bible and opened it at the marked place. 'I'm hardly qualified to be reading this,' he said. 'But as Hagetty was my man, I'll do my best.' He read the burial service, and added a few words about the man himself. Brief, but none the less sincere, the sermon was a tribute to both men, Mary Anne decided. The coffin was then lowered into the earth, and the grave filled. Toby pinched her arm as she stood listening to Bessy talking to Nick, and she turned sharply.

'The man's intent on death.'

'What are you talking about?'

He drew her a little way away, pretending to point out the sweeping gulls near the scattered cottages. 'Your husband, girl! He means revenge, an eye for an eye.'

'He's entitled, perhaps.'

'What are you saying?' He looked at her strangely. 'There's no such right, Mary Anne. The military think they're God, but they're no more than mud on the ground.'

She felt her cheeks colour. 'That's not so! He's not like the military at all. He wants to get out. He told me so.'

The blue eyes narrowed. 'And you believe what he says? Can't you see he's using you? He uses everyone!'

She shook her head stubbornly. 'You're wrong!'

He made an impatient gesture, and spun away. She watched him go, biting her lip. He was only trying to protect her. Why had she been so angry with him? With *Toby*? It was frightening.

'Mary Anne?' Bessy slipped her arm round her waist. She looked tired and old. The lines had deepened about her mouth and eyes, as though suddenly the weight of years were too heavy for her.

'I'm sorry. I was thinking.'

'Of Belle?' Bessy sighed. 'We all do. It was all right, until she came. I mean, we couldn't see then what . . .' She stopped. Nick was watching them, but after a moment he turned on his heel and strode back towards the house. Bessy caught her breath. 'I must go. Take care of yourself, my dear. Very great care.' The words were a warning—she felt it with a thrill of fear. For herself, or for Luke?

Thinking of him, she turned. He was standing by the
grave still, abstracted. She went to take his arm, and he
looked at her as though he'd forgotten her existence. 'If
only I could find Belle,' he said. 'That's the only danger,
Mary Anne. If I knew, I could watch her.'

Simone might know; she must ask her. Luke stooped
to kiss her brow. 'I have to go out to the ship and see the
captain. I want you to go back to the cottage and stay
here.'

'But . . .'

'Belle is still about. She hates you.'

'Very well,' she sighed, submissive.

He scanned her face, and finally nodded. She watched
him walk away before looking again at the grave, dark
against the white of the snow. It had begun falling again,
melting as it touched her face, and she hurried back
towards the cottage.

Toby wasn't there, only McDonald tending the fire.
He smiled at her briefly. He didn't like her, and hadn't,
since their encounter in the Etwalls' garden. He no
doubt felt the Lieutenant had made a sad mistake in
marrying her. Perhaps he was right. She sat restlessly,
trying to concentrate on sewing, and then reading. The
snow continued to fall, coating the ground quicker now
than it could melt, whitening the trees with its silent,
insidious flakes.

Luke came back once, but he was busy with his own
thoughts, and the two men looked over the map again.
Toby came in while they were at it, and ate the meal she
had prepared. But she had no time alone with him, to
ask him about what was happening. When Luke went
out, Toby was ordered out too. 'Like some pet cur,' he
whispered sarcastically in her ear as he went. Laughter
choked her, and when she had recovered it was too late,
and they were gone.

As it grew dark, McDonald presented himself as
escort for her. She was to go to the Etwalls' for dinner,

he said. Outside, the air was freezing. Her eyes watered, and her fingertips ached with the cold, no matter how she blew warm breath on them. McDonald's nose had gone as red as his hair, and they almost hugged Simone when she came to open the door for them.

There was a fire in the sitting-room, and Bessy rose to draw her to the hearth. Nick was there, too, frowning as she came forward. The air seemed charged with something more than the usual unease. Tension and fear, she was sure of it. But were they afraid of her, or Luke?

She watched them covetously. Nick glowering, silent. Ralph more worried than usual, and Bessy drained and old. She felt a dart of pity for them, wondering what was to happen that made them so. How had Belle's murderous act affected them? What had they done to warrant Luke's wrath?

When they heard his voice in the hall, they all looked up. Mary Anne was surprised at the expression on Bessy's face; almost hatred. Lord, what *had* he done!

He came in, cool and commanding. He knew, she thought, watching him observe the room's occupants. A smile played on his mouth, but not of humour. Nick grunted and turned his back. Bessy made haste in her brief greeting, while Simone took his coat. The girl met Mary Anne's eyes with a frown. She, too, felt it, then, and was puzzled and afraid.

'I've never seen snow before,' Mary Anne said in a nervous voice.

Bessy exclaimed dutifully. 'We are often kept inside for days in the winter.'

'I suppose so.'

Nick looked up, blue eyes hard.

The meal itself was worse. Bessy tried, but for the rest there was silence. Mary Anne wished they hadn't come at all. Whatever Luke was doing didn't meet with the approval of the Etwalls. Far from it!

'I saw the Irishman pointing the gulls out to you,'

Bessy said to Mary Anne. 'He wasn't suggesting eating them, was he? He did to me, would you believe it. A pie, he said.'

Mary Anne laughed, 'No!'

'He did indeed. Quite savage, it sounded to me.'

'I'm sure Toby would never be savage,' she blurted out, the relief of having something to talk about making her careless.

Bessy's eyebrows quirked. 'Toby?'

'Toby O'Reilly,' she said, the smile fixed on her face. She felt the colour rising in her cheeks and she squeezed her nails into her palms to calm herself. Stupid, stupid!

'Oh!' Bessy concentrated on her food, and lifted the fork towards her mouth. She put it down again and looking up with a smile that was almost apologetic, said, 'Toby? Isn't that your husband's name, my dear? Your dead husband?'

How gentle the eyes were, how kindly enquiring! Mary Anne longed to wring her neck. There was no other answer she could give but, 'Yes, it was. They're not at all the same, though.' It did sound feeble.

'Naturally not!'

A silence. Nick was drinking heavily, and Ralph stared into space. Luke was staring at her as if she had suddenly turned green. *At least* green, she decided, to warrant that white, strained look, that gathering certainty and wrath in his grey eyes. He had fitted the pieces together in his mind with audible clicks. Another survivor from *Infanta*, the name Toby, O'Reilly's sudden arrival, her plea for work for him. All fitted well, extremely well. And now he would never take her back to New Norfolk, and never grow to love her like a true wife.

He leaned across the table a little, towards her, and said, 'I think it's time we were going.'

'No.' Her refusal was instinctive, self-preservative.

His mouth whitened. 'Yes!'

'I must fetch my cloak,' she said, and rising, almost ran out of the room. The hall was dark, but Simone was on the landing and turned in surprise as she ran up the stairs. She caught the girl's arm, saying in a breathless, frightened voice, 'Run to the cottage, Simone. Tell Toby . . . O'Reilly, that Luke knows. Tell him that! And tell him to hide, for God's sake!'

'Mary Anne?' Luke was at the bottom of the stairs. They were in the shadows, however, and he couldn't see them properly. She gave the girl a push, urgently, and Simone nodded in a bewildered way.

'My cloak?' she mouthed.

'In the parlour, madame, by the fire.'

She went back down the stairs, slowing her breathing by sheer will-power. She felt like the martyr in a play she had once seen, going to the stake. Luke was waiting, white-faced in the gloom. 'It's in the parlour,' she said. 'I must fetch it. I must.'

He made a grab for her arm as she slipped past, but she was too nimble, and hurried away down the hall to the parlour. Give Simone time, she thought. Whatever it costs, Toby must have warning.

At first she thought he had let her go. The fire in the parlour glowed, but there was no other light. The cloak was spread near the fire with Luke's coat, and she went to it, snatching it up with shaking hands. Luke was close behind her, and taking a breath she spun to face him.

His eyes looked black. She had never seen such a war of fury and rage in any man's face. 'Luke,' she whispered, hardly knowing she spoke. His hand shot out, open-palmed, and sent her stumbling back against the chair. Tears of pain smarted in her eyes, and she put her own palm to the stinging cheek. As a child she had received blows with impunity; as a woman she had no defence.

'I'd like to wring your neck!' he breathed. His voice sounded choked and strange, and he clenched his fists as though struggling not to do so. 'You lying bitch! Every-thing you've said. God Almighty, it's like the ground sliding from beneath my feet.'

'Luke, please let me explain.'

It was useless. He looked at her with such contempt that she cowered. 'You'd think I'd learn,' he said in a harsh, measured voice. 'This time is the last time, Mary Anne. Never again.' She felt the tears on her cheeks. He meant it. All the talk of New Norfolk, it was as warm breath on the cold air. Everything was finished, and she'd be worse off than she was before she met him.

'Please,' she whispered, hopelessly, forlornly.

'Go to hell!' His fingers dug into her arm and he jerked her out in front of him. She stumbled, but he dragged her to her feet again, out into the frozen, dark orchard.

'I never meant to harm you,' she said, the tears burning her cold cheeks. 'Toby was dead. I thought him dead until Hobart.'

He didn't reply, just kept pushing her along as though she were his prisoner, less than that even. How he must hate and despise her! All his mistrust had been well placed. All his doubts proved. She couldn't even blame him. There were no more words to mend matters. And tonight was to have been the end of Etwall and the beginning for them both! All lost, all gone . . . She sobbed as she stumbled along, overflowing with misery and self-pity.

The cottage light blinked through the trees, made hazy by her tears. She could smell ash as they approached. Her lungs were aching, her throat burned with the need to howl and scream. He caught her up a few yards from the door, and spun her against him. His breath burned her face as he bent close; his eyes were as dark as the sky and as cold. She caught back a sob, hiccuping.

'After tonight I never want to see you again. Do you understand me? I'll pay you—oh, you've earned a wage! And then you can go to hell, where you belong.'

She was shaking, her teeth chattering, but he seemed to hate her even more for that, and going to the door called out for McDonald. He came, buttoning his coat, his hair tousled. 'Sir?'

'O'Reilly. Where is he?'

McDonald blinked. 'Sir! The girl, Simone, she came to speak with him. From you, she said. They went away.'

There was a pause. 'I want you to remain here until I call you. Understand?' His voice was low, shaking with the control he had over himself.

McDonald saluted jerkily, puzzled by the tension-charged air. Luke turned to look at Mary Anne, and with a cry she fled past him, into the cottage.

The bedroom seemed the only refuge. She ran through and shut the door, leaning her back against it, her breath panting through her lips. There was a pause, and then his steps drew closer. She heard him breathing, as fast and loud as she, on the other side. The bolt slid firmly across, securing the door on the outside.

'You'll stay there until the ship is ready to sail,' he said, quiet now, cold now. The rage had gone, it seemed. 'Spend the night thinking about the lies you've told, and what they have cost you this time, Mary Anne. Not that I think it will do you much good. You've gone too far now for redemption. You don't even know what repentance means.'

'Luke!'

The outside door slammed. She heard voices, and then a different step returned. McDonald. A chair creaked. Mary Anne ran to the window, standing on tiptoe peering out through the high square with its strong wooden shutters. Luke was standing outside, staring in the direction of the harbour. He stood so still, so . . quietly. She opened her mouth to cry out again, to beg to plead . . . But something inside made her bite the words back. It was no use, he wouldn't believe her. And there was still pride.

She watched him for some moments, tears welling again in her eyes and sliding noiselessly down her cold cheeks. And then he walked away, round to the side and out of sight.

CHAPTER FOURTEEN

IT SEEMED a long time later, when she woke. The dream had been unpleasant, something had menaced her. Luke had hurt her, and sent her away. Only it wasn't a dream. Her eyes pricked, and she bit into her lip to stop the inevitable tears. Enough was enough. The man had no right to treat her so. No right!

'Mary Anne?'

She stared a moment in disbelief. The room was empty.

'Mary Anne!' Louder this time, from the window. She stood up, tall as she could, tiptoe. Curly hair and the blur of a face in the dark night. The snow helped to lighten things, but not much.

'Toby? Thank God! Oh, thank God!'

'I doubt God had anything to do with it.' He sounded grim.

'He's locked me in!'

'I wonder he didn't murder you then and there.'

'Please get me out.'

A pause. 'Can you climb up higher? I think I can unfasten the shutters from this side.'

She peered round and, spotting the chair, proceeded to drag it as quietly as possible to the window. She could see Toby clearly now, and he grinned, teeth flashing white in the darkness. 'Now, if I can just remember the old lessons. A push here, a bit of a pull there. That's got it.' The shutters groaned and fell open. He touched her cheek.

'There, my darling, you're free. Can you climb out now?'

She could, but it took time, and the sill scratched her

tomach through her gown. Toby caught her, lowering
er to the ground. The snow smothered their steps, and
hey stood a moment, holding their breaths to listen. But
here was nothing from McDonald, and about them the
orest lay still.

'Oh, Toby,' she whispered, and flung her arms tightly
bout him. 'I'm so sorry! I don't know what came over
ne.'

'Tell me how he found out?'

She did, and felt his breath catch. 'Well, you're a fool,
ut you must know that.'

'I do, I do. What can we do now?'

'I've been thinking about that.'

'I knew you'd know! I knew it. Let's go away, far
way, as far away as possible . . .' And she burst into
ears.

He drew her into the shelter of the trees, and rocked
er a moment, stroking her hair. 'Now what would be
he point of that, Mary Anne? The man's in your blood,
sn't he, and you won't be able to forget him.'

'He hates me!'

'*Now* he does. Give him time to calm down.'

'Toby, he will always hate me.'

But he only laughed.

She sighed, and nestled closer. 'Where are you
upposed to be now?'

'At the camp.'

'Oh God, I forgot about that!'

He shook her. 'Forget the big moment?'

She remembered something else, too, and jerked
way with a sudden breath. 'Toby, the spy! There was
 spy on board the ship. Someone whom Luke was
vatching. I meant to ask you. Who was it?'

'Who?'

'Yes, it's important. Luke said that was the only
langer. Oh God, if he's killed . . .' Her voice rose
ysterically, and he gripped her shoulder.

'Hush. From what I overheard—only by accident mind, I believe the man they were watching was th mate. The young one.'

It was as she had feared. 'The mate,' she whispered No wonder Luke was so angry at her dalliance. 'Wha will we do?'

'I suppose we'd best start up to the camp. That' where the action is to be. No use standing freezing here my girl.'

'Will Luke be there?' she whispered.

'He was to follow someone from the house.'

She was somewhat relieved, and followed him swiftl along the track. He took her through the trees then seemingly in an aimless direction. She asked him once breathlessly, where he was going, but he kept o: through the snow. The icy stillness was eerie, and sh couldn't help glancing back over her shoulder. Th climbing warmed her a little, but her toes were sti frozen and her nose felt painfully numb. The going wa slow, and when Toby at last stopped, she bumped int his back with a squeak.

'Quiet!'

They crouched low, listening, but there was no sound He pointed through the trees. 'The camp should b about there. They'll be asleep now. The Lieutenant's gc men surrounding the place, except for this spot here where I should be.'

'Wouldn't he have filled it?'

'Maybe. We'll just have to hope he didn't have time.

'But, Toby!'

'We'll get ourselves shot if we're not quiet, girl!'

She followed him, half-crouching, through the maz of dark tree trunks. The snow showed them up, but i the shadows they were safe enough. There was a ma ahead. Toby motioned her to stay back, and he made hi way slowly towards the shadows. When the shot rang out she was sure that he had been hit, and screamed ou

his name. But there were more shots, flashing red in the
night, and suddenly an unholy screaming and yelling
seemed to descend upon the place from all sides. Oh
God, what was the matter with them all?

Somehow she was flung back against a rough-barked
tree. A man ran past yelling out obscenities—she
thought she recognised the boy who had slandered her
and been beaten for it. Someone screamed, and there
was a clash of steel and rifles. She ran closer to the
sounds of the fighting, piercing the darkness with
desperate eyes, seeking for Toby. If he was hurt . . .
There was firelight ahead, flames licking hungrily, and as
she broke into the clearing of the timber camp, she saw
clearly what the forest had hidden.

The place was alive with men. Convicts and seamen,
brawling. Another shot, and someone sprawled to the
ground close at her feet. She knelt, putting her hand to
the man's chest, but felt only blood, warm and sticky,
and with a whimper drew back from his staring, dead
eyes. The hut, where the convicts slept, was ablaze, and
close before it, gun in hand, was Belle. She saw Mary
Anne at the same time, and with a soundless cry Mary
Anne fled back into the darkness.

The snow slid under her feet, frozen and slippery, and
she stumbled on tree roots. The feel of the blood on her
hand; the memory of the scene nauseated and terrified
her, and she was sobbing as she ran. Where was Toby?
Luke? Where was Luke?

When the man stepped out before her, she thought it
must be a friend, and ran on. It was Nick Etwall. For a
moment she could only gasp out what had happened,
broken sentences, as she clung to the rough, warm stuff
of his jacket. He held her arms, gazing beyond her head.
Nick?' She shook him, swallowing. 'Nick! Don't you
hear me?'

'I hear you.' He looked down at her. His eyes were
deep and dark, and for a second, an instant, fear gripped

her again. But then he was saying, 'Quickly, come with me!' in a warm, concerned tone, and the fear receded.

She went, willingly. She didn't know this place. There seemed much thicker tree trunks now, and a tangle of scrub in between. They were climbing higher into the forest. Her skirts tore, but he held her hand, and his palm was warm, alive. And she was terrified of what had been happening back there. She longed to be a child, trusting, in his care.

They came to it at last. A gunyah, a sort of native hut. It squatted in a mass of scrub, camouflaged so that she would never ordinarily have known it was there. When Nick tried to pull her after him she resisted, gazing at him in uncertainty.

'Nick? What is this? Shouldn't we get help? I thought . . .'

His fingers tightened painfully. 'It means you'd best follow me, Mary Anne, or I'll have to kill you.'

It didn't seem possible that Nick could have said such a thing to her. People said things like that only in plays and novels, surely? But he had meant it, and now he dragged her, roughly, through the low, narrow V of the doorway, and she couldn't think of a protest. There was a lantern—she heard the rattle of it as he fumbled to light it, and the smell of oil. The wick caught, shining up on to his lined, hard face. Mary Anne shivered, edging towards the door, but he spun about.

'No you don't! I have you safe and sound. What incredible luck! The one thing that bastard won't sacrifice, and I've got it.'

'Sacrifice?' she whispered. Her hands were like ice, and she rubbed them together automatically.

'Hasn't he told you what he's up to?' Her white face said more than words. 'Perhaps I should enlighten you then? Your husband wants my hide. I've quite a profitable little business here, you know. Or would have had if left alone.'

'Timber-getting, you mean?'

He gave a bark of laughter. 'That! Oh no. I mean the other. I deal in . . . in safe conducts. I get money, I provide safety. I have the perfect place for it, haven't I, in this God-forsaken hole?'

'Safety? What sort of safety?'

'What could be safer than Etwall? So isolated, so far from the Governor and his army. Men who want to hide out for a while, men who want to rest up for a while. They pay me, and I see they get just that. Take Brogan, for example. Brogan got out of Hobart with quite a bit of Governor Arthur's treasury. Only Governor Arthur wasn't too keen on people finding out—he would look quite a fool now, wouldn't he? If it was known his secretary could embezzle public monies right under his nose. But Brogan and I were old friends, from army days, and Brogan knew I'd put him up here. He'd be safe at Etwall, isolated as it is. Even from Governor Arthur's long, interfering nose.'

'How *good* of you,' she murmured, sarcastically. He was a bad man, worse than Toby. She despised him.

'Oh, it was for a price! I needed the money, you see. I needed it to set up in Hobart again—to get away from this hell. So it was agreed. I take Brogan under my wing, see he's safe, and in time he makes his quiet way to wherever he wants to go. And, in return, he sees me right.'

It made sense now. The silent conspiracies, the mysterious warnings, that undercurrent of happenings she could never understand. Ralph's tired face, and Bessy's old, grey looks. They, too, had guessed, or were boasted to by Nick. They feared for him, and loved him. How it must have weighed them down, to have Luke billeted at Etwall, snooping about.

'What of Belle?' she eventually asked.

'Oh, Belle knew. And Davey. I had to have someone to take him food and see to his comforts. Someone who would do it for the money, and knew how to keep their mouths shut.'

'And Luke?'

'All that rubbish about being disgraced and coming out to Etwall because of the Governor's displeasure! I half believed it for a time—the army can be like that. But not for long. We've had word from Hobart. We know the truth now. He was sent to catch us out, and to bring Brogan back, quietly, without fuss.'

The spy.

'I suppose knowing the truth made it all the more imperative to get Brogan to safety?'

'There was no chance of getting him out while your husband was here, sniffing about. And now . . . Well, now we have to take the risk.'

Stalemate. Nick had no choice but to act, as Luke had predicted. 'But why the attack on the timber camp? I don't understand it.'

'Your bloody soldier thought Brogan was being kept there. It was to flush him out.'

'Where is he now?' she whispered. There was a pause, and Nick looked up and beyond her with a faint smile. She knew before she turned—the hackles had risen on the back of her neck.

Brogan stood behind her. He was a small man, white-faced, with the blue of unshaven stubble colouring his chin. His eyes were dark, afire in the centres. She had never seen a face with such a dark, bleak look as that. The face of a schemer, a desperate man. Perhaps even a murderer.

'Brogan, my friend, I'd like you to meet someone.'

'Did you know they're killing each other, up there at the camp?' A cultured voice.

'I know, I made sure of it. Someone gave me information on their plans, and I let it be known at the camp that there was going to be some trouble . . . You know the bloody convicts need no excuse for a good fight.'

'So.' He smiled. His eyes went back to Mary Anne, slowly perusing her.

'This is our Lieutenant's wife, Brogan.'

The face split into a grin. 'Belle, have you met the Lieutenant's wife?'

From behind her a rustle of skirts. Jezebel. Mary Anne gazed at her in pure horror. The pale eyes narrowed. 'What is *she* doing here?'

'Doing?' Nick retorted. 'She's our hostage. Rowe won't touch us if she's here.'

'You fool, he'll kill us all!'

Nick scowled, but Brogan was laughing. 'Ah, what a tongue she has . . . No, Belle, the man's right. That's our safe conduct. That pretty little creature there.'

Belle's eyes narrowed, 'You're all fools if you think Luke Rowe will dance to your tune.'

'But, Belle, he'll be frightened to do anything else.'

Nick made an impatient movement. 'Why argue with her? Come on, help me tie her up and we can get moving.'

'Moving where?' Mary Anne whispered. They had rope, and proceeded to tie her hands behind her back and then her ankles together, pulling the cords so tightly they bit into her flesh, making her catch her breath. Nobody bothered to answer her.

'You've a horse?' Brogan muttered.

'A few yards down.'

'Where can you take a horse in this bush?' Belle snapped.

'Where's Davey?' Nick asked suddenly, his dark eyes sweeping up to meet Belle's. The woman tossed her head, hands on hips. She swaggered forward. 'He's greedy. I fixed him.'

'Good God, like you fixed Hagetty?' Brogan whispered, almost admiringly. The pink mouth curved, and the blue eyes slid down to Mary Anne.

'I'm good with a knife. Always was. Had to be.'

Nick had paled, and Mary Anne saw his fingers clench at his side. So he was not so keen on Belle's little ways. Mary Anne didn't blame him. She was not so keen herself.

'And where is your . . . friend?' Nick asked abruptly, turning to Brogan.

'Waiting by the horse, I hope. We can get aboard ship and be off before anyone up at the camp knows anything about it.'

'Guards on board?'

'Yes, but my friend will have some tale to tell. Anyway, who would challenge the first mate?'

Mary Anne shuddered.

'He'll be pleased to see you,' Nick added, chucking her roughly under the chin. 'We'll share you, eh, among ourselves? I've long wanted you, Mary Anne. All the more since you made a fool of me. We'll all be merry together, shall we?'

Brogan laughed. They stood up and spoke quietly together. Then the two men moved towards the door. Belle went too, and they spoke again, glancing back at Mary Anne where she huddled against the wall. Then the men went out, and Belle came back to stand over her. Her eyes were hollows in her face because of the wierd flicker of the lantern, but Mary Anne knew they were full of hatred. She wanted to look away, but found she could not. Her teeth were chattering from cold and fear, and yet she looked up at Belle, bemused by that lovely, evil face.

'They've gone down to meet the spy,' she said softly, and suddenly went down on her knees, pushing her face up close to Mary Anne's. 'They will be gone a little time. And when they come back, you'll be out of the way.'

'You'll let me go,' Mary Anne whispered, but it was not a question, and there was no hope in it.

Belle laughed soft and slow. 'I'll let you go, all right! You've been a thorn in my flesh, and I'm going to put an end to you before you do any more damage. Nick was mine before you turned up, and Luke Rowe before him. And now Brogan is mine, and you'll not have him off me. We're going away together, him and I, and there will be no third party to bitch things up between us.'

There was a knife in her hand. A tiny, wicked thing that winked in the pale light. Mary Anne felt as if all her blood were draining away already. She could not move, and slumped like a rag doll, waiting for the agony of death.

'I'll make you sorry.' Belle's breath brushed her cheek. 'Comin' here and nosing around where you'd no business. You and your fine ways and sparkly emeralds.'

'Where is it?' Mary Anne gasped, struggling against the dark tide threatening to overwhelm her.

'I have it safe.' Mary Anne felt a strand of the long, amber hair tickle her neck. She felt regrets and memories swooping over her, black wings beating, waiting. She thought of Luke, and knew now she loved him as she had never loved another human being. Toby was her friend, her brother, but Luke . . . He was her life, her breath, her being. And it was all too late. She would die with his hatred like a stain against her, and he would never know . . .

The shot seemed like a thunder-clap, deafening her, and reverberating through the gunyah. Belle fell heavily against her, for a moment smothering her, so that she screamed, thinking she was to die. But there was no pain, no thrust of the knife, only the wildly thundering sound of her own heartbeat. Belle lay so still and heavy. Mary Anne became confused and struggled hysterically, trying to throw off the weight with bound hands, her voice whimpering like a child's.

And then, beyond Belle's cloud of red hair, the dark shadow of a figure in the doorway, the whisper of skirts.

'Madame! You are all right?'

Simone.

'Oh God,' she breathed. 'She tried to kill me. Simone, she has a knife . . .'

Simone pushed Belle's body aside, and it was only then that Mary Anne realised the evil woman was dead. Simone's voice was cool and brisk. 'She killed my husband,' she said. 'It was only right. I have avenged him.'

'Simone! Oh, Simone!' The tears were trickling down her cheeks, and Simone found Belle's wicked little knife and quickly cut through the cords which bound her. For a moment they clung together, offering what comfort there was. At last Mary Anne managed to speak in a husky, shaking voice. 'They'll have heard the shot, Nick and Brogan. They'll come back to see what's happened.'

'We must go then, and swiftly.' She was trembling so much that Simone had to put an arm about her waist to help her to her feet. They stumbled to the door and out into the cold darkness.

'Oh hurry,' Mary Anne whispered. 'Oh God, hurry.'

'You will be safe soon, madame. I will take you to your husband.'

Mary Anne gasped, and the tears flowed even faster. 'If he hasn't been k-killed.'

'Madame, please. Hush . . . I hear someone coming.'

They clung together, shaking, peering into the night. The white snow and dark tree trunks mocked them with silence, and then came the crunch of footsteps and the puff of hurrying breath. 'Is it . . .' Mary Anne started forward. 'Oh, Toby!'

His arms were warm and safe and she clung to him, shuddering with cold and emotion. 'Nick and Brogan,' she gasped. 'They must be stopped. They're going to the ship, and mean to escape. They will have heard the shot, and . . .'

'So they mean to escape, do they? That's good to hear.'

'Good? Toby, don't you understand?' She shook him, her voice rising. 'They mean to escape!'

He winced, and put a hand to his upper arm. 'Careful, my girl. I've been wounded. And yes, I understand. But it's just what we had thought would happen, and there are people waiting. Now, where is the delightful Belle?'

Mary Anne put a hand to her brow, bewildered and suddenly very tired. It was Simone who came forward, cool and calm, her chin high. 'She is back in the hut, sir. I will show you. I have known a long time of this place. I've watched that Belle. I've seen her come and go. I've waited. And now I have my revenge.'

'Oh, Simone,' Mary Anne whispered. 'Poor child!'

'Quiet!' Toby cut in impatiently. And then, soft as falling snow, 'Lieutenant.'

They turned round, slowly, like another play. Mary Anne felt reality slipping away as she gazed in elation and dismay at the dark bulk where the man stood, feet apart on the snowy ground. He was holding his rifle, waist high, pointing it in their direction. The rifle he had polished so lovingly. His breath was white, a cloud in the coming dawn. There was a pale grey line along the horizon. The long night was almost over. He had promised her, when this night was over, they would go back to New Norfolk. Now she had no doubt he meant to kill them both.

'Step back, Simone,' he said gently. The girl stepped back, looking puzzled.

'I was bringing madame to you,' she said, gently. 'She has been frightened, but now she is safe. I followed Belle. I knew this place!'

'You're a brave girl. Now, Mr O'Reilly.' He turned to Toby, his voice oddly emotionless. 'I wonder how you come to be here?'

'I heard the shot, same as you.' The Irish brogue was absent.

'I believe you have something that belongs to me.'

Toby stiffened, his hand tightened about his hurt arm. 'Lieutenant, be reasonable.' He sounded tired, but there was no pity in the other man's face. Only a cold, grim determination.

Until this moment Mary Anne had felt a little like a dreamer in a nightmare, a player in a play. But all at once the lassitude which had kept her frozen vanished. He meant to kill Toby, and probably her as well.

'Please,' she whispered. 'Please, you don't understand at all.' And then, her nails biting into her palms until they drew blood, 'He's not my husband. He never was. Nor was he ever my lover. I lied to the Etwalls because it seemed necessary. More . . . more respectable. And now you want to kill Toby for my lies!'

'I don't believe a word you say,' he murmured wearily. The gun barrel was remarkably steady. A tiny, deadly eye. Toby's loud, scolding voice made them all jump.

'Good God, is that how you sweet-talk the girl! No wonder she runs away from you! In fact, man, you seem to lose her all the time. Don't you know better than locking a woman like her up in a room and expecting her to stay there while you go into danger? Sure as hell she'll come after you. Now won't she? And then get kidnapped and nearly murdered into the bargain. No wonder she's a little . . . upset about it all!'

Luke was still, silhouetted against the snow. Mary Anne could not see his expression. She wished Toby would stop his nonsense, but did not have the strength to tell him so.

'You see how white the poor girl is, man? What've you done to her to make her shake so in your presence? I haven't seen her as white since the day she came creeping up to me in Sydney Town twelve years old.'

'Toby!'

'You've no business . . .' Luke began angrily, and now the rifle was not so steady.

'I've every right,' Toby retorted. 'I've been her father and her brother ever since. I've looked after her the only way I knew how. We've had good times, and bad. I think she's been happy enough, in her way. Better than the life she was headed for, on the streets. Better than drink and beatings and old by thirteen, hmm, Lieutenant?'

Mary Anne felt the colour staining her cheeks, and bit back a cry as Toby stepped away from her.

'I heard the shot, and came to kill Nick Etwall and his friend Brogan,' Luke said quietly. 'But it seems they're already off for the ship, where they'll be caught and made ready to be taken back to Hobart. Governor Arthur won't be too happy with either of them. I wouldn't be them for anything. Simone—' He glanced at the girl '—McDonald is looking for you. Go and tell him I'll be along shortly, to see how matters are progressing.'

She hesitated, and then ran lightly over the snowy ground. Perhaps now that her husband was avenged, Mary Anne thought, the poor girl would be ready to start again.

'O'Reilly, get down to the house and have that arm attended to.' Toby turned to go, and then stopped.

'Do you mind, Lieutenant? I think I'll pop in on Belle first. Over here, was it, Mary Anne? No, I'll be fine. You two go on down without me. I'll not be going very far.' He smiled and turned in the direction of the native hut.

Mary Anne lifted her eyes, slowly, reluctantly, to Luke's face. He was looking past her, where Toby had gone. He was as cold and distant as the moon. She saw the rest of her life stretching out before her, empty, without him, and shivered with more than cold. The grey, rosy strip of dawn had brightened. The sun was rising and it was all over, but for her it was still chill and still night. After a moment she realised that Luke had lowered his gun and turned away, back down the slope between the silent tree trunks.

So that was to be it. Not a word of farewell, nothing. She could see how it would be. The journey back to Hobart, separate cabins, meals in the galley but never speaking to one another, and then once arrived going their separate ways. He would pay her, of course, and she would be able to go back to Sydney Town. To what?

With a sob, she stumbled after him, her legs stiff as those of a wooden doll. 'Even . . . Even murderers get a trial!' she gasped. 'You can't just walk . . .' The sobs got the better of her, and she lost the words she had meant to say. A tree rose up in front of her, and she rested her arms against it, crying in earnest.

'You'll turn into a block of ice,' he said coolly, and grasping her hand, dragged her away from the tree and behind him down the slope. She stumbled along, blinded, hiccupping. She hardly realised they were at the cottage until she felt the warmth of the dying fire and the familiar surroundings. Luke pushed her roughly into a chair and stooped to build up the fire, until the flames were crackling greedily over the new wood. He moved away then, and she sat staring into the hearth, shaking now and then, her fingers twisting together. She could not possibly feel any worse than she did now, Mary Anne decided. It was the end of her life.

'Drink this.' A mug was thrust into her hands and she took it, spilling a little of the whisky on her skirt. She mopped at it ineffectually. He was standing beside her chair; she felt him without needing to look. The contempt and impatience radiated from him. He would rather be down at the beach, in the thick of things. He was wasting his time here with her, with someone he did not care about.

It was partly to keep him beside her that she said, 'Nick told me . . . about Brogan, I mean. They thought you were in disgrace, but the spy told them the truth.'

'Yes.' Suddenly he squatted down beside her chair, holding his hands out to the flames. The red reflected in his hair and eyes. 'Governor Arthur didn't want the embarrassment of a public search and capture. He wanted Brogan back quietly. So he sent me out here

ostensibly in disgrace. I wanted to get out of the army,
and after this I shall. We knew Brogan would go to
Etwall and his old friend Nick. It was perfect for hiding
out in, and then getting a timber ship to civilisation when
things had cooled down. But he was well hidden and
cunning. I couldn't corner him. So we decided to let our
secrets be known at Government House. A greedy
friend of Brogan's was sure to send word, for a price. So
they knew our plans, and they were frightened. We
flushed him out with the bait of a ship to safety.'

'Belle . . .' She swallowed. 'Belle is dead. Simone
killed her. But Belle killed Davey. She said so . . . She
was pleased with herself. She had a knife and meant to
kill me. It was then I thought how sorry I would be,
never to have told you how much I love you.'

He said nothing, but his hands were stilled.

Mary Anne sighed, to the depths of her being. 'I can
never make you believe it,' she whispered. 'I see that.
How can you believe me when I've misled you over and
over again? But I wish you to know it before we part
company, I suppose forever.'

'You lied to survive, I understand that.'

She turned to him for the first time, surprised. 'Can
you?'

'It was the fact you couldn't trust me, Mary Anne.
That you were unable to confide your secrets in me. That
knocked the ground from under me.'

He turned then, and met her eyes. She devoured his
tired face hungrily, and clenched her fingers to prevent
her tracing the lines from nose to mouth, and about his
eyes. He began to stand up, as if he could stand the
proximity no more, and as he did so there was a rush of
footsteps at the door.

The trauma of the past few hours, and days, had taken
their toll. Mary Anne had suffered terror at the hands of
Belle and from a world where she had come to mistrust
everything and everyone. The footsteps startled her,

and then horrified her. Nick and Brogan, coming to kill her . . . Worse, coming to kill Luke!

Before she knew she meant to do it, Mary Anne had lurched up out of her chair at Luke, shielding him with her body. Already off balance, he fell to one side, on the floor, and she sprawled over him, her arms about him, covering his body with hers as best she could.

'Look what I've found, round the little beauty's neck. A safe place, I suppose, on a witch? Mary Anne, look!' The voice, loud and shaking with excitement, petered out. 'Mary Anne?'

Mary Anne looked over her shoulder, pushing her hair out of her eyes. Toby stood in the doorway, holding up something in his hand which sparkled and gleamed. The emerald. But his smile was frozen, and he was staring at her in surprise and astonishment.

'Let me help,' he said, and came forward, stretching out his hand. 'You can't imagine what you both look like, peering up at me.'

Mary Anne gave him her hand, and was helped up. She heard Luke behind her, cursing. 'Round Belle's neck,' she said, in a strange voice. 'Fancy! All the time, round Belle's neck.'

'Yes, I . . .' Toby looked from one to the other, uncertain. Luke was smoothing his sleeve, frowning across at Mary Anne, who was avoiding his eyes, her fingers twisting together. 'I think it'll fetch enough to get me to England. I've always wanted to go, and I see myself as a gentleman, indeed I do.'

Mary Anne began to laugh, but the laughter turned to sobs; great racking sobs from deep inside her. She covered her face with her hands and still the sobs went on, tearing at her body.

And then his arms were round her, warm and strong, and his chest was beneath her cheek, a haven. She felt his breath warm on her hair, and then his lips. 'Hush, Mary Anne. It's over. It's all over. It's back to New

Norfolk now, and the peace and quiet of a country farmer's life. Hush now, my love, my dear love.'

'But you don't love me!' Her head went back, and she stared at him from tear-reddened, surprised eyes.

'But I do. I do and always will. I loved you and wanted you when I rescued you from your watery grave. I fought against that love, but it won in the end.'

'But you would have left me in the snow,' she breathed, not able to believe.

'Perhaps. But I would have sent someone to fetch you. I was angry, more with myself. I knew, seeing you, that I couldn't part from you, no matter what I told you. I would take you with me, lies and all, despite the misery you may bring me in the years to come. And now that I realise you love me . . . now there is no escaping, sweet Mary Anne.'

'You know, but . . .'

'A woman does not risk her own life to save that of someone she does not love. Your comic but heroic display just now, sweetheart!'

'Oh. Oh!' Her smile grew, making her face as bright as the dawn outside.

He kissed her on the nose, then the lips, lightly, then deeper. She sensed the deep happiness within him, matching her own. He loved her, and she loved him, and it was for ever. She did not have to ask whether he would abandon her; she knew he never would. She did not even realise Toby had slipped out, the emerald clutched firmly in his hand. Her life had suddenly moved from complicated intrigues and schemes to a few simple facts. She was in love and loved, she was never going to be frightened and abandoned again. The terror of her dreary childhood and her mother's sufferings would recede as the years passed; a sad memory in the glow of new-found happiness.

Mary Anne took a breath, and burst out on the crest of her emotion, 'I promise I'll never ever lie again!'

There was a pause. Luke opened his mouth, met her eyes, and closed it again. With admirable restraint, he bent and kissed her lips, and held her fast. 'And I promise to believe every word you utter, sweet Mary Anne.'

ATTRACTIVE, SPACE SAVING BOOK RACK

Display your most prized novels on this handsome and sturdy book rack. The hand-rubbed walnut finish will blend into your library decor with quiet elegance, providing a practical organizer for your favorite hard-or soft-covered books.

Only $9.95

Approximately 16" x 8" when assembled

Assembles in seconds!

To order, rush your name, address and zip code, along with a check or money order for $10.70* ($9.95 plus 75¢ postage and handling) payable to *Harlequin Reader Service*:

Harlequin Reader Service
Book Rack Offer
901 Fuhrmann Blvd.
P.O. Box 1325
Buffalo, NY 14269-1325

Offer not available in Canada.

*New York residents add appropriate sales tax.

BKR-1R

CLAIM THE Crown

Carla Neggers

The complications only begin when they mysteriously inherit a family fortune.

Ashley and David. The sister and brother are satisfied that their anonymous gift is legitimate until someone else becomes interested in it, and they soon discover a past they didn't know existed.
